UNMASKED IN ARAMEZZO

MURDER IN AN ITALIAN VILLAGE · BOOK 3

MICHELLE DAMIANI

RIALTO
PRESS

UNMASKED IN ARAMEZZO

MURDER IN AN ITALIAN VILLAGE · BOOK 3

RIALTO PRESS

P.O. Box 1472

Charlottesville, VA 22902

michelledamiani.com

CAST OF CHARACTERS

CASALE MAZZOLI

Stella — *ex-chef who runs her ancestral home as a bed-and-breakfast*

Claire and Morton Stafford — *guests and partygoers at the Masquerade*

JOBS IN ARAMEZZO

Domenica — *local bookshop owner*

Matteo — *streetsweeper*

Marta — *sheep farmer, mother of Ascanio*

Leonardo (Leo) — *ex-racecar driver who now operates the family porchetta van*

Cosimo — *antiquarian and expert on local lore*

Don Arrigo — *village priest*

Marcello — *mayor*

Romina and Roberto — *couple that owns Bar Cappellina*

VILLAGERS

Veronica — *the mayor's wife*

Luisella — *frequent customer at Bar Cappellina*

Mimmo — *hunter and former caretaker of Casale Mazzoli*

Giancarlo — *Matteo's childhood friend, visiting*

AT VILLA DELLE ACQUE

Chelsea and TC Durant — *owners of Villa delle Acque*

Judith and Hollis Lake — *longtime friends of Chelsea and TC*

Tripp and Louisa Lake — *son and daughter-in-law of Judith and Hollis Lake*

Gillian Lake — *daughter of Judith and Hollis Lake*

THE POLICE

Luca — *police officer*

Salvo — *Luca's partner*

Captain Tribuzio — *local police captain*

Stella scanned the menu.

Tagliatelle with boar sauce—green lasagna with mushrooms— pappardelle with beef ragù—gnocchi in Sagrantino wine sauce— strangozzi with cherry tomatoes and red pepper flakes.

Sensing her friend's eyes on her from across the table, Stella glanced up.

"What?" Stella asked Domenica. Though she knew.

"Every week. You know the menu. You know what you're ordering. Every week." Domenica chuckled.

Stella shrugged. "It's like a favorite book. Every time you read it, you get something new. Something less . . . obvious."

"Admit it. After your twenty-odd rootless years in America, Aramezzo is turning you into a creature of habit."

Stella lifted her chin. "How can you say that? With all that has happened in the year since I took over the bed-and-breakfast?"

"Not quite a year, *cara*," Domenica corrected, tucking her iron-gray hair back behind her headband. "Anyway, I made no insult. It's a worthy lifestyle, to be a creature of habit. I take pride in it."

Stella cast her eyes heavenward. "Other than cats and books, there's not a habitual thing about you."

"Cats and books. They are enough."

"Throw in flour and butter and I'd be inclined to agree." Stella grinned at Domenica.

Who grinned back before saying, "So, the *pappardelle*?"

"Well, I *almost* ordered the *gnocchi*."

Stella's phone pealing into the warm evening air seared through their laughter. Her stomach lurched, though she could not say why.

Her voice a clipped sing-song, Domenica said, "Don't we have a policy of no phones at the table?"

Stella's fingers trembled as she flipped the phone over to check the screen. She started to explain the frisson of fear but knew how ridiculous she'd sound. After all, she had already tried and failed to articulate the looming dread of something going terribly awry. Instead, she tried for levity. "Matteo said he'd send photos from the Americans' party at Villa delle Acque . . . don't you want to see them? We need a visual on those masquerave costumes."

Domenica shrugged her nonchalance.

"But why is he *calling*? From a *party*?" Her stomach lurched again. "Sorry, Domenica, I need to take this."

Rising, Stella pressed her phone against her ear and hurried from the outdoor restaurant seating into the piazza. For a town of two hundred people, Stella wondered how the piazza could be so noisy. "Matteo? What's up? Did you meet a hot American guy after all and simply couldn't wait to tell me about it?" Stella heard the note of pleading in her own voice. More to distract herself than anything else, Stella turned to wink at Domenica who was deep in conversation with Adele, Trattoria Cavour's chef, and didn't notice.

"Stella!" Matteo's next words sounded garbled, tangled, lost in a cacophony of sound.

Stella clutched her phone tighter. "Matteo? What's going on? I can't hear you."

"Stella! Where are you?"

For a moment Stella wondered if she was supposed to be at the party with him, before remembering—she was most definitely not invited. "You know where I am, Matteo. I'm having dinner with Domenica. It's a regular Friday night for us plebs."

"You're at dinner? How long have you been there? What did you do before? Like right before dinner?"

Stella pulled her phone away from her ear to gaze at it, eyebrows furrowed. Returning it to speak, she said, "Matteo? Are the Americans handing out drugs as party favors or something?"

"Stella! Please!"

She sighed as she fought down rising panic. "Okay, *Dad*. I'll fill you in on my whereabouts. Before dinner, Domenica and I took Barbanera to the vet."

"Did anyone see you? Please tell me someone saw you."

"What did I just say? I took my one-eared cat to the vet. The *vet* saw me, Matteo. And my cat is fine, thanks for asking. Needs to lose a little weight, the vet wasn't into me cooking for him, but other than that, Barbanera is hale and hearty. Like the pirate he's named for."

"And before that?"

"Before that?" Stella cocked her head to the side in thought. "Right. I made an early dinner for the Staffords. Between you and me, I think the missus didn't want her husband drinking on an empty stomach. Which, given what happened last night, is probably a good idea."

Matteo muttered to himself, "Thank the Madonna."

"Why do you need details about my day?" she asked, controlling her breath. "Party that bad?"

Stella could barely make out Matteo's words as he spoke to somebody beside him. "At least they can't implicate her this time."

"This time? What are you talking about? Who are you talking to?" Her knees weakened, remembering the party's guest list. *Please*, she offered up a silent prayer, *not Leo. Not Giancarlo. Not her guests. Not Marta.* Her mind flitted to Marta's son but then recoiled in horror.

She needed Matteo to finish his sentence.

"It's just…" Matteo's voice trailed off.

"Matteo! Say it already!" The couple leaving Bar Cappellina turned at her raised voice.

Stella ignored them.

Listening and waiting.

"Get here, Stella. As fast as you can. Something's…happened." The line crackled. "Again."

Stella set a china saucer, rimmed with violets, in front of Barbanera. He sniffed and looked up at her as if expecting her to whisk a more satisfying option from behind her back.

"Any other cat would be thrilled with carrots and chicken livers," she said, adjusting the red bandana holding back her curly hair.

He blinked, lifting his black chin.

Stella sighed, taking off the chef coat that protected her daily uniform of jeans and a fading t-shirt. "Cat, the vet is going to put you on a diet. Mark my words."

He sat. And blinked again.

Stella stood firm. "You get that or you get nothing."

Barbanera rose and turned to face the window, suddenly fascinated by the swallows displaying their aerial dance across the sky.

Stella fought down an urge to whip up another meal, something a little richer. *This isn't a restaurant*, she reminded herself. I don't have to give him whatever he wants. With resolve, she hung her chef coat, grabbed her shopping list, and closed the door behind her. She opened it again to peek in, hoping to see Barbanera either resigning himself to his least favorite breakfast or trotting to the door to join her. But all she saw was his silhouette, stiff and unmoving, with the suggestion of his tail whipping from side to side.

Distracted, she didn't notice Luca at the bottom of the steps, in his police uniform.

"Trouble in paradise?"

She jumped. At the sudden words, and also the sudden English, which startled her into English as well. "Quite a mouthful! And an idiom no less."

"What?" Luca's face fell. "Speak slower."

"Nothing, nothing," she said, switching to Italian. "I was complimenting your English. It's coming along!"

"Thank you." He smiled, relieved.

They fell in step, walking around Aramezzo's lower ring road. Stella said, "Did you choose an English class?"

He shook his head. "There's no time. The new captain has us doing all these retraining sessions. Apparently, Captain Palmiro kept us on too long of a leash."

"That was the least of his problems," Stella muttered, her gray eyes narrowing.

"I thought you came around on the captain." Luca looked down with a smile.

Stella hated her stomach's irrational swoop at that grin, one front tooth slightly overlapping the other, which, given the fullness of his upper lip, she only saw when his smile grew broad. As it did now. She realized she hadn't responded. "I was not sorry he retired. How's the new guy?"

"Captain Tribuzio? I like him. My shoes have never been so shiny." He laughed, and Stella relished the familiar musicality of it, rising through his deep chest and into the morning air. She said, "Maybe you'll convince him that taking English lessons serves the community. You need some multilingual *carabinieri*, what with tourism spilling out of Assisi."

"Watching American TV works pretty well." He shrugged. "For now."

"Sure, if you want to parrot lines like 'trouble in paradise,' but that's hardly going to get you very far."

Luca hesitated.

"What?"

Luca's dimple flashed as he swallowed. "Stella, I have other ways to practice English."

Stella grinned, relishing the ease of their banter. "Well, sure. You know I'm always happy to help, but we wind up speaking Italian anyway and—"

"That's not what I mean." He ran his teeth across his lower lip. "I . . . Stella, I've been seeing someone."

"Oh!" Stella concentrated on not letting her pace falter. "Oh. Well. That's nice. I mean. I hope she's nice."

Luca's face split into a grin that made his previous one look like a warm-up. "She is! It's early days, you know. But I like her."

Stella tried to figure out a graceful way to ask the question but came up empty, so she just asked it. "Who is she?" Why did it sound like an accusation? She smiled to blunt her voice's edge.

Unnecessary, as Luca seemed lost in a reverie. "Liliana. We were friends in high school, but then her family moved to London. We've been texting. And now talking."

"And . . . *flirting?*" Stella felt relieved that this time her voice landed in a playful tone. After all, she was the one who rejected Luca; why shouldn't he date someone else? How was he supposed to know she'd regretted the rejection as soon as she'd given it? Sure, her track record with men ranked down there with sushi pizza and McDonald's attempting spaghetti, but that didn't mean she had to completely distrust her attraction, did it? People grew and changed. She'd grown and changed. Maybe liking a guy wasn't a sure indicator that he would eventually set the relationship on fire. Or cover it with flaming Cheeto dust.

Well, she'd taken too long to admit her feelings to Luca. This sudden stab of loneliness was her fault. Even so, it didn't make the feeling of being on the outer edges of the schoolyard any easier to bear.

At Luca's expectant look, Stella realized her internal monologue had been so beguiling, she'd tuned out his conversation. To cover her embarrassment, she said, "Erm . . . that's nice."

"I know! She never comes to the Americans' party. Even though her parents do, every year."

"She knows the Americans?" She sincerely hoped Luca hadn't mentioned this while she'd zoned out.

Luca stopped walking and regarded her quizzically.

Stella blushed and stammered an apology.

More slowly, Luca said, "Her father brokered the transaction for the Americans to buy Villa delle Acque. Five or six years ago? I don't remember. In fact, I think they moved to London on the villa's commission. Her family comes back to see relatives and attend the Durants' party. But Liliana, she's always been working, so hasn't joined them in years."

"She's taking a vacation this time," Stella guessed. "For you."

He blushed and ducked his head. "Well, she hasn't seen her grandparents since they stopped traveling to London. Plus, the party is probably a draw. The Durants are going all out this year."

"So I've heard." Stella couldn't help the swell of anxiety at Luca mentioning the party. Ever since she'd heard about it, she'd had a feeling of foreboding. Maybe because the first mention of the party coincided with a funeral. Or perhaps because of the palpable tension between the mayor's wife and Stella's neighbor Louisella at the discussion of who got an invitation. Or possibly because the American guests arriving today booked only last week—even though the Durants sent the invitations months before—which seemed at odds with the rigor and thoroughness of their questions about the accommodations.

Stella shook off the unease and decided to practice a new "one-of-the-guys" role. She play-punched Luca on the shoulder as they slowed outside Forno Antico, Aramezzo's only bakery. "Oh, come on. Don't be modest. How could she resist you?"

"You'd be surprised." Luca chuckled, then gestured to the *forno*.

"What's on the menu?"

Glancing at her list, Stella said, "I need *torta al testo,* to make the American guests' sandwiches when they arrive later today. I think they'll enjoy Umbria's flatbread. I'm picking up a regular loaf, too, for bruschetta. Mimmo brought me a tin of pretty magical olive oil. He wouldn't tell me where he got it, and I didn't press him. I'm just glad to restock without begging a neighbor for their surplus."

"Probably a good idea." He grinned. "Though you can buy local oil, you know; Cristiana has some at the *alimentari.* I picked some up for Mamma last week."

"The cooperative oil is excellent, but not this good. What Mimmo brought me must be single-varietal or something." At Luca's shrug, Stella added, "And you, you headed to work?"

Grinning, he gestured to his torso. "The uniform tip you off?"

She kept her eyes on his, refusing to let her gaze drift across his shoulders. "I'm smart that way."

"The captain has a new code of conduct playbook for us to memorize. I'm going in early so Salvo and I can quiz each other."

"Good times," Stella said in English. Sometimes, there was no Italian equivalent.

"I know that one!" Luca cheered and waved goodbye.

"I bet you do," Stella said softly, watching as Luca strolled to the station. Was his step more . . . *buoyant?* She shook her head, reminding herself that romances were not her genre. She refused to have her internal monologue filled with pink hearts. Still, she couldn't help the questions crowding her head about this Liliana. What was her job? (She instantly berated herself for the total Americanness of the question.) What did she like? Heaven forgive her, Stella even wanted to know if Liliana was pretty.

Stella adjusted her bandana. Her fingers brushed across a fleck of dried batter. The red bandana, and its navy sibling, both needed a scrub. But she was trying to limit their number of washings, as she recently noticed they were threadbare in spots. Great. She'd had an entire conversation with Luca wearing a dirty and threadbare bandana. Perfect.

Not that he'd noticed.

Well, she thought. She broke the eggs, now she had to eat the frittata. "Stella!"

Stella turned at the sound and found Antonio standing in the bakery doorway. "Ciao, Antonio. How is everything?"

He shrugged, "Boh." Stella empathized. "You have guests coming?"

"Yes, Americans. For the party."

"They aren't staying at the villa?"

"I guess not. It seems a last-minute decision. They booked last week. Hopefully, they won't be expecting accommodations as fancy as Villa delle Acque."

At Stella's expression, Antonio clapped his hand on her shoulder. "Stella … *tranquilla*. The *casale* is in better shape than it's been in years."

Stella laughed uncomfortably, imagining looks of dawning horror on her guests' faces later this afternoon. "I'm afraid that's not saying much."

Antonio's red mustache twitched as he tried not to smile.

Stella remembered her errand. "I'm picking up *torta al testo*. And bread."

Antonio gestured with his chin to have her meet him at the register.

"Celeste not here today?" Stella asked.

"She's helping Veronica put together her costume for the party. The mayor's wife, Veronica. Not the woman who sells embroidered napkins at the farmer's market."

Stella had no idea there was any other Veronica in Aramezzo. She felt a spark of surprise, frankly, that the mayor's wife allowed it. She said, "Celeste is helping by choice, is she?"

Antonio's easy laugh filled the bakery. "By Veronica's choice, sure."

Stella smiled, handing over her money—exact change, like the Aramezzo shopkeepers preferred. "I'll see you, Antonio."

He waved her off, already turning to Benedetta, the butcher's wife, dressed in a blue cardigan, blue skirt, and blue crepe heels. The uniform for the women of a certain age in an Umbrian village, Stella supposed. Probably since time immemorial. Did her grandmother shop at the bakery, wearing a similarly proper ensemble? Had she, like Benedetta, exchanged pleasantries with the baker while buying bread for her family's noontime meal?

Or had her grandmother sent her daughter, Stella's mother, to the bakery? Stella envisioned a smaller version of the woman who raised her, only dressed in the elementary school's pinafore and without the bitterness etched in her face, dashing in to fetch a loaf of bread.

Stella thought about all those visits to the bakery, all those loaves of bread, all those easy transactions over the counter, sharing bits of village gossip…all those moments, like pearls on a string.

Strange how the thought of her family living here for generations, incorporated into the fabric of Aramezzo, only made her feel more foreign.

Stella leaned against a stone wall in the parking lot, listening for an oncoming car. Despite herself, she'd grown to treasure this time, waiting for guests to arrive. Yes, it used to fill her with dread—not knowing if the guests would see through her ruse and realize she was no bed-and-breakfast proprietor, but rather an ex-chef pretending to know what she was doing. She employed "fake it till you make it" to good effect, pretending enthusiasm she didn't feel until she'd developed a delight for these moments, when names in her booking calendar became real people. Real people discovering Aramezzo just as she had a short while ago. Even though, as she'd confessed to Antonio, she worried these guests might bristle at her lack of amenities, yet she couldn't help looking forward to their arrival.

Checking her phone, Stella chided herself for not adding thirty minutes to the Staffords' estimated arrival time. Though GPS might prognosticate a landing time suitable for travelers familiar with Italian roads and Italian drivers, non-Europeans took far longer, hitting the brakes at any surprise. Then there was that one family that arrived an hour late and blamed it on the poppies. At first, Stella had assumed they meant crocuses, that they'd gotten stuck in the mire of saffron workers plucking stigmas. But then she'd remembered that saffron farms stretched in the opposite direction.

No, those guests had been waylaid by the spectacle of poppy fields in the plain between Tuscany and this edge of Umbria. They hadn't been able to resist the call of taking photos surrounded by those luminous ruby petals. Stella would have been annoyed, thinking of the ragù she'd left bubbling on the stove while she waited in the parking lot, except those same poppies had entranced her the week before, when she and Matteo drove to Florence for a Caravaggio exhibit at the Uffizi. As she'd helped the Australian family with their bags, she'd delighted in how their lavish praise of the Umbrian valley only ended once they'd climbed the steps through the tunnel that led to Aramezzo's first inner ring road. Then, they'd tripped over each other, pointing out a cat in a flower box, a grapevine spilling across an arbor, a space between buildings that afforded them a slice of view over the sweeping greenery of the valley below, speckled with those same garnet poppies.

Stella sighed. She hoped these Americans would be as easily pleased.

Little by little, the bed-and-breakfast was coming together. Soon enough, she'd be able to sell it and return to her life in the United States. Her old refrain, born of a resolution stated over and over again: *Soon I'll sell it, I'll get back on my feet, and pick up where I left off.*

Suddenly, she wondered why the thought failed to thrill her as much as a simple field of poppies. Her musing evaporated at the sound of an engine.

Stella watched as the car pulled into the lot. The wife, Mrs. Stafford, her honeyed hair swept into an effortless chignon at the nape of her neck, pointed to the town, no doubt noting Aramezzo's unusual town layout—how many other villages were laid out like a birthday cake, with ring roads cinching the layers?

Mr. Stafford climbed out of the driver's seat and gave a cursory glance around before digging into his pocket to pull out his phone.

As Stella approached, she heard Mrs. Stafford say, "Really? You can't put it away for five minutes?"

He grunted, mumbling about the two-hour drive.

"But we're *here*! Look *around*!" Mrs. Stafford gestured around her.

"The markets are still open, Claire."

At a pause, Stella stepped forward, waving a greeting. Mrs. Stafford turned with a dazzling smile. "You must be Stella!" As she leaned to clasp Stella's hand, Stella noticed the bare suggestion of expensive perfume. At close proximity, Stella noticed that though fine lines marked a face on the flip side of middle age, Mrs. Stafford's forehead bore no evidence of advancing years. *Botox*, Stella thought, recognizing the characteristic sheen. With a tumble of words, Mrs. Stafford practically sang, "Well, this place is heaven! Right, Morton?"

Stella turned to greet Mr. Stafford. "Welcome!"

He bent backward to release his stiff muscles and Stella felt awkward with her hand hanging there. As she decided to drop it, he gripped it, squeezing authoritatively.

At her husband's non-answer, Mrs. Stafford tinkled a laugh and waved her hand dismissively, saying in a loud aside to Stella, "Don't mind Morton. He wanted to go to Fiji."

Not knowing how to respond, Stella asked, "Can I help you with your bags?"

Mr. Stafford popped open the Audi's trunk and said, "I'll get them.

You don't look strong enough to carry a shopping bag."

Stella sighed inwardly. Once again with the short jokes. "I assure you, I'm stronger than I look. And we have a walk, with stairs."

Mr. Stafford shot his wife a meaningful look. "A *walk? Stairs?*"

"You're the one who refused to stay at the villa with everyone else," Mrs. Stafford snapped, before turning to Stella with a tense smile. "Yes, thank you, Stella. We'd love some help. I'm afraid I'm a bit of an over-packer—"

Mr. Stafford let out an explosive laugh.

His wife acted like she hadn't been interrupted. "—and of course, for this event, with all the costume options, I had to pack an extra suitcase! I mean, what can Chelsea mean by a '*masquerave*'? Every time I ask, she gives me a different answer."

Stella helped haul all the suitcases out of the trunk and gestured with her chin toward the steps. "It's not far, and the steps are shallow. You'll want to roll the suitcases up the ramps that flank the stairs."

Mr. Stafford squinted. "How do you get service trucks into town without a proper road? Or ambulances?"

Stella's heart shivered, remembering the panic of having the same question bloom into her mind, only less theoretical, as she knelt beside a body. She adopted a light air. "Our service vehicles have wheels that straddle the stairs." She hoped he wouldn't press on the emergency vehicles question. She'd really rather not think about it.

Mrs. Stafford made appreciative noises as she walked, chirping, "It's out of a storybook! How lucky you are to live here."

Stella had never considered herself as lucky. She blinked in thought.

Mrs. Stafford went on easily, apparently not requiring a response, "And our package . . . did it arrive?"

Package? What package? Stella stalled, trying to remember, "Erm . . ."

"I sent you an email. This morning." Mrs. Stafford stopped in the street, the smile dropping from her face as she stared at Stella.

Stella adjusted her bandana, trying not to work the thin area like a wound. She'd never been great with email. Or correspondence of any kind. Then she had a thought. While she might not know what Mrs. Stafford was referring to, she did know no packages had arrived. "Right, right. Of course. No, unfortunately. No package."

Mrs. Stafford and her husband exchanged glances. He cleared his throat. "We were assured it would arrive today. This morning. It's rather important."

Stella wasn't sure what she was supposed to do about it. She wasn't responsible for the mail. But she had a thought. "I'll go to the post office after I check you in. See if it's waiting for delivery." This wasn't a move that would work in the United States—asking a postal worker to hand a parcel across the counter rather than deliver it as indicated—but in small-town Italy, people bent rules they didn't see a compelling reason to enforce. She hoped that was true today. This mysterious package seemed awfully significant to her guests.

Mrs. Stafford smiled a smile that didn't show her whiter-than-white teeth. She looked more pained than pleased, and the expression made her thin face appear gaunt, like skin stretched taut across a skull. A sudden chill clenched Stella and she wished for a sweater. Even as she recognized the breeze as warm.

At that moment, they reached the steps to Casale Mazzoli. Stella had learned early on that guests were not charmed by an unlocked door. So she made a performance out of climbing the stairs to unlock the door, even though when she had no guests, she didn't bother with a key. Nothing ever happened in Aramezzo.

Well.

Until it did.

Stella showed the guests the sitting area where they'd have their breakfast. For now, though, she sat to copy their passport information into her log. She handed them cards she'd had printed with the Wi-Fi information and two sets of keys, before warning them about Barbanera. Yes, she already told them the property came with a cat, and yes, Barbanera rarely went upstairs, preferring his cozy armchair at the kitchen's entrance or curled against her on the sofa as she read her favorite *gialli*, the Italian mysteries with the yellow spines. Still, the cat delighted in taking humans by surprise.

Logistics complete, Stella took her guests upstairs to their bedroom, the larger of her two rental accommodations. Antonio was right, she had done an enormous amount of work. True, Ilaria, the woman she hired to help turn the bed-and-breakfast over between guests, had helped with much of the replastering, the repainting, the refinishing. And Ilaria's family was instrumental with tasks YouTube couldn't help her with, like fixing the bathroom's leaks, which had led to mold and mice behind the walls. Nonetheless, Stella had managed it all. She couldn't help the pride in her voice as she pulled open the cream linen curtains to reveal large windows framing an expansive view of rolling terraces of olive groves, waving wheat fields, and a lingering patch of poppies illuminating the foot of distant mountains.

Mrs. Stafford's breath caught. "Morton. Did you see this?"

He muttered, "Nice," before glancing up. He did a double take, his phone forgotten in his hand.

Mrs. Stafford spun to Stella, her hands clasped to her chest. "It's beautiful," she breathed. "Thank you, Stella. Everything is perfect. Right, Morton?"

His eyes scanned the view unspooling before them. "It is pretty good," he said gruffly.

Stella turned to hide her grin. He reminded her of Barbanera, she realized. Perhaps his bluster, too, hid a soft heart. Hand on the doorknob, Stella said, "I took the liberty of making a platter of *torta al testo*, our local flatbread sandwiches. Not knowing what you might prefer, I made two kinds, one with mortadella and the other with prosciutto. I'll leave them on the dining table on a tray with a pitcher of lemonade I make with a touch of my neighbor's lavender. Please feel free to take the tray out to the patio and enjoy the day."

At Mrs. Stafford's hesitation, Stella added, "While you are settling in, I'll jog down to the post office."

"Thank you, Stella." Mrs. Stafford paused. "How do you say 'thank you' in Italian? Do you know, Morton?"

Stella covered up her confusion at how one could travel to a foreign country without knowing some polite basics with a smile. "It's '*grazie*.'"

"Oh, I knew that! I've heard it in movies. *Glazie. Glazie.* I got it. Such a beautiful language, isn't it, Morton?"

Stella debated correcting her but decided against it. She jogged downstairs, where Barbanera sat waiting. "Fancy a trip to the post office?" She asked while taking the pitcher of lemonade from the refrigerator and placing it on the tray, already filled with the platter of *torta al testo*, a small porcelain pitcher of wildflowers, and a bowl of *brutti ma buoni*, the hazelnut-filled merengues, perfect for a late spring day. At the sight of the nubby, shiny cookies, Stella remembered the day she'd found the recipe. She'd had the cookies before, of course—mostly in Roman and Milanese bakeries—but she'd never made them herself. Which was funny considering not only their tastiness but also how much she'd always delighted in the name which translated to "ugly but good."

Then, a month ago, she and Cosimo, Aramezzo's antiquarian, had gone through her house, top to bottom, emptying all drawers, rooting to the shadowy backs of closets, and lifting all loose floorboards. Their mission? Nothing less than to unearth family treasures—primarily a mysterious medallion that Cosimo remembered belonged to her grand-mother. But also, it seemed baffling that the house would have passed from her grandparents to her aunt to her, and there would be so few mementos. There had to be *something*, tucked away and forgotten.

Barbanera had supervised their work, running back and forth between them, sniffing at old linens, his tail puffing to twice its already enormous size. They hadn't found any jewelry or photographs, which disappointed Cosimo. As for Stella, she found something even better—a handwritten (by her aunt? Her grandmother? Her *great*-grandmother?) recipe for *brutti ma buoni* tucked in a yellowing linen napkin. Cosimo's lined face only briefly noted Stella's glee, before he threw open yet another cupboard with vigor Stella would have assumed possible only in a much younger man. Then again, Cosimo did love his antiques. He'd regretfully offered her a hundred euros for the linens, but Stella refused. She loved the fading gloss of the old napkins, the feel of their history beneath her fingers.

Now she ran her fingers down two of the napkins, embroidered with pink and blue flowers. Barbanera rose and lashed his tail. His single ear perked forward suggested the tail whipping was more anticipation than grudge.

"I guess you've forgiven me for the substandard meal?"

He glared at her balefully, lifting his head.

She chuckled at the sight of the black patch on his chin, the reason she'd named him Blackbeard. Well, that and his one ear. "Dinner will be better, I promise."

He stood and nosed the door. Taking the hint, Stella opened it.

On the stoop, they both stopped to lift their noses. Stella breathed in the tendrils of breeze, carrying the scent of growing olives, cobblestones still drying from last night's brief shower, and a neighbor roasting meaty red peppers. She wondered what Barbanera smelled. Whatever it was, it must be good, given his closed eyes.

She walked the road around to the post office, greeting neighbors as she strolled, Barbanera trotting beside her. No one lifted an eyebrow at the sight of the big cat keeping pace with Stella's steps.

Stella glanced at the police station as they passed. She told herself that she wasn't looking for Luca, not really. No sign of him; though she did see a tall, unfamiliar man striding toward the station, uniform straining against his frame, not the least distracted by the sight of a five-foot-two-inch woman in a red threadbare bandana with a silver-spotted tabby jogging at her heels.

The new captain.

It must be.

Stella dearly hoped she'd never need to interact with him. Captain Palmiro, with his hot temper which made him easy to fluster and divert, had been challenging enough.

Barbanera stopped at the door of the post office and settled in for a flurry of cleaning. Stella stepped into the cramped and stuffy room alone. The postmistress glanced up from stamping paperwork. With a smile, she said, "Ciao, Stella!"

Stella felt a prick of guilt when she couldn't remember the young woman's name, but then noticed the name tag affixed to her uniform pocket. "Ciao, Eleanora. I have a—"

"Oh!" Eleanora spun in her seat to the fabric bins behind her. "You have a package!" Stella breathed a sigh of relief. Eleanora continued, "The carrier brought it back because the street name was misspelled."

Makes sense, Stella thought. Italian words seemed a blur of vowels to non-Italians.

Eleanora rummaged around in the bins before pulling out a small brown parcel. She checked the address and said, "Ah, it came from China! Is it an ingredient for something new you're baking?" Before Stella could answer, Eleanora ran on, "I loved the *brutti ma buoni* cookies you brought to Leo's birthday party. Don't tell my grandmother, but they were better than hers."

Right! That's where she'd met Eleanora, Leo's birthday party. She had been surprised to be included but figured Leo's girlfriend, Marta, must have added her name to the list.

Stella wanted to tell Eleanora that the ingredient that likely differentiated her *brutti ma buoni* recipe from Eleanor's grandmother's, was simple—a pinch of salt. Umbrians' relationship with salt was storied, as she'd been told a zillion times whenever she passed on saltless, Umbrian bread. It made Stella wonder if the relative who'd handwritten the cookie recipe was secretly a culinary rebel.

Before she could tell Eleanora the secret ingredient, the postmistress rushed on, "My grandmother is great with lasagna, but her cakes sink in the middle and taste like sand." She thought for a moment, and Stella wondered if she could now extricate herself. One thing she hadn't gotten used to in Aramezzo, the time it took for even drive-by interactions; no such thing as a quick errand in an Italian village.

But she needed to get this package to the Staffords.

While Stella scanned her brain for a graceful exit, the door flew open. Veronica, the mayor's wife, swanned into the dingy post office as if it were a stage framed by red velvet curtains. As usual, two russet-colored Dachshunds preceded her. One of them cast a look over its shoulder and Stella wondered if Barbanera had taken a cursory swipe at the dog.

"Eleanora!" Veronica crooned. "Please tell me it's not too late to get this into today's mail."

Eleanora worriedly checked the clock and Stella took the moment to slip out with a farewell wave to Eleanora and a bare nod to Veronica, who ignored her altogether.

Barbanera leapt up to follow Stella as she exited, turning over the package in her hands. It *was* from China. What in the world could the Staffords need from China while they were on holiday? Deep in wondering, she didn't notice Barbanera turn in front of her feet. She stumbled over him and into the arms of a stranger.

"Whoa, there," said a gravelly voice as Stella felt a hand steady her shoulder. She backed up at the unfamiliar voice and realized the strange man stood next to a grinning Matteo, not dressed in his usual blue street sweepers' uniform, but rather pressed jeans and an open-throated shirt in a color that resembled terra cotta.

Matteo chuckled. "Why am I not surprised? Stella, I've been looking for you . . . I want you to meet my oldest friend, Giancarlo."

Giancarlo regarded Stella with serious eyes, his hand still on her shoulder. Discomfited by the awkwardness of his touch, Stella backed up, adjusting her bandana before tucking the package securely under her arm. "Ciao, Giancarlo. I've heard so much about you. I'm sorry about your injury."

He regarded her levelly before smiling a slow smile. "It's healing. The surgery went well and I should be back on the pitch next season."

Stella nodded. "Are you enjoying the time off?"

Giancarlo thought for a moment. "Parts of it."

She watched him, waiting for him to say more. He didn't, giving her plenty of time to notice his strong jaw and steady eyes, the exact shade of oregano, which shone particularly against his skin, bronzed from all those hours playing professional soccer. She couldn't remember for what team. Juventus? AC Milan?

Matteo looked from Stella to Giancarlo and said, "Well! Aren't we off to a roaring start? Stella, can you join us for coffee?"

She shook her head. "I wish I could. I have to get this package to my guests." She held it up feebly.

Matteo nodded. "Another time then. Giancarlo is here for at least a few weeks." He glanced at his friend. "It's your longest visit home in years!"

Giancarlo's gaze stayed on Stella as he nodded.

Stella smiled and excused herself. She felt their eyes on her as she strode away. At the sound of laughter, she realized that her visual appeal may have more to do with the cat improbably jogging at her heels, rather than any of her manifold attractions.

Soon enough, she and Barbanera arrived at the house, and she found the Staffords in the garden, both on their phones. She waved the package and called, "Good news!"

Mrs. Stafford glanced at her husband, and when he didn't move, she rose to take the parcel. "Thanks for going the extra mile, Stella. We do appreciate it. Don't we, Morton?"

He grunted, gaze fixed on the screen.

"My pleasure. It must be pretty important to have it mailed while on vacation," Stella said, hoping she'd masked the curiosity in her voice.

Mrs. Stafford shrugged awkwardly and said, "Oh, it's my fault, really. I forgot to refill my . . . .um, medication, before we left."

Medication? Mrs. Stafford did not sound convincing.

"Well, Stella," Mrs. Stafford said, clearing her throat. "I think we'll take a nap. I hardly slept on the plane," Mrs. Stafford said, pulling her husband's arm.

He pulled his arm back. "What now?" he sighed.

"Morton," Mrs. Stafford said slowly between gritted teeth with a glance at the package. "It's time to go upstairs to rest before dinner. Remember?"

He looked confused for a moment before his face cleared. He slid his phone into his pocket and dutifully climbed the stairs after his wife.

"The Staffords aren't terrible," Stella said to Domenica, dropping a plate of leftover *brutti ma buoni* on the desk. "I almost like the wife. But there's some undercurrent of tension between them I can't figure out."

She sat back in the weathered armchair, and a calico cat interpreted this as an invitation to leap up and stretch across her lap. The circle of light from the lamp in the corner grew sharper as the shadows length-ened. Soon she'd have to start dinner for the Americans. But for now, she had a patch of time to sit with Domenica. And Ravioli. Stella didn't like to play favorites, but she had to admit, the patchwork calico, of all Domenica's cats, held a special place in her heart.

Domenica stood at her desk, covered with books and a computer hidden by a blanket and a smattering of scarves. She regarded Stella. "How could they leave even one *brutti ma buoni* behind? The ones you made for the wild asparagus festival..." Domenica's gaze drifted up into the middle distance as she remembered Aramezzo's festival the previous month.

Stella grinned. "Pistachio. Clearly the winner. Even though the nuts didn't make the cookies green like I'd hoped." She remembered setting the cookies down on one of the tables lining the piazza, disappointed at how ordinary they looked.

"Who cares? Everyone loved them so much, they hardly noticed how few asparagus stalks you collected."

Stella shook her head sadly. "I thought I'd have a knack for it. Given how much wild asparagus I've handled in my career. So humiliating."

Chuckling, Domenica said, "Oh, Stella. When will you learn? We like you better for your imperfections."

Stella stroked Ravioli as she remembered how she had practically stamped her foot in frustration when she'd investigated a patch of piney foliage and found not one stalk, only to have Marta come behind her and snap off three. At first the laughter had stung, but when Stella noticed Matteo with his arms crossed in satisfaction, she had seen not only the humor in the situation but also the community that comes from teaching and learning.

"Still. Four stalks." Unlike Adele, Trattoria Cavour's chef, who col-lected a bundle as large as a baby. Stella had started counting Adele's stalks but lost track at a hundred and decided it would be more fun to accept a plastic cup of wine and gaze over the edge of the piazza to the Umbrian valley, holder of so many hidden riches.

Sorting books on the desk, Domenica said, "It's not a competition."

Stella remembered any lingering bitterness from the "hunt" dissipating as she sat at the table between Don Arrigo, the village priest, and Romina, who owned the bar with her husband Roberto. At table, Stella gloried in those blades of purple-green asparagus filling frittatas and adorning freshly cut tagliatelle with their grassy, herbaceous lilt. She'd never forget the moment Adele and her sister took a break from cooking and asked Stella to step in.

Being part of a brigade on a stainless-steel restaurant line, it turned out, had nothing on the thrill of cooking on a battered pan set over a propane tank, as the music of swallows crackled like electricity in the gathering night air, bringing forth the brightest of stars. In those few frittata-making moments, Stella felt at home, surrounded by the burble of village chatter, punctuated by an old woman in navy calling out for Stella to not be so stingy with the olive oil.

And all that before her platter of *brutti ma buoni* got passed around to the increasing hush of the villagers seated along the tables.

A feast.

In every sense of the word.

"Anyway, lucky for you, my guests didn't plow through the *brutti ma buoni* like everyone did at the *sagra*." She thought about that bowl of cookies, hardly touched, alongside the sandwich platter, decimated, the meat eaten out of the middle, the triangles of flatbread lying forlornly on the platter. She sighed. "I forgot how fixated Americans are with their waistlines."

"Waistline? What's that?" Domenica peered down at her generous hips before cackling.

Casually, Stella said, "Say. Have you met Matteo's friend? Giancarlo?"

Domenica glanced up from the books in her hands. Stella prepared for a telling remark from her friend, but Domenica adopted Stella's casual air. "Years ago. Briefly."

Stella nodded, slowly.

"A nice enough looking boy," Domenica said, her eyes sliding to Stella.

Stella was horrified to find herself blushing.

"Though he doesn't read," Domenica said. As if that was that, the young man's worth as a human summed up by his ability to resist the charms of a good book.

Stella tried to work out what to say next when she noticed Matteo and Giancarlo walking up the street. She leapt up, Ravioli falling to the ground with a protesting yowl, and touched her hands to her face, hoping to cool the rising blush. "Oh, Domenica, I need to ask Matteo...something."

Domenica glanced up at the men approaching and chuckled to herself. "I'm sure you do."

Stella burst out of Domenica's shop, landing in front of the young men.

Matteo grinned. "Well, hello there, Stella. Are you in a rush?"

Stella worked on slowing her breath. "Oh! No. I'm...on my way..."

Giancarlo smiled his slow smile. "To Bar Cappellina, I hope?"

Stella blinked. "Yes. Exactly."

Matteo frowned playfully. "But Stella, you don't drink coffee after noon. It makes you not sleep."

Giancarlo said, "She will have wine."

Trying not to grin and hoping her blush was more rosy glow than illicit red, Stella said, "Yes, exactly. Wine."

She fell in step with the men, Matteo hugging her against his side for a moment before letting his arm fall. He told Giancarlo about Stella's history working in New York restaurants, leaving off the unsavory bits, less appropriate for new company—the harassment, the blackballing, the flight to Aramezzo. Then he told his friend about Stella's baking.

Giancarlo said, "It's lucky I'm here now. When I'm playing, I have to be strict with my diet. Hopefully, Stella, I can try something you make?"

Stella cursed herself for giving Domenica all the cookies and mumbled something unintelligible.

Giancarlo gestured for Stella to enter the bar, his hand grazing her arm. Heads turned as they walked in, and then did a double take at Giancarlo. Most people nodded in recognition of their own before turning back to their coffee. But Stella noticed a group of four strangers at the end of the bar. Not locals.

In fact, they could be stamped cut-outs of her guests. She heard Matteo mutter under his breath, "*Madonna mia*. Here we go."

The four blond heads ducked together for a moment before the man strode over, his hand stuck out in front of him. "Giancarlo Casserino? Am I right?" The English words landed like flat boulders into the rolling Italian all around them. Stella hadn't realized until then how this bar, with Romina and Roberto at the helm, embodied everything she loved about Italy. The warmth, the welcome, the smell of coffee, the seasonal offerings in the display case alongside standard favorites like tuna and artichoke sandwiches. How strange to have English echoing among the medieval stones of this former church-turned-cafe.

Giancarlo nodded. Was it her imagination, or did Stella catch a wisp of resignation behind his eyes? Matteo moved to the bar to leave his friend at the mercy of the American man who hadn't introduced himself. Perhaps he thought his identity was obvious. Instead, he said, "That goal you made for Liverpool against Manchester United. Genius."

Offering a wry grin, Giancarlo said in British-accented English, "At a cost. It was my last goal before this…" he gestured to his leg. "And now I'm out until next season."

Stella whispered to Matteo. "He speaks English?"

Matteo frowned. "Of course. He's lived in England for the last five years."

Why had Stella assumed he played for an Italian team? Probably because before this morning, Giancarlo had been a name, a buddy of Matteo's, his claim to fame not so much his career as a pro soccer player but his status as Matteo's best childhood friend. The first person Matteo confided in about his sexuality, the person who stood barrier between Matteo and the other boys who teased Matteo about what they did not understand. With Giancarlo on his team, Matteo had felt strong enough to treat what made him different in a casual way. As if it signified no more about him than his preference for large, cured capers alongside his Aperol spritzes, rather than olives.

Stella tuned back into the performance in the center of the bar. The American, Matteo whispered in her ear, was TC Durant, owner of Villa delle Acque and host of the upcoming party. TC waved over his wife and two giggling teenage daughters. He boomed, "My wife, Chelsea. And our girls, Micah and Shiloh. Come meet Giancarlo." Their voices of introduction and handshaking blurred together as Stella thanked Roberto, who brought her and Matteo glasses of wine, leaving a third for Giancarlo, with bowls of peanuts and chips.

Giancarlo reached for his wine, giving Matteo a meaningful look. Matteo sighed, knocked back a large mouthful of wine, and joined his friend in the middle of the bar. Romina clasped Stella's hand. "What's on tonight's menu?"

"Pasta. With a sausage *sugo*." She checked her phone. "I should get going in a minute."

"These Americans eat so early." Romina patted Stella's hand as she said, "I'll never forget the sausage *sugo* you brought when our grandson was in that accident. The only part of the whole ordeal that felt normal, like everything would be all right."

Stella grinned. "And it *was* all right. I saw your grandson last week at the *forno*."

"He always picks up a loaf when he comes to visit. Roman bread, it's not so good."

"Too much salt?" Stella grinned and sipped her wine. It was an old argument between them. To Stella's mind, Umbrian bread worked for bruschetta, when it was drizzled with green olive oil and sprinkled generously with salt, but little else.

Romina shook her finger at Stella before her face stilled. "He's still riding that blasted motorcycle, though. You'd think he'd learn."

Stella popped a chip into her mouth. "Ah, youth. So irrepressible."

Romina grinned. "He's your age."

Shrugging, Stella said, "I, too, am irrepressible."

Chuckling, Romina moved to the register to ring up customers.

Stella checked the time again. She wondered if she'd made enough sausage sauce for her to have a serving. She hoped so. When alone, she usually ate chickpeas or tuna out of a can. A bit of pasta could do her good.

She heard Mrs. Durant gush, "Oh, you two simply *have* to come to our party! No, I *insist!*"

Giancarlo quickly translated for Matteo and the two exchanged glances, which Mrs. Durant either didn't notice or ignored. "It's a *masquerave!* Get it? Old-style masquerade costumes, touches of neon, or your creative interpretation of the brief. Historic decor, modern music. Everyone is talking about how it's going to be our best blowout ever. Some really quality people are coming from America, you know. And we've invited a few select locals."

Lowering his eyes—Stella tried not to notice the fringe of his lashes resting on his high cheekbone—Giancarlo translated for Matteo. They both started making excuses, a garble of English and Italian. Stella smiled before taking a final sip of wine and tossing the last few chips into her mouth. She handed five euros to Romina at the register and began sidling out of the bar. Matteo yanked her by the arm, pulling her into the center of the room.

With four sets of piercing blue eyes on her, along with Matteo's round brown eyes and Giancarlo's deep-set green ones, Stella's mouth went dry, and she struggled to swallow the half-chewed chips.

Matteo put an arm around Stella and said in halting English. "You have never met Stella?" He knew very well they hadn't.

Stella coughed, chip shards exploding around her mouth as the four Americans ran their gazes over her from the bandana holding back her chaotic curls to her scuffed Doc Martens. They mumbled greetings, and the mother said, "Right. Stella. We've heard about you. The American horning in on the piece of authentic Italy we claimed for ourselves." Her laugh sounded like gears grinding. "I'm joking, of course."

The coughing kept Stella from answering. Which was probably a good thing, as what Stella wanted to say would probably make her a fixture of bar talk well into the next olive harvest. Matteo pounded on her back until she doubled over. Stella caught sight of Giancarlo, who must have read the unsaid tirade in her eyes because he licked the corner of his lip before grinning. Even in her anger and choking, Stella noticed his dimples. Luca only had one dimple. Why was she thinking of dimples now, of all times? Matteo handed her a glass of water Roberto had placed on the bar. Stella gulped while glaring at Matteo over the glass's rim. If not for him, she could have slipped out without this mess.

Finally, Stella stammered out flatly, "It's a pleasure."

Mrs. Durant took Stella by the elbow and pulled her aside. Stella almost began coughing again at the cloud of perfume settling over the two of them. "Listen, I'm sure you're expecting an invite to the party. But we limit the number of Americans to our friends who come all this way. It's not a networking event. You understand."

Stella's eyes widened, but before she could answer, the door opened and Mimmo strode in, dispelling the arching strands of perfume with his heavy musk of dirt and animals and motor oil. Mrs. Durant recoiled to the safety of her husband's side at the sight of Mimmo, his buttons thankfully done up properly today, though it was hard to notice this advantage given the dirt streaks that patterned his already filthy flannel shirt and worn camouflage pants.

Mimmo took one look at the Americans, turned on his heel, and left.

The Americans, as one, lifted their hands to the bottoms of their nostrils. "Well!" Mrs. Durant said. "I see he's still allowed to wander all over Aramezzo."

"Chelsea, I didn't tell you what happened yesterday," Mr. Durant said. "He literally marched up to me and said I couldn't use the pool—my own pool, that I paid for—because there's a litter of wild boar in the forest and the noise would scare them into running across the road."

Mrs. Durant made a clicking noise at the back of her throat. "He speaks English? I must say, I find that rather surprising."

The older of the two daughters said, "One of the gardeners translated. And, Daddy, tell Mom about how he *lost* it when he saw the projectors. I thought the vein in his forehead was gonna pop! That man is so *weeeeeeird*. The way he's always watching us and giving us side-eye."

Stella closed her eyes and concentrated on breathing, tamping down the curl of what must be resentment, but what did she care what anyone said about old Mimmo with his bulbous nose and dubious ethics?

Nevertheless, before any more arms could stop her, she darted out after him. He looked surprised to find her beside him but nodded in acknowledgment. Stella gestured back to the bar. "You couldn't take the heat?"

He stopped and looked around. "This isn't hot, Stella. Wait until July."

She'd forgotten how literal he could be. "I meant . . . never mind. How has the hunting been?"

Darting a suspicious look at her. "You've never cared before."

"Are you kidding? Your hunting means *cinghiale* salami and I wanted to ask what you'd trade for another batch."

Mimmo scratched his belly and studied her.

She lowered her voice. "In all my restaurant work, I've never had better."

He nodded. "I like them cookies you've been making. You brought them to the wild asparagus festival. I only got one."

He said it as an accusation. Nevertheless, a grin lit Stella's face. "*Brutti ma buoni.* You got it. What do you say, a few dozen for a salami? That sound fair?"

"You can't give any to those Americans," Mimmo scowled, gesturing with his chin to the Durant family, still glaring at him through the window. "They should never have come. None of them belong here."

Stella's stomach twisted, though she couldn't say why.

"Never. Just for me." She put out her hand.

He looked at her offered hand curiously before walking away, calling over his shoulder, "I'll have some ready next week. Bring the cookies by."

"Good morning, Stella!" Mrs. Stafford said as she reached the bottom of the stairs.

Stella looked up from setting the breakfast table. "Good morning, Mrs. Stafford. Coffee?" Stella asked.

"Black, please. And none for Mr. Stafford. Coffee makes him jumpy."

Stella had a sudden image of a grasshopper and couldn't quite square it with the ponderous form of Mr. Stafford.

Mrs. Stafford beamed at the tray of warm *cornetti*. "How beautiful! You couldn't have made all this."

"I did." Luckily, within a month of having regular guests, Stella had learned the value of blitz-baking sprees to fill the freezer, making for easier mornings than her previous pattern of folding butter into dough at four in the morning.

"Delightful." Mrs. Stafford pulled a corner off the pastry. She chewed for a moment before saying, "Did I read on your website that you trained in New York?"

Nodding as she put the moka coffeepot back on the range, Stella said, "And Italy. Not for pastries, though. For that, I am self-taught."

Mrs. Stafford tugged a flake off the *cornetto* and laid it on her tongue. "You must be a good teacher." She smiled. "And a good student."

At the sound of footsteps, Stella greeted Mr. Stafford. He nodded at her, his eyes scanning the breakfast table, aglow in the sunlight. Stella thought Mrs. Stafford seemed part of the tableau, her daisy-yellow dress matching the flowers at the center of the table. Mr. Stafford didn't seem to notice the charm of the setting as he sat, drawing the phone from his pocket.

"At the table?" groaned Mrs. Stafford. "The markets aren't open yet."

Mr. Stafford mumbled something about keeping on top of things, but he put his phone away and said, "Are these plain croissants?"

Stella resisted the urge to describe the differences between French croissants and Italian *cornetti*. "They are. But here are jams and Nutella, if you'd prefer them filled."

Mrs. Stafford frowned. "Don't eat too much, Morton. We're meeting the Lakes at the coffee shop. Maybe Chelsea and TC too, if they can get away."

He tore a *cornetto* and shoved half into his mouth. "Already with the Lakes? We're seeing them at the party, isn't that enough?"

Mrs. Stafford frowned. "You said you'd be nice."

"I'm here, aren't I?"

Stella busied herself at the stove before bringing a pitcher of juice to the table. Mr. Stafford's plate was littered with *cornetto* crumbs, while his wife's still held the full *cornetto* minus one corner and one flake.

Mrs. Stafford smiled up at Stella, "Stella, darling. Can I get some cottage cheese, if it's not too much trouble?"

Stella said, "Oh! I'm sorry. I don't have any cottage cheese. It's not very common here."

"It's not?" Mrs. Stafford frowned. "How strange. Well, I'll take some Greek yogurt, then."

Darting a glance at her refrigerator, stocked with many things apparently not on her guest's preferred breakfast list, Stella said, "I have regular yogurt. Plain, or I think apricot." Stella watched as a line appeared between Mrs. Stafford's eyebrows.

Her guest hadn't noted any eating restrictions on Stella's booking form, but perhaps Mrs. Stafford had been dieting for so long, she'd forgotten her particular restrictions weren't universal.

"Have a carb, Claire," growled Mr. Stafford to his wife. "It won't kill you."

At the word, Mrs. Stafford blanched.

His eyes widened. "I'm sorry, darling, I only—"

"I heard you," she snapped.

Stella turned away, trying to settle her breath. Would she ever be able to hear the word *kill* without this sort of reaction?

She cleared her throat. "I'm happy to strain yogurt for you for tomorrow. That will approximate Greek yogurt. In the meantime, can I offer you an omelet, perhaps?"

Mrs. Stafford glared at her husband before shaking her head. He watched her over the rim of his glass as he gulped juice. The eye contact felt charged. What did it mean?

Hoping to steer this boat into smoother waters, Stella asked, "So how do you know the Durant family?"

"Chelsea and I were in school together," Mrs. Stafford said, leaning against her chair. "At Grier. With Judith, who we're seeing this morning. What a crew we made! Chelsea was the darling of our theater program. By our senior year, I'm sure the director was selecting plays to showcase Chelsea." Her voice warmed with pride. "And Judith won every science fair. Plus, she was valedictorian. Why the two of them chose me as their third, I'll never know."

Mr. Stafford's eyes blazed as he muttered, "You are the best of all of them."

"I did okay." Mrs. Stafford waved off his praise, though Stella noticed the last of the tension leave her, her shoulders relaxed to a more normal position.

"Okay? You got a scholarship to Northwestern. That's more than okay.

And you're the only one of them who can hold a conversation."

Stella had never heard him utter so many words in a row, even when he was asking about the Wi-Fi.

"That's not fair. Judith can hold a conversation," Mrs. Stafford said, taking a sip of her coffee before looking up at Stella. "I used to never sit Morton and Judith together at parties. The two of them would start in on whatever smart people talk about, and no one could join in."

He shrugged. Perhaps he'd run out of words.

"The accident changed things," Mrs. Stafford went on softly.

Mr. Stafford shook his head. "Not the accident. Her jerk husband. She should have left him long ago. It's not like she's Catholic or something."

Mrs. Stafford's gaze darted to Stella as if worried about offending her host. Stella kept her face neutral. She wasn't Catholic, though she often attended Don Arrigo's services since she'd discovered how full she felt after an hour in those worn pews, sunlight streaming through the stained-glass windows, the air filled with centuries of incense. Not to mention the painting of the woman who looked eerily like Stella's mother in a far niche.

Mrs. Stafford laughed off her husband's comment. "Just because *you* don't like Hollis…"

He laughed, mouth full of *cornetto*. "He hasn't exactly made me a friendship bracelet either, you know."

Stella looked from one to the other, wondering what happened to sour his relationship with Mrs. Stafford's childhood friend and her husband. Mrs. Stafford's eyes darkened as she pressed her napkin to her lips. She cleared her throat and said, "Stella, I wonder if you'd mind walking us to the bar where we're meeting Judith? I can't remember the name, but I'm sure it's on my phone somewhere." She took out her phone and began scrolling through it.

Stella laughed. "No need, there's only one bar in Aramezzo. I'll happily walk you there." Not quite happily, Stella realized. If the Staffords' relationship with the Lakes was as fraught as it appeared, she'd rather stay home in the company of her one-eared cat.

As if summoned, Barbanera appeared from the bedroom. He curled his body around the doorjamb, his gaze fixed on the guests. Mrs. Stafford remarked, "What a large cat! Maine Coon, I suppose?"

Stella assumed this must be a breed of cat. She shook her head. "There's a story about the cat population of Aramezzo breeding with a small wildcat that lives on Monte Subasio." At Mrs. Stafford's look of interest, Stella added, "I don't know how true it is, especially the part about the wildcats being summoned by a saint named Chiara to rid Aramezzo of the flea-carrying rats. All I know is Aramezzo has a number of big cats, all with silver-spotted markings like Barbanera."

Mrs. Stafford hadn't blinked during Stella's recitation. "How fascinating. Simple country people do love their folklore, don't they, Morton?"

Stella opened the fridge to hide her sudden scowl. Swallowing her impulsive responses was the hardest part of running a bed-and-breakfast. She reminded herself that Mrs. Stafford hadn't meant anything by her comment. Still, Stella couldn't help thinking of Cosimo, who had told her the legend. The candy-floss-haired antiquarian was anything but simple. Stella pulled at the pendant he'd insisted she wear to ward off bad luck. She couldn't love the odd design, but it felt like a part of her, an echo of his care, and her care for the neighbors she'd befriended in Aramezzo. Maybe they were country people. But none of them were simple.

When the Staffords went upstairs to freshen up, Stella set out a mint green porcelain saucer of peas and beef tongue. As Barbanera hunched over the plate, she washed the dishes, thinking about what she'd learned over breakfast. She supposed it made sense that the owner of Villa delle Acque had been a drama sensation in high school, given the theatrics of their annual parties.

The party.

She still couldn't figure out why the thought of it filled her with foreboding. She'd assumed the dread came from associating the party with the funeral where she'd first learned of the event—the mayor's wife waving the invitation around as if to tempt envy when the town just wanted to grieve one of their own. Now, though, she wondered if it had more to do with all this edgy energy—between Mimmo and the Durants, between her guests, between her guests and the Lakes. At least now it made sense that the Staffords had opted to stay with her rather than the Durants' villa, where they'd mingle with people Mr. Stafford found objectionable. It didn't, however, explain why they decided to attend the party at the last minute.

Stella envisioned the partygoers together, all those previously beaten down sparks blazing forth, everyone's inhibitions lowered by alcohol and the masks she assumed they'd be wearing. Stella dried her hands. Maybe it was the masks that shortened her breath. She'd never liked masquerade trappings—even the elegant ones ladies wore, not to mention the disturbing plague doctor mask with the long nose like a malevolent bird.

She wondered if Giancarlo would go to the party. What would he wear? What would he be like without inhibitions? Stella felt a different kind of shortness of breath.

This was silly.

She didn't even know Giancarlo.

Sure, he was good-looking. If one liked knowing eyes and strong arms.

More than that, Stella realized, he seemed unflappable. As someone always flapping, she found that intriguing.

The Staffords appeared, and the three of them stepped into the fresh morning air. Mrs. Stafford breathed deeply. "Wow, the air smells good here, doesn't it Morton?"

Mr. Stafford didn't respond, but he did slip his phone into his pocket. Turning on the spot, he asked, "This road goes all the way around Aramezzo?"

Stella put on her tour guide apron. "It does. The homes on my side of the road face outward, so they have land for raising chickens or growing olives. A little further past the stairs, my friend Marta has sheep and lavender. This part of Aramezzo is kind of like half town, half country. On the other side of the road, the houses hug the mountain, so they have no land. But those are mostly services like the butcher shop, the bakery, the post office."

The Staffords kept step on either side of her. She went on, "We'll climb stairs like the ones we took yesterday to access the second ring road."

"I saw those stairs! Right when we got out of the tunnel!" Mrs. Stafford said.

"That's right. This second ring road is where you'll find more shops plus our one restaurant—which I suggest for your dinner tonight if you'd like a change of pace—and the cafe we're headed to, Bar Cappellina. If we kept climbing the third and last set of stairs, we'd reach Chiesa di Santa Chiara di Aramezzo. That's the church dedicated to Santa Chiara, the saint I was talking about earlier."

"The one who summoned the cats?" Mrs. Stafford asked.

"Exactly," Stella smiled.

"Charming!" Mrs. Stafford breathed, as they came out of the tunnel to the second ring road. "Oh! There they are!"

Mr. Stafford scowled at the group of three people standing in front of the flower shop—a man about his own age, dressed in expensive jeans sitting just so on his hips, dark blue designer shirt with white polka dots cuffed effortlessly to his elbows, his watch gleaming authoritatively on his wrist. On one side of him stood a younger man, dressed so similarly to him that Stella wondered if they'd inadvertently donned clothes they'd purchased while shopping together. Flanking the older gentleman's other side stood a woman in a camel-colored cape of some material Stella longed to stroke.

"Hello!" Mrs. Stafford rushed toward them. "Isn't it wonderful! We're all here!"

A round of cheek kissing followed, though Stella noticed that Mr. Stafford and the older gentleman pointedly ignored each other. Mr. Stafford wandered off to study a poster advertising a meeting of the communist party. Mrs. Stafford pulled Stella closer, announcing, "This is Stella! We're staying in her adorable bed-and-breakfast. Stella, this is my friend Judith Lake's husband Hollis. And her two children, Gillian and Tripp."

Tripp? Must be one of those fancy options for a third son, when parents run out of biblical names. Hollis Lake and his children nodded at Stella without much interest before turning back to the florist, where the light had switched on.

"Aren't we meeting at the cafe? Is Chelsea coming? Where's Judith?" Mrs. Stafford looked around as if expecting her friend to pop out from behind a closed door.

The man shrugged. "We're waiting for the florist to open to confirm the delivery. Judith is coming with Louisa."

The caped woman snorted. "Where is Rebo the Magic Clown, anyway? We've been waiting for ages."

"Would you stop calling my wife that, Gillian?" the younger man said through clenched teeth even as his father chuckled.

Gillian said, "Oh, but it's too good. Leave it to you to marry a girl who used to make her spending money doing magic shows for neighborhood kids. Come on, Tripp. Remember how you'd order the housekeepers to make lemonade for you to sell? It's priceless, the two of you finding each other. Both forever scrabbling for pennies."

He said, "Easy for you to say. For you, Daddy's wallet is always open."

Mr. Lake snarled, "Below the belt, Tripp. That promotion I gave you is new. I can take it away at any time."

Gillian batted her eyelashes at her father. "You tell him, Daddy."

Mr. Lake's eyes flared, with anger or enjoyment, Stella couldn't tell, as he said, "You watch it too, young lady. Or maybe I won't fund your next art spectacle."

Stella watched as Mrs. Stafford shifted uncomfortably.

Finally, Mrs. Stafford said to Tripp, "Does Louisa need help with Judith? Morton and I—"

Mr. Lake waved his hand dismissively. "She'll be here any minute. Dawdling, I'm sure. Go on, they'll be there soon enough."

Mrs. Stafford hesitated, but when her husband started walking away, she called over her shoulder, "I can't wait to see your costumes tomorrow!" Then she muttered softly to Mr. Stafford, "Judith needs to put her foot down. One of her kids should be helping her, not her son's wife."

"Especially not this daughter-in-law," Mr. Stafford agreed.

"It worked okay for a while. Before the baby got colic," Mrs. Stafford said. "It's too much for Louisa, caring for the children and her mother-in-law."

"Well," said Stella awkwardly. "Here we are."

The piazza opened onto a view of rolling olive groves. Beyond them lay fields of foothills and craggy mountains. The vista rarely failed to slow her pulse, beating in an ancient rhythm far from the static of headlines or the press of village gossip. At the moment, though, it couldn't dispel the shadows cast by the walls looming all around them.

As they stepped into Bar Cappellina, Mrs. Stafford's eyes searched the wall above the baristas' white heads. Nothing but liquor bottles and a display of old photographs. "Stella," Mrs. Stafford said, gripping Stella's arm. "Where's the menu?"

"No menu, they offer the same as every other Italian bar."

"Without a price list?" Mr. Stafford huffed. "That's a good way to cheat customers."

Stella pressed her lips together. How could it matter to these people if the bar even doubled their charge from one euro to two? *Patience, patience.* "This is how it's done. How it's been done for forever. There is a price list somewhere, I think . . ." She looked around and spotted it tacked up on the wall, faded by the sunlight streaming in the windows.

The Staffords scanned the list. "It's in Italian!" exclaimed Mrs. Stafford. "Do they have decaf? Morton cannot have caffeine."

"I can have a little. Maybe a latte?" Mr. Stafford said, in a way that suggested he didn't so much want a latte as that he didn't want to be told what to do.

"No lattes here," Stella explained as Mr. Stafford interrupted. "It's right here, *latte*. One euro. That seems cheap." He frowned, as if both Stella and the menu were conspiring against him.

Stella shot an apologetic glance at Romina, who grinned her understanding while foaming milk for Leo's cappuccino. Concentrating on speaking evenly, Stella said, "*Latte* is milk, which you can have warm or cold. In the United States, it's come to mean coffee with a lot of milk, and you can undoubtedly find that in Italian bars that cater to tourists, but here, it's plain milk. The closest thing you'll find to an American latte on this menu is a cappuccino."

"Decaf?" Mrs. Stafford clarified. At her husband's opening his mouth, she said, "I already *had* coffee. I can't have two. And all that milk! Do they have oat milk?" Her eyes scanned the menu.

"No decaf. They have it in bigger cities, but here, if you don't want caffeine, you have tea or hot chocolate or milk. Or wine, if you're into that in the morning." Mr. Stafford's eyes lit up. Stella went on, "And no, no oat milk." Anticipating Mrs. Stafford's next question, Stella said, "It's all from a cow. And it's all full-fat."

"I'm having a cappuccino," declared Mr. Stafford with a glance at his wife.

Stella nodded. "You'll like it. In the States, you need to add all that extra milk to a coffee to hide the bitterness. But the coffee here is so good, a little milk does the trick."

Mrs. Stafford shook her head, sadly. "Only at Starbucks can you get what you want."

Stella's smile tightened. "Shall I order for you?"

At Mrs. Stafford's nod and Mr. Stafford drawing his phone from his pocket, Stella called Romina over. "After much deliberation," she said, noting how soothing it felt to glide into Italian tones, "my guests will each have a cappuccino."

Stella cast a glance over her shoulder and saw the Staffords had moved to the gelato case, Mrs. Stafford pointing out this flavor and that, trying to pronounce the foreign words. Mr. Stafford didn't seem to be listening as his eyes scanned the liquor bottles.

Romina went on, "And for you, *cara*?"

"Just a *latte caldo*, please Romina. I need to settle my stomach."

As she angled the cups under the espresso machine, Romina said, "Feeling okay?"

"Just a little stressed. It's probably nothing," Stella sighed. "At least nothing overt. It's all their . . . little barbs. I feel wrong-footed."

Leo sidled over to Stella. "You know what I think?"

Stella concentrated on exhaling, so Leo's cologne didn't make her dizzy. She liked it better when he smelled like his *porchetta* truck's herbs and caramelizing pork fat. "What's that?" she asked.

"I think you've been here too long," he said.

"Leonardo!" Romina snapped, her eyes darkening.

He held his hands up in a gesture of defense. "I was kidding. You can stay as long as you want. *Love* the cookies. I'm saying maybe you've gotten used to Italy. And now, these people are reminders of the Americanness you'd rather forget."

Stella's mouth dropped open. How *dare* he!

Romina poured the warmed milk into the *latte* glass and the cappuccino cups, sprinkling cocoa on Stella's milk. "There, *cara*, that will soothe your nerves." To Leo, she said, "Leo, *basta*. Enough. Save the mind games for the racetrack."

"I retired too young, remember? Got to get my fun where I can." He chuckled and then turned to Stella. "Stella, you know I didn't mean anything by it."

Stella sat on a barstool and ran her lower lip between her teeth. "The thing is, maybe you're not wrong."

He shook his head and placed his hand on her thigh. "I was teasing. You are nothing like them. And you haven't been here too long. Not at all. In fact, I wouldn't mind seeing . . . *more* of you." He squeezed her leg.

She kept her face neutral as she glanced at his hand and then his face, a small smile playing around his lips. Was he teasing her again? She darted a look at Romina who was placing the cappuccinos on a tray and didn't notice.

Stella picked up Leo's hand with her thumb and forefinger as if it were a cloth soaked in rancid cooking oil. "Leave them where I can see them, buddy."

"Ah, come on, Stella. Can't you take a joke?"

She blinked. Jokes were funny. This seemed like a trap.

To cover her confusion, she corralled the Americans to a table with their tray of coffee. The couple sat down, then Mrs. Stafford leapt back up with a squeal as a young woman pushed open the door and practically shoved an older woman through it. Mrs. Lake, presumably, with her daughter-in-law Louisa.

Mrs. Stafford bolted over to her friend, but then put her arms around her carefully, as if she might shatter like spun sugar. Stella felt a swell of relief and realized that she'd half expected Mrs. Lake to be missing a limb or covered with scars. Instead, she looked relatively normal, just moved with a kind of hitch to her shoulder, which slowed her. Mr. Stafford kissed Mrs. Lake's cheek and brought a chair to their table. He brought another one for Louisa, but the younger woman flipped her honeyed hair over her shoulder and ignored the waiting chair.

Mrs. Stafford waved Stella over. "Stella! Stella, I want you to meet my dearest childhood friend, Judith."

Mrs. Lake clasped her friend's hand with a warm look before turning to Stella. Stella had to step closer to hear her. Mrs. Lake's voice, though clear and well-annunciated, seemed to lack force. "Stella," she said. "How nice to meet you."

"A pleasure." Stella smiled before asking, "Can I order you anything to drink or eat?"

Judith looked around the room, cornflower blue eyes wide. "What do you recommend?"

Stella gestured to Mr. Stafford, who had taken a provisional taste of his cappuccino before his eyes widened and he took a bigger sip. "Your friends have cappuccinos, or I could order you an espresso. And they usually stock something seasonal to eat. Are you hungry?"

Mrs. Lake smiled a slow smile. "Always."

Stella couldn't help smiling back. She stood and scanned the display case. Her eyes brightened. "How about *pizza della Pasqua*? It's common at Easter, but Romina found a supplier that makes it so well, it's still in demand, even though it's out of season."

"Pizza?" Mrs. Stafford frowned. Though whether at the prospect of carbs so early in the morning or at Louisa storming back outside to speak urgently into her phone, Stella didn't know.

"That's what it's called, but it's a puffy, cheesy bread. Like a savory cake, really."

Mrs. Lake said, "That sounds perfect. With a cappuccino. *Grazie*, Stella."

As she rose, Stella heard Mrs. Lake tell her friend. "I'm so glad you're finally coming to one of Chelsea's parties. But why aren't you staying at Villa delle Acque with the rest of us?"

Mrs. Stafford coughed. "Oh, you know. We decided so last minute."

Stella walked to the end of the bar away from Leo and caught Romina's attention to place the order. As she waited for Roberto to slice the *pizza della Pasqua* and Romina to make the coffee, Stella wondered about Mrs Lake's accident. Her eyes flicked to the table. The older woman appeared wan, but otherwise whole.

Stella carried the plate and cup to the table, and Mrs. Lake carefully cut a forkful of the pizza. She closed her eyes. "Well, if that isn't the tastiest thing I've ever eaten." She took another bite. "What kind of cheese is this?"

"It's good, isn't it? Different people have different versions, of course, but they almost always use local Pecorino cheese—young, in cubes, and matured, which is grated like Parmesan."

Louisa stormed back into the bar. "Are you ready yet?"

Mrs. Lake regarded her daughter-in-law with barely concealed fury. "Louisa. We just got here. And Hollis—"

Louisa's snort of contempt sounded eerily like her sister-in-law's. "Oh, Judith. A step behind, as usual. They're not coming. TC invited Hollis to some wine bar in Assisi."

Judith's eyes dropped to her lap. "And Tripp? Gillian?"

Louisa shrugged in resignation.

Mrs. Stafford's lips drew thin. "Really, Louisa. Can't Judith finish her coffee? And don't you want something? You need to take care of yourself, too."

Louisa looked away.

Reading acceptance in her silence, Mrs. Stafford said, "Stella, could you order Louisa a coffee? Or something to eat?"

Mrs. Lake brightened. "Louisa! You must have some of this—"

Louisa stared at the half-eaten bread. "Not in the mood for leftovers. Thanks, anyway."

Shaking her head slowly, Mrs. Lake's voice grew tight. "Seriously, Louisa. This tantrumming is unnecessary. It's hardly my fault—"

"Well, it's not mine either. But somehow I'm once again left holding the bag."

"Louisa!" Mrs. Stafford breathed, her face pale.

No one spoke. The *pizza della Pasqua* and the coffee sat forgotten on the table, the milk bubbles in the cappuccino drying against the side of the cup. Stella's mind darted, looking for an excuse to get up, away from the strained interaction.

Mrs. Lake slumped backward, her eyes closing.

Drawing close to Louisa, Morton Stafford said, "Don't you think it's best to get Judith home? You're both tired—"

Louisa let out a bark of laughter. "Tired does not begin to describe it."

Stella felt a shiver down her back.

All eyes watched Louisa—Roberto, Romina, Leo, Stella, and the Staffords. The young woman flushed, wrapping her cardigan around herself, before staring at her feet.

Louisa looked so fragile, so alone, Stella felt herself walking toward her before she'd formed a decision to move. "Hi, Louisa? I'm Stella. Can I order you a coffee or anything?"

Louisa shook her head, but then said. "Okay. A cappuccino, if you don't mind." With a glance at Mrs. Lake, she added with a sigh, "To go."

Whirling on her heel, Stella asked Romina, "Do you have disposable cups?"

"*Certo.* We use them for passing out coffee at the *sagra.*"

Stella remembered now, the tiny plastic cups of espresso handed round with *panpepato*, an Umbrian spiced fruit and nut cake . . . the sense of contentment as she kicked back after a day of "hunting" wild asparagus, the frittata with tender asparagus, sizzled in olive oil. The green of that evening—the asparagus hiding among the roots of olive trees, the olive oil, still young from autumn's pressing, the blue sky tinged with yellow from the sunset.

She sighed. The peace of that evening felt like a million years ago.

As she handed the cup to Louisa, Stella noticed tears in the woman's eyes. "What must you all think of me? But if you knew . . . I thought being abroad, it would be different, that they'd pitch in." She lifted her chin toward Mrs. Lake, whose head had cocked to the side, eyes closed. Louisa went on, "Because I don't work, it lands on me. But Gillian doesn't work. Why can't she take care of her mother? I'm done with…with all of it."

She let the words trail off and Stella winced, filling in the blanks with Louisa's hopelessness, her desperation.

Seeing Stella's face, Louisa paled. "There I go again, running my mouth. Can we chalk it up to jet lag and the fact that I couldn't get ahold of my mom this morning to check on my babies? I'm a mess. I'm such a mess, I hardly recognize myself."

Stella smiled and handed Louisa the caddy of sugar packets. "Coffee will do you good. I hope you can catch a nap later."

Louisa plucked the blue diet sugar and ripped open a corner before tipping it into her miniature cup. "You're so nice. How did you wind up here? No, wait, I need to get Judith back. Tell me at the party."

"Oh, I won't be at the party."

Narrowing her eyes, Louisa said, "Why not?"

"Not on the guest list," Stella said.

Frowning as she stirred her coffee, Louisa said, "That can't be right. Let me talk to—"

"No, please, don't worry," Stella said. "I have plans, anyway." She knew she was an unconvincing liar and hoped her flush of shame wouldn't give her away.

Luckily, Louisa was walking over to Judith. "Wakey wakey," she said loudly.

Judith jumped and looked around in confusion. "I wasn't asleep."

"Sure," Louisa snorted.

Stella watched them walk out, shuffling slowly toward the stairs.

"Poor Judith," sighed Mrs. Stafford, watching them leave. She licked the tip of her index finger before pressing it onto a crumb of *pizza della Pasqua*. Popping it into her mouth, Mrs. Stafford said, "She wouldn't recognize this version of herself."

Stella ventured, "Can I ask what happened?"

The couple exchanged glances. He nodded, and she took that as her cue to tell the story. "The accident. She had the housekeeper's kids over to swim—Judith is like that, she knew the housekeeper couldn't afford camps. One boy got lodged under a pool toy and by the time Judith got him out, he was unconscious. She resuscitated the boy—what was his name?" she asked her husband.

He frowned. "Did we ever know it?"

"Maybe not," Mrs. Stafford conceded. "Anyway, she ran with him to the house, yelling for help. She slipped on the pool deck."

Mrs. Stafford reached for napkins and pressed them against her eyes before going on. "The housekeeper found her curled around the boy, protecting him as she fell. So she took the brunt of the fall on her head."

Mrs. Stafford closed her eyes and waved for her husband to continue the story as she sniffed. Gruffly, he said, "We didn't think she'd make it. She was in a coma for weeks."

"Over time, she came back cognitively. But not physically. She tires easily, naps a lot. And those headaches are getting worse. They knock her out, sometimes for days."

Stella ran her hand over her face. "What a tragic story."

Mrs. Stafford nodded. "Her kids should help more. But Hollis insists his son be at his beck and call, says it's critical for his advancement at the family brokerage house. What Gillian gets up to all day in what they call her artist's loft, I have no idea." She stood suddenly. "Oh! Chelsea didn't come! And I needed to talk to her about my costume. Let's go, Morton. I'll try on the options and send her photos."

Mr. Stafford rose, though he didn't look thrilled about the prospect of snapping photos of his wife in various costumes. For reasons she didn't quite understand, Stella had a sudden image of those photographs burning from the outside in. Photographs of all the masked guests of the party, burning. From the outside in.

With them gone, the silence in the bar bloomed. Stella could feel Leo's eyes on her. She wondered if he was smirking. Crossing her arms over her chest, she blinked slowly, trying to summon the bar's usual warmth.

Only then did Stella realize she'd been stuck with the bill.

"I'm telling you, Domenica, something is not right with the Americans." Stella insisted, flopping onto the armchair in the corner of Domenica's bookshop.

"So you've said."

"But you don't seem to get it!"

Domenica pushed her glasses higher onto her face. "You mean I'm not bending out of shape like you are? That would be true."

Pulling a long-haired white cat onto her lap, Stella said, "You would be if you listened to a word I said."

Domenica rolled her eyes.

"That's not a response," Stella muttered. "And PS, you're not fifteen."

"*Cara,*" Domenica soothed. "These guests, this party, it's tied you in knots. Trust me, my being tied up in those knots with you wouldn't make you feel better."

Stella muttered under her breath.

"You know it's true," Domenica said, standing to shelve a pile of books. "Everybody is always on edge this time of year. This party *demands*. You're bearing more of the brunt of it, of course, having the Staffords stay with you. But still, maybe there's another reason the situation has gotten under your skin."

"Oh, I don't know," Stella said sarcastically. "Maybe because the Americans are snapping at everyone and sticking me with the bill and there's this undercurrent of resentment and hostility layered on top of everything like a broken sauce?"

Domenica turned to face Stella. "There is something else."

"What do you mean?"

"What do I mean, I mean what I mean. There's something else bothering you."

"Pretty sure that's enough, if I'm honest," Stella grumbled.

"Definitely more there." Domenica nodded slowly before turning to shelve a book. "Have you noticed you keep calling them the Americans?"

"They are." Stella frowned.

Domenica turned to smile at Stella. "Check your birth certificate. Maybe you don't want to consider them part of your own background?"

Stella gasped so loudly that Attila flew off her lap. The cat ground to a halt in the middle of the bookstore to lick himself furiously. "Now look what you did," she accused Domenica.

The older woman kept her gaze on Stella. "A little jolt of adrenaline keeps us young."

Stella sagged back in the chair, remembering what Leo said. Perhaps he said it to get under her skin, but even so. Shivering, she thought of what came after. She'd tried to block it, but should have known the memory would rise, like fat separating from stock. "You may be right. But that's not what's bothering me."

Domenica reached on her tiptoes to shove a poetry book on the top shelf. "Care to enlighten me?"

Stella paused.

"Stella?" Domenica turned to look at Stella over the top of her glasses. Then she asked, in English, "Are your spidey senses tingling?"

"Domenica!" Stella's mouth fell open.

"What?" Domenica pushed her glasses up with a grin.

"Again with the obscure reference! In English! Did you get this one from Hugh while you snorkeled along the Great Barrier Reef?"

"You can't talk when you're snorkeling, dear. Quite dangerous."

Stella dismissed Domenica's remark. "When you came up for

air, then."

"Oh, there wasn't a lot of coming up for air. If you know what I mean," Domenica grinned.

It was Stella's turn to roll her eyes. "Unfortunately, I do."

"I mean we did a lot of lovemaking on the sand."

"No more! This is a PG establishment." They filled the bookstore with laughter until Attila looked back over his shoulder with a stare of resentment. "So, are you going to tell me about the Spiderman reference? In English, a language you keep telling me you can't speak."

"Oh, Stella. Can't a woman have a little mystery in her life?"

"Woman, you *are* a mystery. Full stop." Stella laughed. "You can tell me this one. I promise, your reputation as an enigma will not be remotely tarnished."

Domenica pushed her headband further back on her gray hair. "Raul. We used to read comic books while eating lobster rolls on his dock."

"In Maine?"

"Connecticut. You know there's a whole debate about who has the better lobster roll—"

"Who do you think you're talking to? Of course, I know. I also know the answer." Before Domenica could interject, Stella went on, "If the roll is excellent and the lobster is pulled fresh from the ocean, then Connecticut with melted butter. If either of those is substandard, go for the lobster roll with mayonnaise and celery. Which really should be called a lobster *salad* roll, if you ask me."

Domenica suppressed a smile and turned back to the shelves.

"Domenica! You derailed me! Who was this Raul?"

Biting her lip, Domenica said, "Raul. I haven't thought about him in years. I wonder where he is now."

Stella waited for the faraway expression to leave Domenica's face before saying, "How did you have so many relationships go sideways?"

"They didn't go sideways, dear. They ran their course. Now," she said, rubbing her hands together as she returned to her chair. "Who is getting us off book?"

Stella smiled. "It seems to be our habit, doesn't it? You're getting worse than Matteo."

Shaking her finger, Domenica said, "Don't start again. Now, tell me what's bothering you."

Stella patted her legs until Attila decided it was safe to return. "It's probably not a big deal. It happened so fast and then came all the drama with the Americans, which, yes, bothers me because I see the parts I hate about myself in them. Even while I feel so different from them, I can hardly believe we're cut from the same cloth."

"You're not, though. Your mother was as Italian as they get."

"An Italian who hated Italy. I'm not sure how much that counts."

"But she kept Italy alive, *cara*. Your mother hung onto Italian cooking and Italian language and Italian holidays and Italian customs of generosity. Not to you, perhaps," Her voice softened, seeing the shine in Stella's eyes. "Not enough generosity to you by half. But the way she'd feed the immigrants who lined up outside her shop. Stella, you see how you do the same, hefting tureens of soup and sauce all over town to whoever needs nurturance. You *are* Italian."

Stella wiped her eyes irritably.

Domenica went on, "Anyway, these Americans are not like all Americans. They are spoiled and entitled and are so used to getting their way, they assume something is deeply wrong when they don't. These Staffords and Lakes and Durants, and all the rest coming for this party—they certainly don't match the American in you and they don't match what you told me about your father. They lack your tenacity, your creativity, your striving to innovate. They don't match my American lovers either." Domenica said with a saucy wink to make Stella smile.

Stella smiled.

Finally, Stella said, "Anyway, while this was all going down at the bar,

I talked to Leonardo."

"Leo? Okay. And?"

Stella inhaled and said carefully, "It's probably nothing. I know it's probably nothing. But he put his hand on my leg and didn't move it and then said something about wanting to see more of me." She hurried on, "Even as I'm saying it I feel ridiculous. I know Italians are more affectionate than I'm used to. I shouldn't have read anything into it." She dropped her eyes and watched her fingers appear and disappear in Attila's white fur.

"Stella." Domenica commanded.

Stella said nothing.

"Stella. *Cara*. What are you saying?"

"I know! I said I was wrong. Ignore me. Tell me more about Raul. Was he a fisherman like whatever his name on the Chesapeake Bay?"

"Won't work this time," Domenica said firmly. "Stella, listen to your own words. Leo's hand on you felt inappropriate. Which means it crossed a line. Why second guess yourself?"

Stella shook her head, not trusting herself to speak, and stared at the cat in her lap.

"*Cara*." Domenica moved forward until her eyes met Stella's. "I'm sorry this happened. Leo is a huge flirt, always has been. And that means he crosses boundaries without the awareness or insight we would wish for him. I'd hoped—rather erroneously, as it happens—that being with Marta had steadied him."

Stella's phone buzzed, and she tugged it from her pocket. She glanced at it and frowned. "Speak of the devil."

Domenica clapped her hands over her mouth and peered around before whispering between her fingers, "*Leo?*"

"Come now, Domenica," Stella tried to smile. "You know too much about hacking and surveillance to assume anyone is bugging our conversation. No, I meant Marta. She wants me to help with her costume for the party."

Domenica said, "You're going?"

Stella's fingers trudged across the screen. "She's my friend."

"Will you tell her? About Leo?"

The swooping sound of a sent message filled the bookshop. "Are you kidding? Right now, the last thing I need in my life is more bitterness."

"Maybe give her a clue?" Domenica suggested.

Stella rose and reached for the lint roller on the desk behind her. "You know how bad I am at that. My subtext is mostly text."

Domenica smiled. "It is what I love about you."

"Oh, Stella, thanks for coming," Marta threw open the door, and immediately a blue-striped blur skidded around the corner and flung itself onto Stella's legs.

"Hello there, Ascanio," Stella said, lifting the little boy into her arms. "I've missed you, too."

"Mamma is going to a party and I can't go because it's in the nighttime and nighttime is too scary," Ascanio announced.

Stella glanced over at Marta, who shrugged. "He added that last part. I told him he couldn't come to the party because it's past his bedtime."

"I sleep at night," Ascanio nodded sagely. "So I don't see the bad things."

At the sound of Marta's great white Maremma shepherd dog galloping into the living room, Ascanio bucked out of Stella's arms. "Let me down! Orlando and I are playing! I'm a robber outlaw and he's my trusty steed!"

Stella pressed her lips to his forehead with a smacking kiss before setting his feet on the ground. Ascanio ran off with a whoop. Watching him, Stella said, "That's new."

"The outlaw thing? He's been playing Cinicchio the bandit since

Cosimo told him the story. We can't go for a walk on Monte Subasio without Ascanio checking every crevice for signs of outlaws. Orlando is thrilled. It's like I have two boys. Or two puppies. A little of both, really."

"That I remember. I mean the nighttime fear."

Marta said, "Leo stayed with him last week when I had a doctor's appointment and apparently they read some books I wouldn't have chosen for another few years."

Stella darted a look at Marta. "You're okay with that?"

"Leo's right, I have a habit of coddling the boy." Marta's lips pressed to a line. "Anyway, with the storms in Sicily, I'm more worried about Ascanio's grandparents getting home tomorrow in time to babysit. Leo insists I can bring Ascanio to the party, but I keep telling him the Durants invited him, not me. What is that American expression…plus one? I'm his plus one. Who cares about a plus one's childcare challenges? Besides, it *is* past Ascanio's bedtime."

Stella inhaled. "Marta…I'm not sure how to—"

"The lemonade!" Marta said suddenly. "I left it outside. I'll grab it. Want a glass, Stella?"

Stella shook her head, but Marta didn't see as she hurried out. " The dress is in my room. Tell me what you think?"

She hadn't been in Marta's room before, but the house was small, and the room was easy to find, past a toy-strewn room and a closet-like bathroom. The dress hung outside Marta's wardrobe, a beam of sunlight shining on it like a stage light. A pale periwinkle, it glowed, gilding the air around the draping folds that fell to the floor.

Stella reached out to touch it, letting the silk slide through her fingers. Marta appeared at her side, offering a glass of lemonade. Stella took it without thinking and said, "It's exquisite, Marta. Try it on?"

Marta smiled in relief. "Really? You mean it?" She removed the dress from the hanger and began flinging off her clothes as she chattered. "I mean, what's a masquerave, anyway? Leo says it's like Carnevale with a modern edge. I didn't think I had anything ball-worthy, but then I remembered this dress I got years ago for a friend's wedding. It's more formalwear than costume, so I made a headdress to fit the theme. But I'm worried it's ridiculous."

Marta slipped into the strapless dress. It fit her perfectly. She looked as magical as the lavender she grew. She reached for what looked like a simple violet-colored mask, until Stella noticed the wires coming off of it, each one ending with a butterfly. Marta took out the braids wound around her head and her gleaming hair waved past her shoulders. Stella had never seen Marta with her hair down. With it framing her face, her cheekbones seemed higher, her eyes more luminous.

Marta adjusted the mask over her eyes. "Making this with a bandit in the house . . . not easy. What do you think?" She turned to face Stella, the butterflies arcing over her head.

Stella backed up to take in the full look. Almost perfect. "You need heels."

"Oh!" Marta tossed clothing off a chair to get to a shoebox hiding beneath. She slipped on cream heels, and, with the extra two inches of height, the dress flowed effortlessly to the ground.

"It's perfect," Stella breathed.

Marta turned to examine herself in the tiny mirror. "Do you think Leo will like it?"

"How could he not? You are a vision." Stella put down the lemonade. Now or never. She made her voice easy. Nonchalant. "How are things going with you two?"

Marta removed her mask and glanced at Stella, her face a frozen sea. "Why do you ask? I mean, fine. But why do you ask?"

Stella adjusted her bandana. "I saw him earlier today, and, I don't know. I got a vibe."

"He told me," Marta said, the words clipped.

"He *told* you?" Stella asked, her voice heavy with incredulity.

"Yes." Marta brushed her t-shirt down. "It's the reason I wanted to see you. I like to think it was a misunderstanding."

Stella blinked. "I'm lost."

"Me, too." Marta dropped onto the bed. "Leo hasn't been himself. Mr. Durant has been holding some TV or film deal in front of Leo like a carrot for years, saying a man like him, with his history and his looks, belongs in the limelight. So poor Leo keeps showing up to these parties, performing for them. I know it upsets him, but he won't say more than that. He doesn't want to worry me."

"Doesn't that worry you more?"

"Yes," said Marta. She smiled. "Anyway, so I know, or at least I *think*, this tension he's carrying, it's the reason he misconstrued today. You were probably being friendly. I know how affectionate Americans can be."

"Americans are affectionate?" Stella asked, remembering how she used the "Italians are affectionate" rationale with Domenica.

"Sure," Marta shrugged. "Aren't you? Or they? I never know how to refer to you," she added with a kind smile. "But I see it on TV, in the movies. Even the Americans that come every year. So much hugging! So much body-to-body contact!"

"Italians kiss all the time," Stella said.

"That's cheeks. Much less intimate."

Stella didn't know what to think. Her brain felt staticky. "What did Leo tell you?"

"He wasn't telling tales, really. He was edgy when he came back from the bar. I asked what happened, and he wouldn't tell me. But finally, he admitted you were flirting with him. That you . . . put your hand on him."

Stella said nothing as her mind's churning storm upgraded to a hurricane.

"Don't be angry at him for telling me."

"I'm not angry," Stella said. She had no idea what she was. But angry didn't seem the right category, let alone the right word.

Marta rose to stand in front of the mirror, braiding her hair. "Stella? You seem thrown. Did you … is it possible … *were* you flirting with my boyfriend?"

"No."

Marta turned and frowned. Her hands stilled at their weaving hair back into braids. "I certainly hope not. I know you're probably lonely. Things didn't work out with Luca and I'm sorry." Stella winced. "But Leo and I are happy. I hope you can respect that."

The words flew out of Stella's mouth before she could bite them back. "He put his hand on me."

Marta's head whipped toward Stella so quickly, the braids came loose. "What are you talking about? He told me what happened."

"No, I'm telling you what happened. He put his hand on my leg."

"He didn't," Marta decided.

"He did."

"He didn't. He said that Romina saw you, with your hand on his."

Stella didn't understand until she did. "Yes. To take his hand off my leg."

Marta turned back to the mirror. She kept her eyes fixed on Stella's reflection as she returned to braiding. "Look, Stella. This would be easier if you admitted it. You were a little lonely, and you got flirty. It happens. I could let it go if you stopped lying." She snapped the rubber bands in place and began winding the braids around her head.

"But I *didn't* get flirty. I *didn't* touch him. He put his hand on *my* leg. Not the other way around."

Without a hair out of place, Marta turned to consider Stella. "This is not at all how I thought this would go. I thought I was making it easier, being open-hearted, like Don Arrigo says." She frowned, tears coming to her eyes. "Lying like this. Stella, don't you see? It makes everything worse."

Stella stood. "I guess there's nothing more to say."

"I guess not." Marta strode out of the room.

Stella followed, her mind spinning. As she approached Marta, she said, "Actually, there is more to say. Does me hitting on Leo match what you know of me?"

"No," Marta said. "But Leo explained how I sometimes believe the best in people, even if it's not deserved. He said you're jealous of me."

"I am."

"You are?" Marta stared, dumbfounded, before saying, "So you see, he's right!"

"No, jealous isn't quite the right word." Stella thought. "Marta, I admire how you've taken this battered history and made a beautiful life. But I want to celebrate it, not take you down. You know I adore you, I adore Ascanio. I'm proud to know you." Marta blinked, tears in her eyes. Into the silence, Stella added, "Leo, though, I'm not loving. To be honest."

Marta said, "He didn't want to tell me, Stella. But what could he do?"

"Not lie to cover his tracks. That would be a start."

Ascanio ran into the room, Orlando loping at his heels with the rocking horse gait he used when trying to throttle down his speed to follow the boy. Throwing his little arms around Stella's knees, Ascanio said, "Stella! You can't leave! Orlando and I need to tell you about…" he lowered his voice to a loud whisper, "How the bandit fooled the rich farmer!"

Stella tousled the boy's hair. "Next time, okay?"

He scowled. "You'll forget."

"I won't."

A grin pulled up the edges of his mouth. "Maybe I'll forget."

"I'll remind you," Stella promised. "Now, be good for Mamma and Orlando, okay?"

"No! I'm the bad bad bandit, Cinicchio!" A cloud marred the sun of his smile. "But I'm not a very brave bandit. Mamma, I don't want to stay here alone when you go to the party."

"You won't be alone, silly. Nonna and Nonno will stay with you."

"But you said! I heard you *said*! They might not come in time."

Marta shook her head. "I would never leave you alone, *caro*."

"You'll take me to the party?"

Marta said, "Ascanio—"

"I wear my Cinicchio costume! Then I be brave! So brave, I fight the nighttime! I show you! Come on, Orlando!"

Stella watched him leave, a shiver of frost threading through her ribcage, despite his funny slipping run as he waved an imaginary sword and made swooshing sounds. Pretending to fight demons, cloaked in darkness to blend with the night.

Lost in thought, she startled when Marta said, "Leo wouldn't lie to me, Stella. He's opened up to me like he's opened up to nobody else. I know him. I know his heart."

Stella paused. "Marta. I love you. So I hope you're right. I hope he forgot himself, put his hand on me, and then only recognized it when my hand met his."

"Maybe," Marta conceded. "I suppose that's possible."

"Because if it's not," Stella said, "then Marta, I'm afraid he's not the man you think he is."

Marta straightened. "I think it's best you leave."

"I'm already gone," Stella said, walking out into the fading light. She shivered, despite the warm air. She shivered like she'd been plunged into cold water and didn't stop shivering until she found herself at Matteo's doorstep.

"Stella! What are you doing here?" Matteo threw open the door. Over his shoulder, he called, "It's Stella, Mamma."

Matteo's mother popped out of the kitchen. "Stella! Can you stay for dinner?"

Dinner! For a moment she panicked about getting it on the table, but then remembered she'd successfully convinced the Staffords to try out Trattoria Cavour. Only by agreeing to meet them at the restaurant to help them order. She checked the time. Twenty minutes.

She inhaled. *Mmm.* "I'd love to, but I only have a few minutes. It smells amazing, are you frying artichokes?"

Matteo's mother laughed. "That nose of yours. Yes, I am. Sure you can't stay?"

Stella shook her head regretfully. "I wish. Love the little sprinkle of oregano you added to the batter. Matteo, do you have a minute?"

Matteo put his arm around her shoulder and shepherded her to his room. "Of course. Giancarlo and I are going through my closet, trying to figure out what to wear. And also trying to figure out how we can get out of going to this thing."

Giancarlo looked up from fastening a black cape around his neck. "*You* are trying to get out of it. I've decided to enjoy the night out."

Matteo lifted his eyes heavenward. "This guy. You go to enough parties with the glitterati and suddenly any event with free-flowing booze becomes an opportunity."

Stella tried to smile at their banter. At her wan expression, Matteo dropped his voice. "Hey. What's going on?"

Hearing the seriousness in Matteo's voice, Giancarlo stepped toward the two of them. Stella could feel the intensity of his gaze and dropped her eyes.

"Nothing, it's nothing," she mumbled.

Giancarlo lifted her chin gently to search her face. At his touch, Stella felt her stomach swoop ridiculously. Giancarlo said, "What's happened, Stella?"

Stella steadied her body and then cleared her throat. "No, really. It's nothing." She barely knew Giancarlo. What would he make of her fight with Marta? "I'm being stupid."

A slow smile crept across Giancarlo's face. "Impossible." He looked from Matteo, whose eyes were fixed on Stella, to Stella, whose eyes blinked back tears. Nodding to himself, Giancarlo said, "I'm going to see if your mother needs help pounding the veal."

When the door closed behind Giancarlo, Matteo put his hands on her shoulders and rested his forehead on her own. "What is it? You're scaring me."

At the kindness of Giancarlo's exit and the warmth of Matteo's hands on her shoulders, Stella felt a tear slip down her cheek. "I'm sorry, I don't want to ruin your fun time."

"Please. Ruin away. Only please break my arm while you're at it."

Stella attempted a smile. "You'll have a blast. You always do. Matteo, you bring the party."

"Ha!" Matteo's laugh exploded for a beat before fading. "Now are you going to tell me or do I need to arm wrestle it out of you? Thereby serving two purposes as you'd likely win, and maybe I'd break my arm after all."

She breathed for a moment. "Something happened today at the bar. With Leo. He said this weird thing and before I knew it, his hand was on my leg."

"He told you about the—wait, his hand was on your leg?"

"Yes. And Domenica said I should tell Marta, and I wasn't going to, but then it came out. But I guess Leo had told her a twisted version of the story, making me the instigator." Matteo let out an expletive and Stella blushed. "Matteo..."

"Sorry, Stella, sometimes the situation calls for swearing. Much as you hate it. That *jerk*."

"Is it possible, though, that he's not? Maybe I—"

"Stop it, Stella. Just. Stop. We both know Leo. You didn't make this happen."

She ran her teeth over her lower lip. "What do I do now?"

He paused. "Can you let it be? See what happens next?"

"Matteo—"

"Yes, I know that's not your style. To sit on your hands."

"I don't like this dark space between me and Marta. Maybe I should apologize. I don't want to lose her friendship."

"You won't."

"But—"

"Stella. Really. She's been dating Leo for a few months. That's a few months longer than any of his past relationships. Combined, probably. It's got an expiration date that is around the corner. She'll see him for what he is soon enough."

"But maybe this will go the distance. Maybe they'll get married and I'll be an outcast from her forever."

"Ah, Stella. The drama," Matteo smiled. "It hasn't lasted a long time because they're made for each other. It's lasted this long because Marta is trusting and sweet. So trusting and sweet, she can't see what's right in front of her. He's getting restless, as he does. That's his pattern. Soon the pattern will be inescapable."

Stella listened.

Matteo squeezed her shoulders. "They will implode. Probably in spectacular fashion. At any moment."

Stella's mind flicked to the party tomorrow. She shook her head and said softly, "I can hardly root for her to suffer."

Matteo wiped her tear with the pad of his thumb. "Don't you think she's suffering now? She has to feel the distance growing between them, his wandering eye. Better to know than be deluded. Which is just knowing without knowing you're knowing."

"That's a mouthful," Stella smiled tremulously.

"Tell me about it."

Stella breathed. "Thanks, Matteo. What would I do without you?"

"Let's never find out."

She had a thought. "You know, this party might not be so bad. Maybe you'll meet an American hottie. Someone perfect for you."

He guffawed, his long face mirthless. "I'm pretty sure any American at this party wouldn't be remotely interested in a garbage collector."

Stella smiled. "Then they don't know what they're missing. You're too good for any of them."

Matteo grinned. "You need my support in this trying time. I don't know why Giancarlo wants to go to this stupid party so badly, but I can tell him—"

"You'll tell Giancarlo no such thing. I'm having the usual Friday dinner with Domenica tomorrow. We'll miss you, but we'll toast your good fortune, hobnobbing with the rich and famous."

"Madonna, save me," Matteo grumbled. Growing serious, he said, "You going to be okay?"

She nodded. "I'll keep my mind on the long game. Like you said."

"There you go. Marta will come around. You'll get past this."

Her hand on the doorknob, she said, "Now, you have to promise to live-text me from this shindig. I want photos, commentary, all of it."

Nodding, Matteo said, "You got it."As she turned to go, Matteo added, "Not to minimize the situation with Marta, but I have to tell you, I'm a little relieved. I thought for sure you were going to say you found a body."

Stella smiled wanly. "Those days are behind me."

The day of the party dawned fresh and beautiful, the sky a kind of fragile blue that made Stella want to cup it in her hands. She hummed as she made a *crostata alla marmellata*, a common breakfast and dessert in Italy, filling the buttery crust with an orange jam she'd made over the winter with a bit of star anise. She left the crostata, along with the yogurt she'd strained, and a salami. The salami seemed out of place, but she figured carb-fearing Mrs. Stafford might appreciate the protein.

As she made her way through her olive grove to the ring road, she noticed how the trees transformed light, from stormy-skied days when their brilliance could be blinding to clear days when they softened the sun's rays to a muted glow. To now, when they rustled with shifting shadows, casting streaks of darkness in her wake, like dark confetti.

A tumble of restless thoughts churned within her, leaving her short of breath. She shook her head to clear it.

Walking toward the park, a fluttering in the bushes pulled her attention. She gasped at the sight of a miniature hummingbird flitting around and between the bush's flowers. But no, she was sure she'd heard that there weren't hummingbirds in Europe. Besides, hummingbirds couldn't be this small, could they? The size of a nutmeg berry! She leaned closer and startled at the sight of a coiled tongue shooting out of the wee beast.

A hummingbird moth! It must be! She watched it for a moment, wishing she could share the moment of one animal disguised as another with her sister.

A passing cloud cast Stella in sudden shade. She shivered, and the moth darted away. Stella sighed. The coldness followed her through the tunnel. Somehow, she felt the dankness coming off the stones in a way she never had.

She crested the stairs and ran into Luca, his arm around a young woman."Stella!"

She stretched a grin across her face. "Luca!" she said, though her eyes kept returning to the woman. A woman who would have drawn her gaze even if not with Luca, with her tall and willowy bearing and her hair so straight and shining, it fell, gleaming, down her back. Though the color of her hair wasn't more than a shade or two different from Stella's dark chocolate brown, it seemed made of water and light rather than anything as ordinary as keratin.

"Stella, I want you to meet Liliana," Luca beamed.

A flash crossed Liliana's face before she held out her hand. "Stella. I've heard so much about you."

"Thanks, er, same. And welcome home," Stella said, trying to smile.

Liliana wound her arm through Luca's as she grinned at him. "You're right! Her accent is so cute!"

Stella's smile froze on her face.

Luca laughed uncomfortably. "Okay, then. We've got loads to do before the party tonight. We'll catch you later, eh, Stella?"

"Sure," Stella said, watching them stroll up the next set of stairs. She caught sight of her reflection in a window and groaned. Her hair looked wild from the morning walk. Not at all tamed by the garishly red bandana that was now, heaven help her, so threadbare, some of her hair escaped through the holes like errant wires. Stella leaned forward, confused about the marring on the reflection of her neck. Oh, no. Yogurt. How had it gotten on her *neck?*

She sighed and made her way to Domenica's. "*Buongiorno,*" she called, more cheerfully than she felt.

Luckily, Domenica was half in a closet and didn't notice the artificial note in Stella's voice. "Stella. Ciao. I'm trying to get this…ugh! This one cat carrier for Barbanera's appointment. But it's stuck back here. Hold on."

Stella sat down, her hands reaching into her curls. She smoothed a lock of hair. Then another. Finally, she called, "Any carrier will do, Domenica. We're not fussy."

"I got it!" Domenica announced triumphantly. She emerged from the closet with an enormous carrier in her hand. "And not just any carrier will do, Stella. Not with that cat. You need one fit for a small dog."

Dusting the carrier, she set it in front of Stella. "How did the Staffords like Trattoria Cavour?"

"Signor Stafford must have at least enjoyed the wine. In fact, they must have ordered a second bottle on their own because he made an unholy noise coming home. I had a hard time going back to sleep. Then I got up early to make a *crostata.*" Stella yawned theatrically as she smoothed another curl.

Domenica peered around the bookshop.

"I left the *crostata* at home because I went for a walk, but I'll bring you a slice when we take Barbanera to the vet."

"What kind?"

"Orange."

"Which orange?"

"The ones my neighbors brought back from Sicily when they went to their niece's wedding. To thank me for looking after their chickens."

"Is that the orange jam you added star anise to?" Domenica asked.

"The same."

Domenica made a noise of satisfaction. "That's my favorite."

"Me too." Stella smiled.

"Don't you think it's wasted on these guests?"

Stella shrugged. "I find it easier not to think that way. I figure I'm feeding their humanity. Better food, better humanity. Provided, of course, they eat it."

Domenica chuckled and then looked toward the door as it opened, sending the bell jingling merrily.

Stella recognized Tripp Lake, with an Italian gentleman she couldn't place. Once they passed the desk without greeting Domenica, Stella shot her friend a questioning look. Domenica leaned forward and whispered, "Gino Bernardi. He used to live in Aramezzo but now lives in London. Big in real estate."

Stella's eyes found the man's back. *Liliana's father.*

From the back of the stacks, she heard Gino tell Tripp in clipped English, "Try not to mind the smell. Cats and old books. The worst. But, batty as she is, she does have a pretty good selection."

Anger flooded Stella. She found herself rising until Domenica pulled her arm with a bare shake of her head, mouthing, "No."

Gino kept talking. "You'll find flipping through books much more satisfying than scrolling the internet. Wives love to make a dream board from the clippings, which can help define what you both want in your own Italian paradise."

Sitting back down, Stella inhaled lustily. What smell was he talking about? Old books, yes, but who would classify that as a bad smell? The air smelled more of coffee than anything else. Stella darted a look at Domenica.

Her friend insisted she spoke only Italian and a little Spanish, but trotted out enough idiomatic English that Stella wondered. Especially since she'd anticipated Stella's impulsive reaction. How much of the insult did she understand?

She shot a look at Domenica, who appeared unfazed as she organized the books on her desk into piles and then rearranged them distractedly.

Maybe she understood more than she let on.

Stella realized Gino was still talking. "Once we get a sense of what you're looking for, I'll curate some options in your price range. If you've established…" He let the words trail off, a broad hint.

Tripp said, "Let's not worry about the cost."

"All right then," Stella heard Gino slap his hands and rub them together. "It pays to be the son of a Wall Street tycoon, eh?"

Chuckling, Tripp said, "Well, not yet. Right now I can't even buy my wife a Tesla. But I'm on the fast track, in a manner of speaking."

The men laughed heartily and brought a stack of books to the desk. Domenica offered a bland smile and started clacking the prices in her ancient calculator. Which Stella always found amusing, since she knew Domenica could add any string of numbers in her head. Tripp said to her, "I assume we get a discount. I mean, we're buying almost all your architectural books on Italian homes."

Domenica looked up and blinked. "*Come?*" What's that?

Reaching into his pocket, Gino said in Italian, "Surely you can offer some incentive."

Domenica blinked as if confused before slipping a bookmark into a book. Then she totaled the amount. "It's on me," Gino said magnanimously and reached into his wallet.

As they turned to go, Domenica whispered to Stella. "Sometimes it's more efficient to play the part they expect."

"With them specifically? Or with anyone?"

Domenica smiled enigmatically.

Before the men reached the door, Marcello, Aramezzo's mayor, strode in. "Ah, Gino, I thought that was you! Here for the masquerave, eh? Glad to have you back!"

Gino nodded, "Have you met Signor Lake, one of Signor Durant's guests?"

The mayor turned to Tripp and said in English, "Welcome me! We are happy to keep you in our city."

Gino winced.

Undaunted, the mayor rolled on. "It is beautiful to see you buy the things and spend the coins here. Oh! Here it is Cosimo. He have a shop where it is possible to buy many things, old things!"

Cosimo nodded to the men and ambled to Domenica's desk.

Gino shifted uncomfortably. "Well, Marcello. We'll see you tonight! I have a feeling it will be one for the books."

Tripp shot a confused look at the mayor before allowing himself to be led away.

Marcello watched them go. To Cosimo, Domenica, and Stella, he said, "Fine men. A credit to our town." With that, he swanned out of the bookstore.

Stella ran her fingers over another curl as she said, "What was all that?"

Domenica chuckled. "You haven't heard our mayor practice his multinational tongue? It's always a treat."

Picking up a pencil-lead gray cat, Stella said, "This party certainly is bringing characters out of the woodwork. Is it always like this?"

Cosimo leaned against the desk as he said, "To some degree. Any occasion at Villa delle Acque is an event, of course. There aren't many three-story villas in the area, especially built in the 1700s. And none built on Roman baths."

"Now, Cosimo," Domenica cautioned. "The baths. That's speculation. You don't know that's true."

"You don't know it's not. I myself have found remnants of an aqueduct leading to the villa."

"Villa delle Acque!" Stella sat straighter. "Villa of the Waters! I get it!"

"Brava," smiled Cosimo. "I wouldn't be surprised if they found mosaic tiles during the renovation and didn't think anything of it. Anyway, you can see how the history would lend an occasion, well, a sense of occasion. For all we know, this is not the first masquerade ball at the villa."

"Wait, it's an actual *ball*?" said Stella.

"What did you think a masquerade was, child?"

"I don't know," Stella scowled. "But this is also a rave and I'd never call a rave a ball."

"A rave?" Cosimo looked at Domenica, as if for clarification.

Stella, assuming Domenica to be as in the dark as Cosimo, opened her mouth to respond but then Domenica said, "A rave is a dance party. Often in an industrial space like a warehouse at midnight. With electronic dance music."

He frowned. "Do people dress in costume?"

"Not as such," said Domenica. "But there's a lot of colorful clothing. Glow-in-the-dark jewelry. Things like that."

Cosimo paused. "I wonder if the darkness of a rave and the masks of a masquerade serve the same purpose."

Stella and Domenica exchanged glances.

At their silence, Cosimo added, "Of course, I don't know about raves. But Venetian partygoers at masquerade balls reveled in the anonymity of the masks that allowed them to indulge in behaviors so wild, so estranged from their normal standards, it would risk scandal should they be identified."

Remembering her earlier reflections, Stella mused, "Masks . . . masks and darkness. They both allow partygoers to release their inhibitions."

"The thrill of adopting a new persona," Cosimo said, nodding. "Therein lies a kind of liberation."

"I have to say, it sounds kind of fun," Stella said, still running her curls through her fingers.

"Pssh," Domenica said. "It's just a party with a different kind of hangover."

"Well," Stella said, lightly, as the cat leapt from her lap to sniff the carrier. "I certainly hope they all have a very good time."

"My hope," said Cosimo, "is that Mimmo gives them a wide berth. I ran into him on my way here. Apparently, they've got some sort of light show going at the villa and he's incensed."

"Light show?" Stella said. "Sounds tacky."

"I wouldn't know," Cosimo said. "But if he gets underfoot, I don't think they'll be too happy."

Stella thought about the Americans. Many of them didn't seem too happy to begin with. She shook her head. Not her problem. Her only worry was the Staffords. Mr. Stafford seemed to enjoy his introduction to Umbrian spirits a bit too much, if last night was any indication. She could see him losing his inhibitions, his perspective. His coordination. Stella sighed, wondering if she should offer to drive them home from the party.

"All right then," said Stella. "Some of us have homes to sweep and linens to iron while the lucky few prepare for the ball." Stella chuckled at the image of herself as a modern-day Cinderella. "Domenica, meet you in the parking lot with Barbanera?"

"You'll need help. He won't go easily. I'll ring before I come over."

As Stella waved and walked to the door, she heard Domenica say, "You looking for ancient religious texts, Cosimo?"

"As ever."

"I got something in last week I thought you'd appreciate." Their voices faded as they disappeared into the back of the shop.

Stella walked home, her nerves jangling. Not even the sight of Don Arrigo, the village priest, surrounded by teens teaching him dance moves, soothed her nerves. Maybe she needed to bake something. But what? Running through the items in her larder, she didn't notice Luca and Liliana until she practically bumped into them.

Luca's eyes widened. "Stella? Are you okay?"

"Sure. Why?"

He shifted. "No reason. Just…wondering."

Liliana snorted and looked away. Luca tugged her arm, and they continued walking, Luca calling over his shoulder, "Get some rest, okay, Stella?"

Stella watched them go.

Then she ran the rest of the way into her house, hoping the Staffords were out or safely lodged upstairs. Thankfully, only Barbanera acknowledged her return. Did Stella imagine the way his eyes narrowed at the sight of her?

She rounded the corner into the bathroom and came face to face with her reflection. Her curls, rather than straightening under her ministrations, had separated. She looked like that classic *Saturday Night Live* character from old clips, Roseanne Roseannadanna. The one who said, "It's always something."

Stella sighed. It was, indeed, always something.

She couldn't wait for dinner with Domenica. This day needed to end. A plate of heart-nourishing *pappardelle* was sounding pretty good.

"Get here, Stella. As fast as you can. Something's . . . happened." The line crackled. "Again."

The line went dead.

What did Matteo mean? He couldn't possibly mean . . .

No. Not another . . . body. It would be too bizarre. Most villages didn't see as much homicide in a centenarian's lifetime as Aramezzo had since her arrival. Was it her? Was she bad luck? Her fingers clutched her lucky pendant.

Simmer down! Stella ordered herself. Matteo probably called because the lava cakes were overcooked or something. Her friend would no doubt use that grave voice for a lava cake with no molten center. Still, it's not like she could cajole the caterers into a better product. Why would Matteo call now rather than complaining about it tomorrow?

And what could Matteo have meant by "again"?

Deep in thought, Stella didn't notice Domenica appearing at her side. She yelped and leapt backward.

"*Cara*, what is it?" Domenica leaned forward, searching Stella's face for evidence of whatever had caused her to deflate.

Stella shook her head. "I don't know. Matteo said to get over there. That something has happened. Again."

"Again? What again?"

"I don't know!"

"Well, why didn't you press him?"

Stella practically stamped her foot in impatience. "You don't think I tried?"

"A death?" Domenica breathed, her eyes wide.

Stella shook her head, "I don't *know*. How could I *know*?"

"A *murder*?" Domenica's eyes widened further until her pupils looked like spinning balls. Or maybe, Stella reasoned, that was her own reflection.

"Domenica. I. Don't. Know." She closed her eyes and concentrated, trying in vain not to summon the faces of partygoers, who should have been knee deep in Prosecco and dancing by now. "But whatever it is, they'll call the police, right? If it's urgent. The police will sort it out. Let's get back to dinner. I definitely am going to order the gnocchi this time. No time like the present."

"I ordered you *pappardelle*, which I'll cancel."

"No. We'll eat. It's none of our business what happens at the villa."

Domenica peered at Stella over her glasses until Stella felt like she was being chided by her second-grade teacher. "Stella."

"What?" Why did the word come out as a whine? She coughed and deepened her voice. "What?"

Crossing her arms over her broad chest, Domenica said, "Matteo called you. There must be a reason. You know you have to go."

Stella opened her mouth to protest, but a series of faces flashed across her mind. Too many people she loved at that party. She sagged in resignation.

Domenica fished around in her purse. "Take my keys."

"I can walk."

"In the dark?"

"It's not dark."

"It's dark and getting darker," Domenica said, gesturing to the sky growing inkier by the moment. "Get gone, Stella."

Stella snatched the keys and strode away.

"Stella!"

She turned at Domenica's call.

Domenica hesitated, then said, "Be careful."

Stella bit her lip and nodded. "Thanks, Domenica. I'll see you soon."

Domenica took a few steps after her and then paused, watching as Stella turned the corner.

Stella concentrated on walking steadily until the memory of Matteo's voice—thin and panicked—prompted her feet to hurry, hurry, hurry. She jogged down to the parking lot and found the car where they'd left it after taking Barbanera to the vet. Stella threw the car in gear and then paused.

Part of her wanted to peel out of the parking lot. Get to whatever drama was unfolding at the villa. And part of her wanted to slow down. Whatever waited for her couldn't be pleasant. Maybe if she slowed a little…it would all be resolved by the time she got there. Her foot hovered over the accelerator. Then she remembered Matteo's voice, breaking. She saw him, bent over the form of someone she loved. *Please, please, please…*

She gunned the engine and sped into the gathering darkness.

Stella rehearsed her entrance as she drove. The Americans had made it quite clear she wasn't invited. How could she explain her appearance at their door? Then again, if things were in as much of an uproar as it seemed, a party-crasher might go unnoticed.

She tried to remember how far the villa was up the road from Aramezzo. Before the old amphitheater where ancient Romans had staged naval battles (if Cosimo could be believed, it still seemed too fantastical to be true). Ah, the trees! She remembered the line of cypresses lining the villa driveway. Those should be easy enough to spot, even as the sky grew darker. It should be just another three or four turns in the road, she thought to herself.

The engine stalled.

Then quit.

"*Cavolo*," Stella muttered. She had never developed a salty tongue but appreciated that in Italian, "cabbage" stood in for the racier swear words.

Just her luck, not only did the engine die, but it died where there was no shoulder. Stella popped the transmission into neutral and got out to push the car to the side.

The car began rolling downhill as soon as she opened the door. She slammed the brake, her heart beating in her ears. "*Cavolo!*" More colorfully this time.

How could she hold the car in place without engaging the emergency brake, which would keep it from rolling backward but would also prevent her from being able to push the car to the side of the road? Then again, she wasn't sure she could roll it forward at all, given the hill.

Stella squeezed her eyes shut in frustration.

Hoping nobody came up the road, yet already sensing the slam of the car into her, Stella set the parking brake. She popped the hood and climbed out of the car. Gazing at the inner workings of the engine, she wondered what she was supposed to be looking for.

At the sound of an approaching car, she jumped.

Then realized it was the wind in the trees.

Staring at the unfamiliar territory under the car's hood, Stella supposed she'd hoped for a big cartoon arrow pointing at a loose, vividly colored wire in the engine. No luck. Nothing pointed to a problem. The engine looked like an engine. No cartoon arrow or even a wisp of smoke.

Her heartbeat raced, knocking wildly against her ribcage.

All she could hear, the thumping of her heart in the darkness.

Maybe Domenica would know what to do! Of course.

With relief, Stella drew out her phone and selected Domenica's contact. She paced around the car, waiting for Domenica to pick up. Her friend always turned her phone off in the evening, but she couldn't have tonight, could she?

Stella pulled the phone away and stared at it. Was it, too, broken? She felt a flash of paranoia. Had someone messed with the engine and destroyed her phone to get her out here in the dark?

But no, her eyes locked on the total absence of bars. Nobody had done this to her. Except, possibly, fate. She was out of range, which she should have remembered. Every time she hiked around here, she lost her signal within a few turns of Aramezzo.

She gritted her teeth in frustration. Blast these pockets in the hills where sunlight had a hard enough time filtering through, let alone a cell signal.

Matteo needed her. Could she leave the car here, on the road? She had to, didn't she? No choice. Her eyes searched into the shifting darkness ahead of her. How much farther up the road?

She remembered Cosimo's stories of mysterious happenings in these woods. Or she tried to, but they blended with the campfire stories her father used to tell when he took her and Grazie camping—people suddenly going mute when crossing a fairy circle of mushrooms, gods and goddesses sending wild animals with bared teeth to punish wanderers who strayed too far into hallowed territory, tortured spirits that rose from the ground when an ill-fated traveler stepped over their shallow grave. The stories wove together, bound by the pain of remembering Grazie. Her eyes shining in the firelight, gripping Stella's hand with her s'mores-sticky one as she whispered, "Papa is fooling, right, Stella? *Right?*"

Stella swallowed, the grief at the little coffin linked with most memories of her little sister—forever innocent and full of lost promise. How could one moment change everything? A drunken driver ripping away her father and sister in one fell swoop, leaving her with a mother who barely tolerated her in the best of times and, in these worst, seemed to blame Stella for being the family member left standing.

One moment, and everything changed.

One police officer at the door.

The harder Stella tried not to think it, the more pulsating the answering thought became: one phone call shattering the easy joy of a weekly dinner in Aramezzo's piazza.

What would be the consequences of tonight's broken moment? Again, like a deck of cards, she felt more than saw the images of Giancarlo, the Staffords, and Marta fluttering around her. She wrenched her mind to the present before she could acknowledge the card with Ascanio's image. *No.* His grandparents must have arrived in time. She would have heard if they hadn't. No way Marta would have brought him to the party.

Stella remembered Ascanio, hair tousled in his striped pajamas, waving an imaginary sword. Would he have tried to get to the party on his own, battling the dark like the bandit he admired?

She had to get out of there. Not only did she need to get to Matteo, she couldn't stand being on this road, vulnerable, waiting for an unknown something to happen. Flipping the hazards on, Stella hoped a car wouldn't careen around a corner too fast to notice the signal. The lights from the hazards pulsed against the trees behind her, hopefully enough of a warning to slow an approaching driver.

Stella suddenly remembered. The triangle! She was still using her international driver's license, and had only started studying for her Italian one, but she remembered that Italian law said every car must carry a reflective triangle to prop in the road.

Quickly, she wrenched open the trunk and pushed boxes of books aside until she found the triangle. Jogging down the road fifty meters, surprised she remembered the law's specifics, she found a likely spot. She arranged the reflective triangle, offering up a prayer to an unnamed god of cars, and strode back up the hill with a confidence she couldn't quite feel.

When she rounded the first turn, the lights from the car disappeared as if a heavy curtain had fallen over the road. Stella's ears longed for the sound of insects, frogs, even a scurrying in the underbrush. But she heard nothing. Only an aching silence.

In the quiet, the shadows seemed to clot and take form. She felt something lurch next to her, and she jumped with a squeal that died quickly as she realized she'd drifted too far over in the road, alongside the bushes that seemed to appear from nowhere.

She felt like an idiot as she remembered her phone flashlight. Stumbling, not wanting to pause her momentum toward the villa, she kept her eyes on the road and on her screen, bumbling for the flashlight. Before she could tap the button, a sound behind her stilled her movement.

Her heartbeat cantered, gaining speed until she felt it might choke her.

The sound disappeared into the distance. Maybe a fox running through the trees? Or the brook, she suddenly remembered. Water ran alongside the road here, supplied by the same spring that supposedly once filled the amphitheater and perhaps Roman baths. Maybe all she heard was the sound of water sliding across smooth stones.

Animals liked to congregate at water. Maybe a *cinghiale*, a wild boar. They could be dangerous, she knew. Mimmo loved to tell stories of novice hunters thinking they'd gotten the best of a wild boar, only to be gored by one attacking from the side. He described it like a scene from Jurassic Park.

A thought occurred to Stella.

Maybe what she heard wasn't a wild animal.

Maybe, whatever prompted Matteo to call her, maybe it had slipped away into the shadows. Maybe her appearance would startle it, force it out of hiding. Maybe it would be none best pleased.

Maybe it had a weapon.

Her fear rose, choking her. She didn't notice the roar until it pulled alongside her with a yawning screech.

"Stella!"

She jumped, her heart in her throat, blinded by the sudden head-lights, her ears full of the engine's reverberation.

The glare forced her to shield her eyes. "Luca?"

"Is that Domenica's car back there?" He leaned out of the police car window, head craning into the darkness behind them.

"It stopped. Out of the blue. I didn't know—"

"Probably the fuel pump. I heard the engine sputtering yesterday and told her to get it looked at," Luca said. "Tow truck is on its way. I'll have them take it to Rocco's."

"Rocco's?"

"The mechanic. At the gas station on the way to Assisi."

Stella nodded, uncertain.

"Well?" Luca said. "Get in."

"Into the police car?"

"Do you see another vehicle?" Luca grinned. "Let's go. We're already late. It's good we ran into you."

Stella hesitated, confused, and then opened the back of the car. "Hey, Salvo."

Salvo nodded, his mustache twitching.

Luca stared ahead grimly. "Matteo called you, I suppose?"

"Yes. But that was like a half hour ago now. What's going on?"

"Captain Tribuzio's been trying to track down an English-speaking officer since the one in Assisi is on holiday in the Canary Islands. Usually, we'd ask an English speaker in town if necessary, but they are all at the party, and we can't have a witness translate. It's a good thing we ran into you because it turns out that tonight, I'm the closest this police department has got to someone who speaks English." Luca turned around to offer her a wry smile. "Pathetic, I know."

"Shouldn't you be at the party?" Stella frowned. "Didn't it start an hour ago? Or two?"

"Yes. I, er, lost track of time. It took dispatch a bit to . . . locate me."

Salvo made a whistling noise. "Why go to a party when you got the best kind of party, right, Luca?"

Stella felt glad of the darkened backseat to hide her blush as she realized Luca had been with Liliana. *Indisposed.*

Luca laughed uncomfortably. "You could say that."

"So you weren't at the party," Stella summed up, firmly. "Then what do you know? Matteo didn't say."

Salvo turned into the long driveway. Spiraling blue lights reflected off the villa ahead. Luca nodded. "The ambulance. Matteo said he called them first."

Stella realized. "The ambulance, it's not moving. Shouldn't it be moving? What do you know? What *happened*?"

Luca climbed out of the car. "I guess we'll find out."

Stella followed the officers to the door. At least, she tried to—she kept growing distracted by the twinkling lights in the trees. Her breath caught at movement over the front of the house. It looked like falling, jewel-toned confetti. Her eyes scanned for the source of the brilliantly hued blue and red and green confetti and found projectors set up along the lawn, throwing images of confetti and now masquerade masks that turned into butterflies that beat their wings to fly off the top of the house into the indigo sky.

This was the light show Mimmo objected to.

She realized the officers had reached the door, and she ran to catch up. Before they could knock, the door was thrown open by Chelsea Durant, the villa's owner, in a black dress with cuffs, collar, and crown that appeared made of vintage playing cards. All the cards were hearts. Ah, she was the Queen of Hearts. Wanly, Mrs. Durant said, "It's about time."

Stella stepped into the villa.

Villa.

She had thought it a pretentious word. But once inside, she realized this edifice needed a grander term. It felt like a palatial hotel, with its entryway spanning almost the entire length of the house, the ceiling high above. So high, Stella noticed, her neck craned backward, there was a railing on the second floor that looked down onto the long foyer, which had been turned into a ballroom. To the right of the front door, shiny white squares had been arranged on the floor for dancing. To the left, Stella spotted a sitting area furnished with the same luxuriously covered couches and settees that lined the cream-colored foyer. Stella could imagine the serenity of curling up on one of those sky-blue chairs along the parchment-colored entry room, gazing out through one of the three sets of glass double doors, thrown open to a courtyard. For a moment, Stella assumed the courtyard to be another room, thanks to the glow of lights wound around every tree limb creating a twinkling canopy, and the set tables, covered with gold damask linens, elaborate candelabras, and crimson dahlias. But then she felt the cool air drifting in from the French doors and noticed the change in flooring from the marble foyer to what looked more like stone.

The villa was a cream and azure-tinted wonder. Not at all the McMansion she'd planned to mock. No recreations of famous frescoes, no ostentatious statues, not one gilded surface. No, this was elegantly executed without being over the top.

Stella tried not to gape, fixing every detail to recount to Domenica.

As she came further into the long foyer, she had to work harder not to gape. A riot of fabrics in different colors and textures flanked the edges of the room. The costumes, she'd forgotten it was a costume ball. She felt like she'd walked onto a set with a patchwork curtain. Black taffeta and gold ruffles and red velvet and pink tulle. Some partygoers still wore their masks, adding to the decadent visual cacophony with feathers and lace and horns and steel wings. She caught a glimpse of violet butterflies and remembered that Marta should be here, somewhere.

A clutch of teenagers in the courtyard outside the French doors had opted for more of the rave aspect of the theme. They resembled a handful of highlighters with their neon, slinky ballgowns, a few suits in lime green and disco pink, and their neon sneakers, flat for the boys, platform-heeled for the girls. Had they all gone shopping at some high-end rave store?

Her eyes couldn't focus. She tried closing them, but that made it worse. So much sound—rustling fabrics and the delicate chandelier tinkling in the breeze and the whispering in two languages and someone weeping at the back of the room. Worse than all the sound, so much *scent.* Apparently, when people wanted to become someone else, they also doused themselves in perfume. A confusion of smells assailed her— gardenias and musk and pine and vanilla, mixed with whatever the kitchen was producing, gorgonzola and baking bread and shrimp and something with saffron and olive oil. Stella felt lucky that the candles strewn over every surface were ones with electric wicks. She couldn't imagine how strong the smell would be with melting candles added to the mix. Especially scented ones.

She felt a tug at her elbow and opened her eyes. "Matteo. What the world—"

He shook his head and pulled her closer to the officers who had entered the middle of the foyer. The chatter all around her faded.

Matteo whispered furiously, "I called you a half hour ago. What took you so long?"

"Domenica's car broke down."

"Probably the fuel pump."

"That seems to be the prevailing theory." She scanned the sea of ashen faces. Leaning close to Matteo, Stella whispered, "Will you finally tell me what's going on? Luca and Salvo didn't say."

Luca materialized beside them. "Because we don't know. Matteo?"

Matteo nodded grimly. "I didn't know how to explain properly. You better come see." He walked toward the grand staircase, the quiet party-goers parting before them in a swirl of taffeta and velvet and lace. Matteo turned to Luca. "You found Stella."

Luca nodded tightly, his eyes on the staircase rising in front of them.

Stella followed, trying to look as if she belonged alongside the police. She half expected an American to yank her back, accusing her of not being invited. But as she scanned the room, she felt a different kind of uncomfortable. So many masks, so many capes, so many feathers, so many wires suspending halos and horns and insects and birds. Eyes glittered emotionless in the holes of the masks, or above furred collars. Everything felt a beat off, as if she'd arrived late to a planet she didn't know existed.

She noticed she'd fallen behind and raced to catch up, listening to Matteo. "The party was in full swing, but barely. Someone noticed he'd disappeared." *Who disappeared?* Stella wondered, castigating herself for her distractibility. She tried to stay focused as Matteo went on, "His daughter went looking for him." Stella quickly calculated who had a daughter here. Not her guests. Instantly, a flood of relief washed over her shoulders. She hadn't realized how much anxiety she'd carried about something happening to either of the Staffords. They were often infuriating guests, but they were *her* infuriating guests. She scanned the room for them and caught sight of the two of them talking to Louisa Lake in a black bodysuit and a pink boa.

At the sound of Luca's voice, Stella jogged forward to listen. "And she alerted the rest of you?"

Matteo inclined his head. "In that she screamed, yes. Then everything was in an uproar. I was coming out of the bathroom when it happened, practically tripped on Mrs. Lake asleep on the chaise."

Matteo paused at the landing that overlooked the ground floor and then gestured that they had one more flight of stairs to climb. Stella could hardly catch her breath, though from all the stairs or the anticipation, she couldn't decide.

Luca said, "Who has been in the room?"

Matteo said, "His children. Both of them. Obviously not his wife. Oh, gosh, I can't remember who else, though I closed the door to keep everybody else out as soon as I could." As they crested the stairs, Matteo nodded at a group of men standing at the door. At least Stella thought they were men, she couldn't tell amid the costumes. She and the officers swept into the room.

At first, all Stella could see was highly polished, black leather shoes jutting out from behind the bed. Other than those feet, nothing seemed amiss in the room. The linen duvet, sprigged with china-blue flowers, was pulled up over the bed. No items marred the surface of the dresser or nightstand. Only, Stella noticed, the lamp's shade looked knocked askew.

She hesitated in the doorway. The officers greeted the ambulance workers standing by the bed with their medical bags. She heard one say, "He was dead when we arrived. Nothing we could do."

At a nod from Luca, Stella approached the men, her eyes trained on the spot on the floor between the bed and the window, at those highly polished leather shoes. As she rounded closer, more of the body came into view. The knees, the belt, the black velvet cape spread across the floor. A mask lay alongside the man's hip, a gold plague doctor, the beak broken. At his other hip, Stella saw his hand, clutching his phone, the charging cord still attached, though the charger itself was pulled from the wall, probably when he fell to the ground. She came farther around the bed—the starched white shirt, the onyx buttons, the high cape collar, flourished with a trim of mechanical gears, forming improbable swirls and flourishes. Finally, the face.

She struggled to place him. But then the man's identity swam into focus. After all, she'd only met him briefly outside the flower shop. Back then, he'd been dressed like a wealthy Wall Street tycoon on vacation. Back then, he'd been full of restrained energy. Unlike this man before her, in a black suit and a black velvet cape spangled with gold trim.

Motionless.

She didn't know how it could be the same man, but it was.

Hollis Lake.

Dead.

Dead, with his mouth open in surprise, his glassy eyes staring at the ceiling.

Luca said, "Who is he?"

Matteo answered. "Signor Lake. Hollis Lake. A guest. From America," he added irrelevantly. Obviously, the man was no local.

Hearing some bustle at the doorway, a medic went to stand in the hallway to keep curious eyes away.

Stella stared at the body. One, two . . . three. Three bodies in her short tenure in Aramezzo. Why was it not easier? No less disturbing? Life snuffed, ended. And once again, the question: Was there a killer in their midst?

Luca asked the other medic standing by, "Any chance it was a heart attack?"

Stella exhaled. Yes, people died of regular things like heart attacks. Why did her mind go to murder? Her eyes drifted back along his arms.

The man said, "Someone from the medical examiner's office will make that determination. But I'd say there's a good chance. No wounds that we can see. It looks like it was sudden. It has heart attack written all over it."

Stella muttered, "But his hand."

The medic frowned, and Stella felt all the men's eyes on her. She shifted, suddenly uncomfortable. She'd gotten used to sparring with Luca and Salvo—they had reached an easier place. But new people to baffle with her hodgepodge Italian accent—a relic of learning Italian at her mother's knee but refining it in high-end kitchens in Florence, Milan, and Bologna—it felt too tiring to begin. She shook her head.

Turning to Luca, the medic said, "Who is she?"

Luca said, "Stella. Buchanan, but her mother's people were Mazzoli. She owns the bed-and-breakfast in Aramezzo."

The medic frowned, letting his eyes rake over Stella from threadbare red bandana to clunky black boots. "She's not an officer." It wasn't a question.

Luca and Salvo exchanged glances. Finally, Luca said, "She's a civilian with specialized skills we often find useful."

Stella tried not to smile, a task made harder by seeing the corner of Salvo's mustache twitch as he drew out his pad and pen. Her specialized skills ran mostly to flaky pastry and a light béchamel, but who needed to be the wiser?

"She speaks English," Luca said, firmly.

Salvo looked up from his notepad. "Plus, she has a nose for this stuff." Stella's eyebrows flew up, despite herself. She'd always thought Salvo barely tolerated her presence at crime scenes. His praise made her straighten her shoulders.

"A *nose*?" the medic scoffed. "Go on then, Signorina Nose. Give it a go. What do you smell?"

Stella glowered for a moment. But then couldn't help saying, "Shrimp."

"Shrimp?" Salvo winced. "What do you mean, *shrimp*?"

"I don't know," Stella shrugged. "I smell shrimp on him. Burned shrimp. They must have served it at the party." Her eyes narrowed in thought. "But I didn't smell anything burned when we walked in."

"Shrimp." Luca smiled his crooked smile, "Not sure how we can use that."

"I'm not sure either, but he has shrimp on him as much as he has this costume, so I figured I'd mention it."

The medic rolled his eyes. "I'll wait for you to take photos. Then we'll take him to the medical examiner."

Salvo lowered his voice and said to Stella hopefully, "You mean maybe he had a shellfish allergy? And that's what killed him?"

She shook her head, angry at herself for saying something stupid before she could work out why it might be important. Her eyes scanned the body on the ground and got hooked once again on the off-kilter lampshade on the nightstand. She gestured, "I'm guessing everyone noticed the lampshade."

The medic shook his head, chuckling. "Umm, yes? It's kind of obvious."

Stella drew closer to the nightstand, gingerly stepping over the body. Salvo reached to pull her back, no doubt regretting his previous estimation of her skills. "Glitter," she said, pointing.

"Where?" Luca said, coming closer.

"Just a dusting, you see it? It looks like it fell where the phone was, right here." She looked back at the phone in Mr. Lake's hand. "Yes, see, there's the barest bit of glitter on the phone. Glitter must have fallen over the phone on the nightstand, and when Mr. Lake picked up the phone, it left a glitter outline of the phone."

"I don't see it," Salvo said. Luca pointed, and Salvo peered closer. "Oh, yep. There it is."

Salvo shot the medic a triumphant grin, but the medic shrugged. "It's a costume party. He's in a costume."

Stella pointed to Mr. Lake. "Do you see any glitter on his costume? He's dressed like a steampunk plague doctor." To herself, she added aloud, "Pretty clever. Maybe this theme was more interesting than I thought."

Salvo wrote furiously in his notebook.

Meanwhile, Luca said with a tight laugh. "And to think I almost showed up in the same costume. How embarrassing would that have been?"

Stella looked up at him.

"Kidding," he said apologetically, before sighing. "Sorry. I—I suppose I should be used to this by now, but...I'm not."

She shook her head. "Tell me about it."

Salvo looked up from taking photos. "Make it three."

How strange, Stella thought. Aramezzo was so small and—before this last year—so sleepy, she had roughly as much experience with dead bodies as these two officers.

Stella said, "I wonder how it happened?"

They all looked at the body, the hand still gripping the phone. Stella ran her gaze from the phone to the charging cord to the charger on the floor. She said, "Looks like he was unplugging his phone. Or plugging it in?"

She hunched closer to get a better look, unsure of what she was looking for. Then rose. "The burned smell. It's on him. On the body."

Both Luca and Salvo crouched beside her and inhaled. Salvo muttered, "What are we supposed to be smelling?"

Stella said, "Close your eyes."

Salvo complied. Luca watched for a moment and then closed his own eyes. Stella could hear the medic shifting behind them with a huff of annoyance. "Ignore him," Stella murmured. "Empty your mind. Don't think about the body or this villa or the costumes. Don't even think about what I said it smells like. Just inhale and tell me what comes to mind."

She smiled in satisfaction as she watched both Salvo and Luca draw in a deep, complete breath with an intent look of concentration on their faces.

In a soft voice, so as to not break their concentration, Stella said, "Tell me. Not what you smell. Tell me what comes to mind." For herself, it was a history of accidentally leaving rubber spatulas over a gas flame. Metallic and acrid, as well as slightly sweet.

"Country train tracks in summer," said Luca as Salvo said, "That restaurant in Campo Imperatore, the one where they light coals with flame throwers and you cook lamb skewers over the embers."

She didn't know what Salvo meant, but she could picture it. "Right."

They opened their eyes.

"Wow," Luca said. "I smell it now. How did I miss it before?"

The medic let out a noise like a leaky radiator. "Talk about the power of suggestion."

Stella scanned the body, the wall, the outlet. "Do you think he could have been electrocuted?"

Luca got to his feet as she said, "Based on the smell of burned shrimp?"

Stella shook her head. "I think those are different smells. The burned smell happened here. The shrimp, he brought that from downstairs. I smelled shrimp when I entered the villa."

"Electrocution," Salvo muttered, rising to write in his notebook. "Is there any evidence?" He caught sight of the medic opening his mouth and said, "Besides the odd smell, I mean."

Stella gestured to the phone in Mr. Lake's hand. "Well, that's what got me. When people die, don't their muscles usually relax? Not clench?"

The medic scoffed, "Ever hear of rigor mortis?"

Stella frowned. "Sure, but that doesn't set in for a couple of hours after death."

"So he's been dead a couple of hours," shrugged the medic.

"And didn't drop his phone in that time?" Stella said. All eyes went to the phone clutched in Mr. Lake's hand. "When people are electrocuted, don't they get stuck to the source of the electricity? Like a fork in an outlet?"

"In cartoons, maybe," the medic said, rolling his eyes.

Stella continued, "Plus, there's something funky about this charger. I can't think of what it is, though."

"Electrocution," Luca muttered. "I'm calling the captain. We're going to need help here."

While he called, Stella investigated the charger more carefully. It looked like a regular charger—a cube of white plastic housing some sort of wiring within—but something felt off. "This could be what's rubbing me wrong."

"What's that?" Salvo leaned to see what she saw.

"This charger. It fits an Italian outlet."

"What do you mean?" Luca slid his phone back into his pocket.

"Well, Mr. Lake arrived from the United States. Our outlets are different, so when tourists bring phones or hairdryers or whatever, they have to bring an adapter that converts the plugs to ones that fit Italian outlets. But this doesn't have an adapter. It's a European charger."

"We give them to everyone," came a voice from the doorway.

Stella whirled to find Mr. Durant, his face white above his red cape with a collar that resembled furry dice. Stella remembered his wife's costume. Maybe he was the King of Chance, if that was a thing. "We offer European chargers so our guests can charge their iPhones without having to bring adapters for our outlets."

Luca and Salvo looked at Stella, confused. With a start, she remembered her role and translated.

Salvo wrote this information in his notebook as Luca said, "That's very thoughtful. To provide chargers."

Stella relayed this to Mr. Durant, who shrugged. "It's a simple amenity our guests appreciate."

In case this proved relevant, Stella translated and then continued serving as a mediator for the back-and-forth.

Luca asked, "How recently was the villa's wiring redone?"

The medic guffawed. "You can't take the electrocution theory seriously? Based on a *smell*?"

Luca kept his eyes on Mr. Durant as he said, "The odds seem low. But it doesn't hurt to investigate all leads."

Stella translated Luca's question about the house's wiring.

"About eight years ago. When we renovated the villa." Mr. Durant frowned. "You can't think this has anything to do with our wiring."

Through Stella, Luca said, "I'll need the name of your electrician."

"I assure you—" Mr. Durant said.

Stella interrupted. "This is standard procedure, Mr. Durant. I'm sure there's nothing wrong with the wiring, but the police will need to know exactly what your electrician did and may want to check the rest of the house. To avoid another accident."

He paled and shook his head. "We have a renovation binder. I'll get it."

As he walked away, Stella turned to Luca, "You think the house wiring could have zapped Mr. Lake?"

Luca paused. "I thought that's what you thought."

Stella shrugged. "I don't know. Maybe. But something else about the charger seems off to me. Maybe it's still that there's no adapter. Or maybe it's the phone." She got on the ground and looked more carefully. Slim, the newest model. "Do you think one of you can remove the phone from his hand?"

Luca said, "With this many question marks, I want to wait for the captain to do anything."

"Even though Salvo's been taking photos of the scene?"

He nodded, a warning look in his eye cautioning her from pushing her luck.

She nodded and got down on the floor, turning her head upside down to take photos of the phone from all angles. "Huh," she said.

She straightened and shook her head to correct for the blood flow angling to her head. "No phone case. Don't you think he'd have one? And the sides of the phone, they're scuffed. Don't most phones wear on the back? Not along the edge. It's peculiar."

Stella turned when she heard Mr. Durant reenter the room but then startled to find . . . not Mr. Durant. Instead, Gillian and Tripp Lake stood in the doorway. Gillian wore a skin-tight, vivid aquamarine dress with a flared bottom and a sheer bust covered with strategically-placed appliquéd seashells. Tripp wore a sparkling tuxedo with a matching top hat and a vivid green dress shirt under his vest.

Stella frowned. Gillian was a mermaid, but what was Tripp? Tripp caught her questioning gaze and muttered, "It makes more sense with my wife's costume."

Gillian shrieked.

A sustained sound that made Stella want to cover her ears.

Stella looked at Luca. Wasn't Gillian the one who found the body? Why the surprise?

But here was Gillian, pointing at her dead father. "His watch! His watch is gone!"

Stella leaned closer; Mr. Lake's wrist revealed a tan line that suggested a watch, worn fairly regularly.

When Gillian took a breath, Stella touched her arm. Gillian recoiled and rocked backward. "What! Can't you *see*? Someone took my father's watch! I remembered, I didn't see it on him when I . . . found him. And it's true, the watch is *gone*!"

"Maybe he wasn't wearing it tonight?" Stella suggested.

"No," Gillian said. "He always wore that watch."

Tripp nodded. "Let's check." They started throwing open drawers.

Luca and Salvo shouted for them to stop, but Gillian had already pulled the top drawer of the dresser open. She staggered back, her fist in her mouth. "There, see? No watch. His wallet. His Tiffany bracelet. No watch."

At Luca's roar, Stella put a hand on each of the siblings' arms. "Please. This may be a crime scene. You can't leave fingerprints."

"You bet it's a crime scene," Gillian crowed. "My father probably walked in on a robbery and the thief attacked him."

"With . . . what?" Stella asked, raising her hands. "There's no wound. No sign of a struggle."

"With . . . with . . ." Gillian looked desperately at her brother. "I don't know! That's *your* job."

Stella said, "Is it possible he could have put the watch somewhere else?"

Tripp shook his head. "He was very particular. It's an Omega. It always went with his valuables." He turned to his sister. "I told Dad we should have brought lockboxes. The Durants need safes in these rooms."

Mr. Durant appeared in the doorway. He looked from Gillian to Tripp to the officers to Stella. "Is there a problem?"

Gillian rushed to him. "Daddy's watch! It's not on him, and it's not in the drawer! It's *stolen*!"

"The Omega?" Mr. Durant paled. His eyes flicked to the feet jutting out on the floor.

Gillian said, "I bet I know who took it."

Mr. Durant said, "Now, Gillian. You can't know that."

"Ever since we got here, I've said there's something wrong with him."

"I'm sure we'll find the watch. Maybe he left it in the bathroom or something." Mr. Durant put an arm around Gillian and held out a business card to Stella. "Here's the electrician's card. I also found the bill for the work. I assure you, we paid top dollar. It passed inspection with flying colors."

She passed the card to Salvo, translating the scene for the officers. Luca's eyes widened, and he stared at Stella. "So there could be a motive here. Like, robbery. Which means this becomes a murder investigation."

Stella watched the question rise into his eyes, registering her improbable appearance on a dark road, alone, around the time of death. He breathed, "Stella . . . please tell me . . ."

She nodded curtly. "I went over this with Matteo. I've been around countless people all afternoon and evening."

He closed his eyes and exhaled.

Stella ignored him. Goodness, he acted like she was always the most obvious suspect in a murder. She asked Mr. Durant, "The chargers you give to your guests . . . where do you get them?"

"I don't know. My wife does that hospitality stuff." He put his arm around Gillian. "I'll take her downstairs. I think she needs to sit down." The three of them walked out.

Stella translated for the officers.

Luca said, "I believe it's time to interview the guests."

They nodded slowly. Nobody moved.

Luca's smile tugged at the corner of his mouth. "Stella? That means you're up."

Stella and the officers filed past the medic, standing silent now with his bag. Over his shoulder, Luca said, "Make yourself comfortable. I don't want the body moved until the captain offers his assessment."

They descended the stairs. Stella once again heard the wailing coming from a corner of the large corridor that seemed more properly a parlor stretching the length of the house.

Matteo appeared, Giancarlo beside him. In a low voice, Matteo asked Stella, "Murder?"

"Possibly. It's unclear," she said.

"Something about it seemed off. That's why I called."

Stella lowered her voice further, "One thing is for sure, the whole thing is a dark kind of strange."

Stella noticed Giancarlo tense. Perhaps he had as little familiarity with death as she recently did.

Matteo inclined his head toward Luca. "What does Luca think?"

She shrugged. "How are things here?"

"A mess." Matteo looked around the room. "Luckily, I didn't have to work too hard to prevent anybody from leaving. Most of the Americans are staying here, and no way the locals were going anywhere with this drama playing out."

Mr. and Mrs. Stafford rushed up to Stella, dressed in matching gold capes over their black formal wear and holding sun and moon masks. Mrs. Stafford wailed, "Stella! What is happening? No one will tell us anything! Is it true, is Hollis...dead?"

Stella nodded grimly.

Mr. and Mrs. Stafford exchanged glances. Stella noticed something shift behind Mr. Stafford's eyes. The crowds parted, and Mrs. Stafford glimpsed Mrs. Lake, dozing in the chair closest to the stairs that divided this part of the house from, if the scents were any indication, the kitchen. "How can she be sleeping?"

Mr. Stafford looked up from the phone he'd drawn from his pocket. "Doesn't stress bring on the headaches? And the meds..."

Mrs. Stafford clutched her husband's arm. "Oh, Morton. Someone told her, didn't they? About Hollis?"

He scanned the room. "I should think so."

Mrs. Stafford looked down the hall to where Gillian sobbed in TC Durant's arms on what was supposed to be the dance floor. Her voice flat, Mrs. Stafford said, "They treat Judith like she's a child. I bet nobody bothered to tell her."

She pressed her lips together and strode to her friend. Crouching next to her, she said, "Judith? Judith. Honey, are you awake?" Mrs. Lake's eyes fluttered behind her nose-length black lace veil.

"What? What's going on?" She asked slowly, her hand reaching to her head to adjust the headband that held the veil and propped up the lace cat ears atop her head, lined with neon pink silk.

Stella turned from the scene, not wanting to witness the grief. Grief was the worst part of finding a body—even if you didn't care about the person, knowing that someone else did, and someone else would soon be landing in a grief-framed alternative reality.

Stella remembered.

Even now, sometimes, when her phone rang, her heart leapt,

thinking it could be her father. Or something funny would happen and she'd think to herself she couldn't wait to share it with her little sister. In grief, the mind can't process a world without the one or ones taken away. Mrs. Lake's pain felt all too familiar to Stella. Even before she heard the hiccuping sob.

Mrs. Lake rose, shuddering. "Let me go to him. He's a deep sleeper. He's sleeping. You don't know."

Mr. Stafford put a hand on her arm. "Judith, you know you can't climb all those stairs. It's why you have your room on the ground floor. Emergency services have been here, the police are here. You can ask Stella."

Mrs. Lake's eyes landed on Stella, and Stella felt pulled into the swirling emotion on the older woman's face. "Stella. It's true? It's true what they say?"

Stella nodded grimly. "I'm so sorry."

"But," Mrs. Lake's voice lifted querulously, "how? Was it his heart?"

Stella said, "Did he have heart trouble—"

But her words were cut off by Marcello, the mayor, striding up with Luca and Salvo. "How is exactly what we'll need to find out," he said importantly. "Stella. I can't imagine why you're here."

Luca's jaw worked, and he said, "We brought her. We'll need her help to interview witnesses."

The mayor puffed out his chest. "I assume you've forgotten that I'm fluent?"

Stella stared at her feet.

"You're a witness yourself," Luca said before turning to Salvo. "Salvo, can you gather all the guests into a private space?"

"I can do that!" The mayor trumpeted. "This is my job!"

Though the Americans didn't understand his words, they still faded backward, Mrs. Stafford leading Mrs. Lake to one of the loveseats lining the parlor. Stella heard Mrs. Stafford murmuring something about positioning her friend to catch the fresh breezes drifting in through the double doors. Fresh breezes and also the sounds of the teenagers' voices: "Give it back, Sterling!" and "I told you not to tell him!" and "What do you *mean*! I'm *so* not *that* girl!"

Meanwhile, the mayor stopped Mrs. Durant as she passed. He plastered an enormous smile across his face and in English said, "Pardon you, Madame. Is which you have a rum for these nice main to be speaking?"

Mrs. Durant stared at the mayor. Stella smothered her grin. She cleared her throat and said to Mrs. Durant, "Is there a room we can use for interviewing?"

Mrs. Durant gave a faltering smile at the mayor and gestured to the end of the room. "At the end there, where we had the dance floor set up . . . to the right, you'll find our sitting room. If you'll excuse me, though, I need to speak with the kitchen staff."

The kitchen staff.

Stella had a thought.

"What did she say?" demanded the mayor.

Stella told the officers about the sitting room and lowered her voice to say to Luca, "I have an idea. I'll just be a minute."

He grabbed her arm before she could walk away. "Where are you going?"

"To the kitchen."

Luca's eyebrows lifted. "How would they know anything? They didn't know Signor Lake."

Quickly, Stella internally cataloged all the murder mysteries she'd read where an enemy of a victim got a job as waitstaff to poison a drink. But she didn't want to get into another discussion with Luca about how closely her *gialli* paralleled real life; this was not the time. Instead, she shrugged. "Background information, I suppose. Timing." A thought occurred to her. "The shrimp. I can find out when it was served, that might shrink our window of when Mr. Lake went upstairs."

"How?" the mayor asked. "Stella, don't you think you should do what the officers ask instead of inserting yourself into everything?"

She looked at Luca, who nodded, "Go. Thank you, Stella. Good thinking."

She brushed past the mayor, who stayed rigid, glaring at her. On her way to the kitchen, she also passed Mrs. Durant, who'd been pulled into an animated conversation with her husband and Gillian.

As Stella entered the kitchen, she stalled. Given the rest of the house, she expected the kitchen to be top of the line—all stainless steel appliances and copper pans and a wall of kitchen tools, perhaps with a marble island in the center for working dough. This, though. Few resources had gone into renovating the kitchen. Her eyes went to the outlets, expecting them to be hairy with cords, the faceplates falling off like in the kitchens where she'd started out. But the outlets alone seemed modern. Well, those and the lighting, harsh florescent tubes that flickered uncomfortably, like a modern, if low-tier, office space.

Why spend all this money renovating a home and give a kitchen such short shrift?

If she had this space, oh, what she could do with it!

The looks of the chefs and waitstaff, whispering in the far corner, recalled her from dreams of sleek surfaces intermixed with Italian country sensibilities like battered tin strainers and ceramic mixing bowls and linens woven by cloistered nuns. She cleared her throat and made her way toward them, trying to keep her mind on her task and not grow distracted by the jots of savory mushroom sauce on the island and the sheet pan of caramelized baby tomatoes with wands of thyme. She couldn't help, though, pressing her finger against a shard of tart dough, delighting in the satisfying crackle, and popping it into her mouth.

While Stella had hoped she'd know what to say once she approached the staff, she arrived in front of them, her mind still blank. But then she realized. She knew exactly what to say. These were her people. "*Buonasera*, all of you, I'm Stella. I have to say, I've worked in kitchens in Florence and Milan, as well as New York, and your pastry crust is perfection."

A woman in a toque flushed with pleasure. "That's mine."

"Ice water in the dough?" Stella asked. "Or vodka?"

"Vodka?" The chef grinned. "That's so old school. No, I use ice water but fold the dough like I'm making puff pastry. And I use a spray bottle to wet the dry bits of dough at the bottom of the bowl, rather than dribbling water."

"Keeping moisture down," Stella grinned back. "Neat trick."

The chef shrugged. "You know how it is, you pick up this and that along the way."

"I do indeed know that." She looked around. "And the mushroom sauce? I didn't even have to taste it. From the smell and the shine alone, I can tell it's incredible. Nadia Santini couldn't make it better."

All eyes turned toward a young man with a goatee. In a voice rich with pride, he said, "I trained with Santini."

"So did I," Stella smiled, warmly. "Though only for a week. The restaurant I was apprenticing with in Milan loaned me to her for a weekend function." She looked around at the faces that had visibly relaxed. "Quite a talented crew. You guys are a catering outfit?"

The first woman nodded. "Out of Perugia."

"I have a bed-and-breakfast in Aramezzo. I'd love your card. As tourism grows around here, I know I'm likely to get inquiries from people planning events."

The woman reached into her pants pocket to draw out a man's wallet. Stella smiled. She too had carried a man's wallet in her pants, under her chef's coat, when she worked kitchens in NYC. The turnover in restaurants was so high, you couldn't trust that a stranger wouldn't go rummaging through your locker or the coat on your hook. And women's wallets didn't fit pockets. Stella would have worn men's jeans, as this woman seemed to, if they came in her size. But she refused to shop in the boys' section, reasoning that was a bridge too far. She accepted the card, noting the large font for the company name, Rosmarino, and the smaller name below it.

She tapped the card against her fingers. "Bianca, that's you?"

The woman nodded.

"Wonderful. The important stuff out of the way," Stella smiled, and the staff shifted uncomfortably, tensing for what they'd been waiting for. "I suppose you know what's going on out there?"

Most heads nodded, and some didn't move.

"A guest has died," Stella said, summoning more authority than she felt.

Bianca said, "Was . . . was it . . . his time? Or an accident? We've heard . . ." She looked at the others, who looked around the room.

Stella understood. "Of course, you've been listening in on the conversation. The rules for keeping focused on your work don't matter when there's a death at the gig."

Nods.

Stella went on. "Where were you in the line-up when someone alerted you to stop cooking?"

Eyes flicked to Bianca, who not only seemed to be the executive chef but also the spokesperson. "Nobody told us. Pietro," Bianca gestured to the young man with the goatee, "heard someone shrieking and running downstairs and then a bunch of commotion. People had been moving from drinks on the lawn to their seats in the courtyard, but then there was this stampede into the house. We heard people yelling and running everywhere and then someone corralling everyone into the main room that runs along the house."

"What time was that?"

"We were just getting ready to serve the soup, so about 20,00."

Even though Stella had lived in Aramezzo for this long, and lived in other cities around Italy beforehand, she still found herself having to subtract 12 to get to standard time. Eight o'clock, she thought to herself.

"And before dinner, it was passed *hors d'oeuvres*?" It occurred to Stella how strange it was that the global culinary world used the French nomenclature for passed small bites. At the table, they'd be bite-size appetizers and, in Italian, they'd be called *antipasti*.

Bianca nodded.

Stella went on, "Something with shrimp?"

Bianca's eyes widened. "You heard about the grilled shrimp with confited tomatoes?"

She hadn't, of course, but no use trying to explain she smelled shrimp on Mr. Lake. Though this explained those heavenly tomatoes in oil she'd seen as she'd passed through the kitchen. Stella nodded.

Slowly, Bianca said, "Funny. I didn't think they came out as good as usual."

"What time were those served?" asked Stella.

Bianca stepped to the counter and picked up a yellow legal pad, covered with notes, the first quarter of the page crossed out. It must be the order of tasks, everything completed up until the served meal. Bianca ran her hand down the page as she said, "We were running behind. The American guests did photos on the lawn first. Nobody told us that was happening. We started moving out with Aperol Spritzes they had requested for the start of the party, but they waved us back to the kitchen like we were interrupting."

"Let me guess," Stella said. "You had to hold everything back."

"Which is fine for the *hors d'oeuvres*. Those were all cool or room temp. But slowing down the mushroom sauce?" said Pietro. "Not pretty."

"How long did it set you back?"

Bianca scanned the room. "Enrico, do you remember how long they were taking photos?"

Enrico, a curly, dark-haired chef cocked his head to the side for a moment. "Ten minutes? Maybe twenty?"

Bianca turned to Stella. "Sorry to be so vague."

Stella closed her eyes, imagining the scene—guests in vivid costumes hurrying outside, confused waitstaff trying to hand out drinks that got waved away. A man dressed as a steampunk plague bearer taking photographs with the rest. She opened her eyes. "Fascinating costumes out there, I noticed."

Bianca nodded. "I didn't see much, I've been in here. But when the chaos started, I went out like everybody else and was confused. I'd forgotten it was a costumed event, and thought I'd wound up backstage in somebody else's dream."

Stella chuckled at the image. Then she said aloud to the room at large, "Any of you happen to take a photo of partygoers?"

Bianca instantly understood and chimed in. "You won't be in trouble. We need to get a sense of timing."

A thin server, the trim uniform billowing around her, tentatively raised her hand. "I'm sorry. But when I told my girlfriend what I was doing tonight, she didn't believe me. I wanted to send her proof."

"Thank you, Coralina. Anybody else?" Bianca asked.

Heads shook. Stella approached the waif-like server. "Can I see the picture?"

Coralina shot a look at the head chef, who nodded. She withdrew her phone from her pocket and tapped on the photos. More like ten images, Stella noticed, shot from the corner of the courtyard to the lawn where the Americans—the Staffords, the Durants, and the Lakes, and about twenty more people she didn't know—were taking photos of each other or themselves on the lawn. The adults stood in clutches of two or four, taking traditional photos, like they might appear in a newspaper Style section, while the teenagers alternately pouted and looked surprised at whatever camera was aimed at them.

The groups didn't change much between photos, though in the second to the last one, Stella noticed Louisa in a bunny costume leading

Mrs. Lake in a lace black cat ensemble to the courtyard and presumably inside. In the last photo, both were missing. Stella looked up, "You stopped taking photos because they were approaching you?" She pointed to Mrs. Lake and Louisa.

Coralina flushed and stammered, "I . . . I didn't want to get in trouble."

Bianca looked over Coralina's shoulder at the photo. "This is when you came running into the kitchen, Coralina?"

Coralina nodded.

Bianca said, "Okay. About a minute after Coraline came back in, Signora Durant came in and said it was time for the spritzes."

Stella checked the time stamp. "So just a shade past 18,15, then."

"Sounds about right."

Stella nodded, flipping through the photos again. Something seemed amiss, but she didn't know what. She wished she could take over the kitchen and bake something to organize the thoughts swirling like whipped cream around a whisk. "Is it okay if I send these to myself?"

"Sure, I guess," Coralina said, at an affirmative nod from her boss.

"*Grazie.*" She turned back to Bianca. "I'm trying to get the chronology down here. So, you began at 18,15, fifteen minutes behind. When would you have passed the shrimp around?"

Bianca reached for her yellow legal pad. "Those were second. After the prosciutto wrapped asparagus."

Stella said, "Any chance I can see your menu rundown?"

Bianca handed it to Stella, who scanned it. There was the shrimp, the second passed dish to hit the party. She read on past beef carpaccio with *cavolo nero*, pancetta crisps with fig, Cannara onion tartlets, and finally gorgonzola cheese puffs.

Gorgonzola.

She felt like smacking her forehead. Of course.

"The gorgonzola cheese puffs. When would they have been served?"

Bianca checked her notes. "Based on how we stagger the new dishes,

I'd say around 19,00. Or a little before."

"Would you mind if I took a photo of your menu rundown?"

The chef's face grew stiff.

Stella realized. "Not for ideas. Just in case it helps establish when Mr. Lake went upstairs."

"Won't you get a time of death or whatever from some medical office?"

"We should, yes. But it could be important to know when Mr. Lake separated from the group. Which is hard to know at a party."

"But how would this help?"

Stella hesitated. "This is going to sound crazy, but I smelled shrimp on him."

The chef said, "How is that crazy?"

Grinning, Stella said, "Right. Who am I talking to? I'm sure you would have smelled it, too. But see," she pointed at the list, "about forty-five minutes later, gorgonzola puffs go out."

Bianca's face furrowed in thought for a moment before she smiled broadly. "And you didn't smell it. The gorgonzola. On the . . . guy."

"Right. So I can assume he went upstairs sometime between the shrimp and the gorgonzola. So," Stella calculated, "Sometimes between 18,15 and 19,00," she guessed.

"Wow," Bianca smiled.

"Right?" Stella said with satisfaction. It was such a relief to not have to explain. "Better sleuthing through sniffing. Anyway, that's the first thing that occurs to me as I look at this, but I want the chance to mull it over some more."

The chef hesitated before nodding. "I'm being silly, I know. Last year, a waiter I hired last minute shared my menu with another caterer. A caterer, I should add, that had badmouthed me as a hack for the previous year. It took me three months to perfect a new menu. I guess it's made me paranoid."

Stella put a hand on her arm. "Listen, I've been there. You're right to watch over your shoulder. But you can trust me. Chef to chef."

"The guy who stole my menu was a chef," Bianca said. "But okay. Go ahead."

Stella snapped the photos, making a show of skipping the pages with recipe notes. She looked up with a smile. "Ciao, *ragazzi*. Thank you so much. If you think of anything else, I run Casale Mazzoli in Aramezzo. Call me."

Bianca straightened. "Yes, chef!"

Stella saluted Bianca and her brigade. She turned on her heel and strode toward the swinging door. Before she put a hand out to push her way through, she cast a look over her shoulder.

She caught Bianca's eye. The chef smiled and nodded at Stella as if she knew how hard it was for Stella to leave the warm kitchen with its easy camaraderie. She'd forgotten how good it felt to work with other chefs—that tingle of pulling together as a team, united by tasting spoons and a hard press to the pass.

Stella sighed and pushed the door, into a room lit by electric candles.

Stella spotted Matteo waiting by the stairs. "Why haven't they turned the lights on?"

"They are." Matteo pointed down the parlor area. "Only not in this room. Atmosphere, I guess."

Stella closed her eyes.

"You okay, Stella? I know this is . . . a lot." His eyebrows contracted and flew up his long forehead, like they did when he was worried or surprised.

"Yes. I'm fine. Where is everyone?" She gestured to the guests milling about the long room. "Not everyone. I mean . . . Luca and Salvo, specifically."

"They started the interviews." She opened her mouth to ask the question, but before she summoned the words, Matteo added, "The Italians. No need for translation."

"Oh," her face fell as she hurried to the end of the hall. "I didn't want to miss anything."

"Lucky for you, I volunteered to go first. They're interviewing Giancarlo now." He kept pace with Stella, slowing as they approached the end of the hall, an alcove that led to a bathroom straight ahead and the room that Mrs. Durant had indicated to the right.

"And you promise to tell me everything you told them?"

"Later. Now, go on." Matteo practically shoved her into the room where Luca and Salvo sat with Giancarlo, though it sounded more like Luca and Salvo were grilling Giancarlo about his appearance in the Champions League final than the body upstairs.

At her appearance, the officers seemed to remember themselves. She caught Giancarlo's eyes, and he held them, pulling her forward into the room. His face warmed as he searched hers. "Stella. Are you all right?"

Luca stared from Stella to Giancarlo. "You two know each other?" Before they could explain, he said, "Right, Matteo. Of course."

Salvo, catching a note of ire in his partner's voice, said. "Stella, you're late. We had to start without you."

Luca shook his head. Did she imagine his jaw clenching? "It's fine, Salvo. We didn't need her for translations yet."

Luca and Giancarlo moved to bring a chair to the circle around the coffee table. At a glare from Luca, Giancarlo sat back down. Stella sank into the proffered chair, and Luca returned to the large armchair at the end of the coffee table.

Salvo cast Luca a curious look and cleared his throat. "So, Giancarlo. You said you arrived at the party at 18,30 and noticed nothing amiss."

"Correct."

"Did you see Signor Lake when you arrived?"

"I did not."

Luca frowned. "Do you know who he is?"

Giancarlo nodded and said tightly, "We've met."

Salvo said, "Matteo said you both ran into Mr. Lake and his son outside Flavia's."

"Flavia?" Giancarlo frowned.

Luca looked exasperated. "Flavia. Our town florist? Have you forgotten?"

Giancarlo regarded Luca for a moment. "I have, actually."

Luca asked, "What was he doing? Mr. Lake."

"Directing the flower delivery. That's what he told us. For the party."

Luca shook his head impatiently. "No, what was he doing when you saw him at the party?"

The three of them stared at Luca.

Finally, Salvo cleared his throat. "Giancarlo said he didn't see Mr. Lake at the party."

Luca took out a notebook and started writing furiously.

Salvo watched him for a moment and then turned to Giancarlo. "Can you tell us anything that seemed off or out of place during the party?"

"Well, I mean all the shrieking. That was weird."

"You're referring to Gillian, Signor Lake's daughter, when she found the body?"

"I guess. Shrieking. That's all I can tell you. It was so high, so long. It didn't sound," Giancarlo searched for a word, "human. It didn't sound human."

Stella's stomach knotted. She knew what Giancarlo meant. It was the sound she'd made when the police showed up at her door and told her mother that Stella's father and baby sister would not be coming home.

"Do you remember what time you heard that shrieking?"

Looking at the top right corner of the room, Giancarlo said, "About 20,00. Maybe 20,30."

Luca grumbled. "Matteo didn't know either. Does no one carry a watch anymore?" He rose from the large chair, indicating the meeting was over. "Stay on the premises. We may have more questions later."

Everyone followed suit. Giancarlo reached for Stella's hand and pulled her a fraction closer to say, "Play simple, Stella. You've got this," before walking out.

Luca stared at Stella's hand as if it had turned into a robotic appendage, before saying in a stilted voice. "So, Stella. I hope you learned something in the kitchen."

She nodded and explained how Signor Lake must have gone upstairs between the shrimp and the gorgonzola course, so roughly between 18,15 and 19,00. Assuming he'd died right after he went upstairs, and hadn't had a protracted discussion with someone or done a spot of business, he probably would have died soon after he went upstairs.

Salvo smoothed his mustache. "I don't know. Can we narrow it down by smells and cooking times? If so, my nonna should be a detective."

Luca stared at Stella and said softly, "You're sure, Stella? About the gorgonzola?"

"Yes." She considered. "Though I suppose if he declined a gorgonzola puff, he could have been present, but wouldn't smell like it." She shook her head. "No, he'd have the scent on him if he was anywhere close to them. It's powerful cheese. I have a hard time getting the scent off my hands when I work with it. Which is why I never serve it at the bed-and-breakfast. Impossible to get the scent out of the linens."

Slowly, Luca said, "Well, it's a start. We can ask the next guests if they were with Signor Lake between the shrimp and cheese." To Salvo, he said, "We'll need the daughter next. Hopefully, she'll be calmer by now."

Salvo opened the door, and the mayor stormed in. "Let's get this over with."

Salvo looked at Luca, who said, "Signor Sindaco, we're not ready for you."

"What does that have to do with anything? I need to get my wife home. Now. This has all been far too much for her." At the silence, the mayor went on, "So? Begin."

As the mayor spun to sit on a chair, Luca touched his arm. The mayor yanked his arm back and spat, "Don't you touch me! I'm not the criminal here. You all need to do your job and do it right this time. Or I'll be having words with your captain."

Stella wondered if he had the same rapport with this captain as he'd had with Captain Palmiro.

"One step at a time," Luca said. "We have some statements to take first."

The mayor's mouth dropped open. "You must be kidding."

"I'm afraid not," Luca said without a trace of emotion. "And even after we take your statement, not one of you can leave until we release you."

"What! You'd hold me hostage here against my will! This is an American party. With *American* suspects. What do I have to do with it?"

Luca set his jaw. "Everyone here is a potential witness, and none of you can leave."

Stella squinted into the corner of the room, pretending to be invisible.

"I'm going to have to speak with your captain!"

Luca took the mayor and led him to the door. "Please do. He's the one who gave the order."

The mayor gawped like a landed fish. "He couldn't have meant me!"

Luca inclined his head and showed the mayor to the door. Stella saw Matteo lean in, scanning the room until he saw her. "You okay?" he mouthed.

She nodded.

He listened to Luca for a moment and then turned into the crowd. Luca said, "He's getting the daughter."

Salvo flipped through his notes. "What's her name again?"

"Gillian," said Stella.

Salvo muttered, "Why can't Americans give their kids regular names?

What's wrong with easy-to-pronounce ones like Anna or Maria? Or even Anna Maria?"

Mr. Lake's daughter appeared at the door, mascara streaking her ashen face. Stella's heart ached for her. To find her father like that. Stella couldn't imagine.

Gillian ignored the chair that Salvo pulled out for her, instead flouncing into the large armchair that dominated the space. Luca watched her for a moment and then settled into the chair Salvo had been offering Gillian.

Stella wondered how her sympathy for Gillian could evaporate so quickly.

They all sat down and Luca began by saying, "I'm Officer Luca Borghi and this is—"

"I can't understand you," Gillian broke in, her voice so loud, Stella wondered if all the crying might have plugged her ears.

Stella leaned forward. "Hi, Gillian. I'm Stella. I didn't get to, er, reintroduce myself upstairs. We met the other day outside the flower shop."

Gillian looked as if she'd gotten a whiff of something malodorous. "And?"

Stella inhaled slowly. "The officers here have some questions for you, and I'm translating until an official translator arrives with the police captain."

"You're Italian? You don't sound Italian. You don't look it either with those freckles." She lifted a hand and shook it in the direction of Stella's offending nose.

"Nevertheless, I am. Half." She remembered what Gillian had been through. If anyone deserved some slack, it was her. "First, we want to offer our condolences. I'm sure this has been extremely trying."

Gillian lifted a wadded-up tissue to her face. "*Extremely* trying. *Thank* you."

Stella nodded and translated quickly to the officers. She then began translating back and forth, losing herself in the rhythm until it hardly felt like she was present at all, but more existing in the space between them, shining the light of understanding on their conversation.

"Thank you for agreeing to talk to us, Signorina Lake. We know how hard this must be," said Luca.

Gillian sniffed.

"Can you tell us when you went upstairs?"

She shook her head. "Not exactly. We were called to the courtyard for dinner and I didn't see my dad. I couldn't find my brother to ask him, and Louisa was helping my mother to the table. Neither of them had seen him. Then Claire said—"

"Claire?"

"Yes, Claire Stafford. She's staying somewhere in the village. I don't know why," Gillian's said. "Anyway, she told me that my dad had said he was going to his room to grab his phone. We'd all been taking photos earlier, and he realized he must have left it upstairs. Claire said he'd decided to go up and get it before dinner. So he left. He told her he'd be right back." She frowned. "That's what she said."

Gillian closed her eyes. The only sound in the room was Salvo's pen furiously moving across the page to keep up with Stella's translated words.

In a voice hardly above a whisper, Gillian went on, "I waited a few minutes, but he didn't come back. At first, I thought maybe he'd gone to the bathroom. Or no, I didn't think that. Morton Stafford, Claire's husband, made a rude joke about it. My brother figured Dad must have checked the numbers and gotten distracted. But I had a bad feeling. I . . . I went upstairs. It was so quiet. I called him. He didn't answer. The bathroom door was open, so I knew he wasn't in there. I pushed the door to his room open. At first, I thought he'd tripped or something. Maybe bumped his head. But then I came around the bed and I saw his face."

Gillian's head fell in her hand. "I've never seen a face look like that before. His eyes so wide. Like the last thing he saw, or maybe the last thing he thought, was something terrible."

The room once again went silent. When it seemed Gillian had run out of words, Luca asked, "Signorina Lake. Do you know if your father had any enemies?"

She looked up, her voice full of wonder. "You think he was murdered."

"Not necessarily. But we need to be prepared for whatever the medical examiner may find."

Gillian didn't seem to hear Stella translating Luca's words. "Good. I'm sure he was murdered." Once all eyes were fixed on her, Gillian said, "And I know who did it."

"You . . . you do?" said Stella, even before she'd translated. But Luca's informal English studies must have paid off because he said, "Who?"

"That guy. That homeless guy."

Stella and the officers exchanged looks.

Stella said, "Homeless guy?"

"Yes! You know the one! He's always here harassing us. It's obvious he wishes he was one of us."

Butter hit the hot pan. "Mimmo?"

"How the hell should I know his name? I'd be surprised if he had one."

Stella quickly translated and then said, "A hunter?"

"That would explain the gun."

Why didn't she mention the gun in the first place? Were so many people in the United States strolling down Main Street with guns that it no longer occurred to people to mention it? Stella said, "You saw him in the house? With a gun?"

Gillian rolled her eyes. "Like we'd let that happen. But I've seen him with a gun before. He waved it around like it would scare us."

"Why do you think he killed your father?"

"Are you kidding? Come on. He's been casing all around, shooting us looks of death. He came to rob us, nabbed my dad's watch." She looked around. "Well? What are you waiting for? Go arrest him!"

Stella translated and watched as the officers communicated wordlessly, before she said, "Mimmo is … well, he's a particular sort. I get that he might have made you uncomfortable, but that's more than a hop, skip, and a jump away from murder."

Gillian's lips thinned to a straight line. "I see. Writing me off because I'm a hysterical woman. Got it."

Stella didn't bother translating. "What? Absolutely not. Believe me, I'm the last person … I mean, there's no way …" Stella wondered where all her words had gone.

Gillian rose. "I'll speak with your superior, if you don't mind."

A small shake of his head let Stella know that Luca understood. Stella said, "That's not possible at the moment."

Gillian flounced out with as much flounce as one could manage in a skin-tight mermaid dress. Over her shoulder she trilled, "I'll be letting him know about this!"

Interesting that she assumed the superior to be a man. Especially after her little speech, thought Stella.

Luca said, "Who should we call next?" as Salvo said, "Is she possibly right? Could it be Mimmo?"

Luca said, "In what universe? First of all, how could he have 'snuck' into the house without anybody noticing? He hardly fits the brief."

"Plus," Stella thought aloud. "I don't see Mimmo figuring out how to electrocute a person."

Salvo shook his head. "We don't know that's how he died."

"We know it wasn't a knife or a gun," Stella said. "Which are the tools of Mimmo's trade."

Luca sighed. "We have a ballroom full of people to interview. Mimmo can wait. Who should be next?"

"Signora Durant," Stella said firmly. "As the hostess, she'll be the most aware of the dynamics of the party." True, but not entirely. Stella didn't want to press her charger theory until she had something substantive to go on. Hopefully, the officers wouldn't notice her steering the conversation in that direction.

Luca turned to Salvo. "Agreed?"

Salvo shrugged. "Why not?"

Luca opened the door and called for Matteo, who appeared so quickly Stella wondered if he'd been lurking in the hallway. "Get Signora Durant?"

Matteo disappeared into the crowd for only a moment before he returned with Mrs. Durant, resplendent in her Queen of Hearts costume. Stella wondered if the aged playing cards on her cuffs, collar, and crown were actually vintage. Stella remembered Mrs. Lake mentioning her friends' history in the theater. That certainly made sense given her ensemble. On closer inspection, Stella realized the gown's shimmer came from tiny, neon pink hearts. She wondered if the hearts had lights in them to make them glimmer, but then decided they were crystals, catching the light. She couldn't imagine how much it had cost. Probably enough to rebuild the crumbling Aramezzo schoolhouse.

Mrs. Durant sank into the chair that Luca gestured to and he sat in his original armchair. Perhaps the throne-like chair was Mr. Durant's chosen seat and therefore Mrs. Durant harbored no motivation to claim it, but Stella suspected her obedience had more to do with her fatigue. The woman looked washed out, like a wrung-out cloth. She looked up at Stella as if seeing her for the first time. "Stella, right?"

Stella nodded.

Mrs. Durant let out a shuddering breath. She seemed to have faded in the time since she'd opened the front door for them. What could have happened? Or perhaps it all finally caught up with her. "Can you even believe all this?"

"I can't, no." Stella waved her hand in the direction of the officers.

"These are Officer Luca Borghi and Officer Salvo Paviotti. They are conducting the interviews and I'm helping translate until the department can bring in a translator affiliated with the police. Are you okay if they ask you a few questions?"

"Sure," Mrs. Durant said.

Stella turned to the officers, and they began their questions.

Mrs. Durant answered them in low tones, her hand repeatedly wiping her eyes. She hadn't noticed anything amiss at the party. In fact, a few minutes before Gillian came shrieking down the stairs, she had told her husband that she thought it was their most successful fete. The costumes had added the spontaneous, ebullient tone she'd hoped for. Everyone was in great spirits. She'd been too distracted to notice Mr. Lake heading upstairs.

Stella said, "Your husband mentioned you provided the guests with phone chargers." She took a breath to form the question. "Have you ever had any problems with those chargers?"

"No. Why?"

"Do you buy them yourself?"

"Yes." She frowned. "I don't understand."

"And do you order them, or buy them in a shop?"

Mrs. Durant stared at Stella. "Did Hollis's death have something to do with his charger?"

Stella said, "We're gathering as much information as we can."

"I order them from the Apple store in Rome and have them shipped here."

Stella's thoughts clarified with such force, it left her breathless. Luca seemed to understand she was onto something and, blessedly, let her continue without asking for a blow-by-blow translation. "You order chargers from an Apple store?"

"Of course. That way if a guest brings an android phone, they can still use the charger. Chargers for android phones won't work on

Apple products."

"Any chance you might have ordered them from another site set up to mimic an Apple store?"

"Are you suggesting I'm an idiot? I know the difference between Apple's website and an imposter."

"Of course," Stella said, and translating to buy herself time to ask the next question, which was forming in her mind. "Could we please see the chargers you gave your guests?"

"Wh-why?"

Softly, Stella said, "Mrs. Durant. If there's something wrong with the manufacture of the charger, that's hardly your fault. But we wouldn't want another accident, would we?"

If possible, Mrs. Durant paled further. She rose and ran out of the room. Stella explained to the officers. Salvo frowned. "Who cares about the other chargers? I'm not sure why we even care about this one."

"Stella?" Luca said softly. "We're giving you latitude here. You going someplace specific?"

"I thought of something. I'll explain after," Stella said, unable to shake herself of Mr. Lake's hand clutching the phone, the faint smell of a rubber spatula set over a gas flame. She picked up her phone and scrolled to find the photos of Mr. Lake's phone and charger.

Mrs. Durant strode in, dropping a basket of four chargers on the coffee table. "Here's what I have out for guests. Those who need one take one."

Stella looked at the chargers on the table, reluctant to touch them. She got down on the floor to see them at eye level, her eyes scanning back and forth between the photo and the chargers. She looked up. "Is there any chance you gave a different charger to Mr. Lake?"

With a furrowed brow, Mrs. Durant shook her head. "No. Our housekeeper and I opened all the boxes and left them in a basket for guests to take what they needed on arrival."

Luca said softly, "Stella? Care to fill us in?"

"They're different. I mean, they all say Apple, just like Signore Lake's. So maybe these differences are nonsignificant. But there are differences. His, the one that fell out of the wall, it's not the same as these." She snapped photos of the tangle of chargers on the coffee table.

Luca said, "Any chance Mr. Lake brought his own?"

"It would be an American one. It wouldn't fit," Stella said.

"Not if he brought one he'd carried to Europe in the past."

"Good thought," said Stella, pleased that he reasoned so clearly, even without knowing her direction. She turned to Mrs. Durant. "Do you remember if Mr. Lake took a charger you offered? Or perhaps declined because he had his own?"

Mrs. Durant bit her lip. "I can't say. I feel like he took one because I remember him commenting that not even European hotels offered this kind of service. But I don't remember for sure."

Stella turned to the officers and translated, then added, "His wife might know. Signora Lake."

Salvo wrote furiously as Luca said, "Let's get her in here next."

Salvo looked up. "Will she be in any state? She lost her husband an hour ago."

Stella noticed the muscle in Luca's jaw work. "We'll have to see. Stella, before we release her, ask about Signor Lake's relationships with the other guests."

Nodding, Stella said, "How did Mr. Lake get along with the other guests? Any tension or friction that you know about?"

Mrs. Durant's eyes widened. "You think it's murder?"

Stella shook her head. "We need background information. While we have you."

Mrs. Durant smoothed her dress. "Hollis was charming. At first. But he was a hard man to know. It's not easy to explain. He can be . . . intense. I enjoy his company in small doses. But after a while, well, he sort of expects everyone to wait on him the way Judith once did. I always chalked that up to her accident. It impacted different people in different ways. Her daughter went a little wild. Her son stopped being wild and buckled down with dreams of taking over the family business. And Hollis? He started acting like the world owed him."

It took Stella a full minute to realize she needed to translate. Mrs. Durant's words seemed more insightful than she would have expected. Maybe she'd sold the woman short, seen everything about her through the lens of being rejected by the established American lady who felt at home seemingly everywhere whereas Stella felt at home nowhere.

In a rush, she explained what Mrs. Durant had said and then turned back to her. "Anybody you can think of who he especially rubbed wrong?"

Mrs. Durant darted a look over her shoulder.

Stella caught her meaning. "This is confidential."

"I feel awful saying this. I mean, I'm sure he didn't do anything. But Morton and Hollis have been at war for years."

"Do you know why?"

Shrugging, Mrs. Durant said, "Morton claims that Hollis cheated him in a multi-million dollar business deal. They're both investment managers for their own houses, it can be pretty cutthroat. Morton never forgave him. Judith and Chelsea and I warned them this might happen if they brought business into our social circle. Any freshman econ major would have said the same. And now you see why. We three women are still tight, but we can't ever do anything as couples anymore. In fact, I was surprised when Morton agreed to come. They never have before."

Stella passed this information on and thought for a moment as Salvo's pen scratched across the page. "How did Mr. Lake and Mr. Stafford get along tonight?"

Mrs. Durant hesitated. "Again. I hate saying anything. I'm afraid it looks like I suspect Morton of some wrongdoing and I do not. But there was a . . . moment." The room stilled. "Judith needed help getting to the bathroom. Not using the bathroom, you understand, just walking there. She's often weak, especially in the evenings. She asked her family to help her and they ignored her. I'm afraid that's common. It's frankly a little hard for Claire and me to watch. We have loved Judith since we were girls."

"Mr. Lake, he was cruel to his wife?" Stella's eyebrows went up.

"No, no. Never cruel. Only sometimes … dismissive. Again, I think seeing her so altered is hard for him to bear. He resists her … disability. Which makes it seem like he's resisting her. We can understand that."

"But you don't. Resist her disability."

"I suppose that's true." Mrs. Durant cocked her head to the side. "Yes, I suppose that's true."

Stella translated and then on a whim asked, "How altered is Judith from how she was before?"

Mrs. Stafford shrugged. "The best of Judith is still there. Have you heard her tell a bawdy joke? No, I don't know how you would have. Goodness, she keeps us in stitches. Her body is weakened, but her mind is unchanged." She paused, thinking. "And what's more important?"

Stella offered the words in Italian. Luca said, "So what happened between Signor Stafford and Signor Lake?"

Stella nodded. She'd gotten off track and hadn't even noticed. Taking a beat to silently praise Luca's steadiness of mind, Stella translated for Mrs. Durant, who nodded and said, "Hollis sent Louisa to assist Judith. That's when Morton snapped that maybe Hollis should take responsibility for his own one of these days. Only I think he used the term, 'grow a pair.'"

"How did Mr. Lake respond?"

"Well, everyone laughed. Even though it wasn't funny. Hollis turned pretty red. He grumbled something I couldn't make out and stormed away."

"To help his wife?"

"No. Louisa did that."

"I'm guessing she wasn't too happy with that."

"Can you blame her? But what can she do? Hollis is her husband's father. He holds the purse strings. So she needs to keep the peace." She sighed. "I feel for Louisa, I do. It can't be easy. She has her children to raise, and I can tell she'd like to move away from the family business, to have the four of them be their own unit. But Tripp, he can't quit working for his father. No other job has the same financial potential. So they're stuck."

Stella had a thought. "They *were* stuck. But now, won't Tripp take his father's position?"

Mrs. Durant went white. "No. It's not true. What you're thinking is simply not possible."

Shrugging, Stella said, "I hear you. It's hard to believe. And remember, we don't even know if this was intentional or not. But there have been tales of a son killing his father for gain since time immemorial."

"Oedipus," said Mrs. Durant.

"Oedipus, sure. But there are more. And not just in mythology."

Mrs. Durant shook her head. "Those are stories. Tripp could never. He idolizes his father. You wouldn't think it to look at him, but he's always been a sensitive little boy."

"He's not a little boy anymore."

"Yes. Yes, that's true." Mrs. Durant thought for a moment before shaking her head with conviction. "But it's not possible."

Stella consulted with the officers and then asked, "Back to Mr. Stafford. Can you confirm he was downstairs with everyone the whole night?"

Mrs. Durant chewed the corner of her mouth. "I didn't see him leave. But I can't say he didn't. Hosting a party…you know. Or maybe you don't?" She narrowed her eyes at Stella as if in appraisal. Stella felt a leap of indignation at the assumption but then realized it was fair. With her uniform of a t-shirt and threadbare bandana and Doc Martens, she could hardly be presumed to be interested in party planning.

Stella translated and then Mrs. Durant looked around. "Is that all? I'm sure everyone is starving. I need to ask the kitchen if they might prepare plates from the meal we didn't eat, but someone keeps pulling me into conversation."

Luca listened to Stella translate and rose, thanking Mrs. Durant for her time. With her hand on the doorknob, she turned. "I should add, though. There's a guy, local, who has been hanging around a lot lately. He is none too pleased with any of us being here. Honestly, if someone…m… m…did something bad, he's a more likely candidate than anyone here."

"Mimmo, you mean?" Stella asked.

"Yes, that's right, that's his name." She frowned. "It's a wonder you'd know it, dear. I don't know why you'd fraternize with his type. People might get the wrong idea."

Stella pressed her lips together. "This isn't Mimmo's style."

Mrs. Durant lifted an eyebrow. "Honey, there is no style about this. Don't tell me that's news to you." With that, she whisked back into the hallway.

Luca said, "Let's get Tripp Lake in here. Sound good?"

Salvo said, "Not Morton Stafford?"

Luca looked at Stella, who shrugged. Luca sighed. "Son of the victim makes more sense as a starting point. Let's not tip our hand to alarm the Staffords."

Stella said, "Right. Good thinking."

"Salvo?" Luca asked

Salvo confirmed with a nod.

Luca leaned out of the room. "Matteo, can you get us Tripp Lake?" He shut the door. "Okay, Stella," said Luca, closing the door behind Mrs. Durant. "Now, what is all this about the chargers?"

Stella took a breath. "Okay. It might not be relevant at all, but when she mentioned the Apple store, I remembered this time, years ago, when

I was between restaurant gigs and hoarding every penny. Back then, I told a friend of mine who worked at an Apple store that his chargers were overpriced. I said anyone who bought them were fools, since you could buy a perfectly good charger online for like a tenth of the price."

Luca and Salvo looked at each other. Luca said, "Stella. While I'm enjoying your walk down memory lane—"

Stella held up her hand. "Humor me. I'm almost there. Grant told me horror stories of faulty wiring in knockoff chargers which allow too much electrical current to move through the cord. So when a person plugs their phone into the charger, *all* the house's power goes through the charger, through the phone, and through a person, to find the earth. I remember Grant said, 'Power seeks ground'. Like lightning."

She hoped she was explaining it right. Science, aside from anything she could use for culinary purposes, had never been her strong suit. Luca's and Salvo's eyes widened and Stella felt her shoulders drop a fraction. They got it. She went on, "Grant told me a faulty charger can allow a surge of electricity to be delivered to the phone. Turning the phone, essentially, into a grenade."

"It explodes?" Salvo asked, his voice hushed.

"It can. But usually it delivers an electrical shock. Sometimes mild, like static electricity. Sometimes more. Like enough to stop a heart."

Luca said, "But wait, wouldn't we see that? Like with fire and smoke?" His voice faded. "The smoke. We smelled smoke."

"Right. That was my missing link. The smoke. When Grant was trying to scare me away from knockoff chargers, he said sometimes they can cause the phone to explode, if there's no place for the electricity to go. But if the electricity can ground by moving through a person, it will. Which will..." Stella took a breath before going on, "cook a person. Inside. Or maybe outside? I admit, at this point, I wasn't asking Grant any more questions."

Luca said, "This can't be common. And even if it was. It can't be intentional."

Stella nodded. "It's not common. I think it's only happened a handful of times. But it does happen. With faulty chargers."

Salvo darted a look toward the chargers on the coffee table. "Are they faulty?"

"That's the thing," said Stella. "I see the Apple logo on all of them, the one in Signor Lake's room and the ones Signora Durant brought us. But his seems different from the rest. Maybe a different model? Or maybe something else."

The three of them stood in thought for a moment before Stella remembered. "Oh! Luca. About what you said, about it being intentional. I don't know. I mean, I guess if chargers can be faulty then someone can make them faulty? But here's something else weird." She pulled out her phone and showed them the photo of Mr. Lake's phone, clutched in his hand. "The scuffs on the side. Like it's a few years old. But this model was released in November."

Salvo said, "Your friend at the Apple store again?"

Stella shook her head. "Domenica. You wouldn't think it to look at her, but the woman internet shops when she's angry. Or not shops, really, since she buys nothing, but she combs tech websites to get the sense of what new stuff is hitting the market so she can rage against it and forget her original anger."

They stared at her. Finally, Salvo said, "Domenica? Who owns the used bookshop? And wears like fifteen scarves?"

"I don't know what to tell you, it's true." She realized that Domenica's technological talents were likely not for public consumption, so best not to say too much. She ran on, hoping to distract the officers from this tidbit. "Anyway, see? Signor Lake's phone is scuffed hard. A weird pattern. Check your phones."

They all drew out their phones, except Stella, who turned hers so they could see the sides. "Look at the wear patterns on our phones. All older than Signor Lake's. See how it's different?"

Salvo frowned. "Ours are in cases."

Stella said, "Right! That's the other thing. How can someone have a top-of-the-line phone with no case?"

Luca shrugged. "Maybe if you have a ton of money, you don't feel the need to protect your expensive devices."

"Maybe. Still, the wear pattern is strange, right? It looks like . . . scrapes around the edging, rather than regular wear. Like somebody took the two halves of the phone apart. Or tried to."

"Why would anyone do that?" asked Luca.

Stella frowned. "I don't know. But—"

A knocking at the door cut off her words.

Before Luca could open the door, Salvo muttered to him. "We're not seriously considering this a murder investigation, are we?"

Luca twitched rather than shrugged. "I didn't think so. But it is strange about the chargers. Why would only Signor Lake have a different one? Unless he brought it."

"But Stella even said: It has an Apple logo. This feels like a wild goose chase."

Luca closed his eyes. "Sorry, Stella. But it does. A bit."

She turned away, and he reached for her arm. "We'll do the interviews. Better safe than sorry, and all that. But let's rein it in a little, okay? Consider this our information gathering for any scenario, without getting locked into one."

Stella saw the wisdom. Still, she gritted her teeth. "I get it. We'll move on."

Tripp Lake stepped into the room, nodding at the officers and Stella. "I saw you upstairs," he said to them.

Stella nodded and gestured to the seat Mrs. Durant had recently vacated. He gripped his hands between his knees and looked up. "I can't believe it. I can't believe he's . . . gone."

Stella sat in her seat and introduced the officers and her role in the proceedings. "We're so sorry for your loss."

"But . . . it doesn't even make sense that he's dead." Tripp winced at the word. "I guess everybody says that. The hugeness of death, it's hard to comprehend. That someone can be here with us one minute and in another . . . *poof*." He whispered "poof" as if were a small explosion rather than a word.

Stella nodded. "We have a few questions for you." She looked at Luca, who asked the question and then Stella translated. "Do you know why your father went upstairs?"

He nodded. "To get his phone. It was missing."

"Do you know how long it was missing?"

He shook his head. "No. He didn't have it when we took photos on the lawn. I remember he complained about all the pockets in the lining of his cape. He figured it was in one of those, but he couldn't tell because the ornaments were so heavy, he couldn't tell what was phone and what was costume decor. He gave up when I told him we'd use my phone and I'd send him the photos."

"So he didn't have his phone during the party at all."

"I guess not." He thought for a moment. "Wait, when he was searching for it, he mentioned that he'd thought he had it earlier when we were drinking scotch, waiting for the women. I remember because he made that old joke about the gremlins. But he must have been mistaken. Because it was upstairs, right?"

Stella translated and ignored Tripp's question. She asked Luca about her proposed next question and he sighed, but nodded his assent. "Do you know if your father packed his own charger or used the one provided by the Durants?"

"Why would he bring his own charger?" He frowned. "What does any of this have to do with a charger?"

Stella waited.

Tripp deflated a bit. "No, I don't think he brought his own. It's not like I packed for him, so I can't say for sure. But he made a big deal about how classy it was for the Durants to provide chargers. And I think I remember him taking one. Then again, my father will take anything offered, even if he has no need or want of it. That's the kind of guy he is." Tripp swallowed. "I mean was."

After a conference with the officers, Stella went on. "Did you notice anything off during the party? Anything that gave you pause? Any tension or distress?"

Stella noticed his hands whitening as he gripped them harder. "Not really. I mean, I noticed the Staffords arguing. But everyone knows Morton didn't want to come. You've probably already heard how his wife held something over his head to get him to agree to make the trip."

Stella frowned. "This is common knowledge?"

His eyes slid sideways. "I shouldn't have said anything. Probably rumors."

"Did you see any negative interactions with your father?"

He thought for a moment. "No."

Stella exchanged looks with Luca. Either he was lying, Mrs. Durant was lying, or Tripp wasn't present for the interchange between Mr. Lake and Mr. Stafford. "Were you close to your father all evening?"

"I'm not his shadow, if that's what you're implying," he bristled.

Stella softened her tone. "We want to know if he might have disappeared at any point without your noticing."

"Oh. No." He affected a laugh. "I mean, yes. I was pretty close to him. He likes me near, in case he gets an idea he wants me to write down or research." He swallowed. "I mean, liked. Does this ever get easier?"

Stella translated and nodded when she understood Luca's next question. "So, you didn't leave the party for any reason? Not with your father or without him."

He shook his head. "No."

"Not to go to the bathroom, or—"

"No. I mean, I brought my mom a drink. But that wasn't leaving the party, right? She was in the parlor. And anyway, I only made it to the threshold when my wife told me she'd already taken care of it." He paused. "Why aren't you asking me about that guy who's been lurking for days?"

Stella sighed. "We'll look into it."

"I mean, the guy had an agenda. He wants us off what he thinks is his land. Like he's some kind of Indian or something." Stella coughed back her correction of his language and his assumptions. Tripp didn't seem to notice as he added, "We're here, get used to us, am I right?"

Stella didn't bother figuring out if he included her in that we, she needed him out of the room. Once he left, Luca said, "I think we need to talk to the wife. Signora Lake. Sounds like she sat in one spot, inside, for much of the party. She would have seen if anyone went upstairs."

Stella said, "Plus, she might know if her husband packed his own charger."

Luca frowned. "Stella, remember. *All* information. We're not to get boxed in here."

Stella shrugged. "I bet you forty euros she didn't spy Mimmo sneaking up the steps."

Matteo appeared in the doorway. "Who's next?"

"The wife," Luca rubbed his hand down his face. "Signora Lake. Does she seem in any shape to talk?"

Matteo glanced over his shoulder. "I think so? She's shaken. But people are taking turns sitting with her."

He left and returned a few minutes later, leading Mrs. Lake. Her hair was in disarray, her clothes were mussed, the sheen on her nails marred, and her cat headband now hung halfway on her head. But she seemed composed enough for the interview. Matteo walked her in, keeping pace with her shuffling steps. It seemed she could hardly lift a foot, let alone move it forward. But in typical Matteo manner, he did not rush or hurry, walking as if this was his normal strolling speed. Stella's eyes smarted at his kindness.

Once they reached the seat Salvo held out for her, Matteo gently lowered her into her chair. She gripped his hand between both of hers and looked into his eyes. "*Grazie*, Matteo. *Grazie*."

"*Piacere*, it's my pleasure." Matteo ducked his head before backing out of the room.

"Such a nice boy," Mrs. Lake said. "So obliging. A friend of yours, Stella?"

Stella nodded.

"I can see why. You have a similar sensibility."

Stella blinked. She always thought she and Matteo's bond was the way their differences dovetailed—her impetuousness brought out his fun side, his steadiness encouraged her to look before leaping.

At a glance from the officers, she realized they didn't know she and Mrs. Lake had only been exchanging pleasantries. Luca's English couldn't possibly extend to a word like "sensibility."

She translated, and then to Mrs. Lake, she explained her role in the proceedings, hesitating only once as the woman lifted her handkerchief to her eyes. "I'm sorry," Mrs. Lake apologized. "I can't believe he's gone."

Stella waited for Mrs. Lake to compose herself.

"When you get to be my age, of course, you understand that death is not a tragedy. Death is an inevitable conclusion. It comes for all of us. And yet. You don't think something as ordinary as death could bring down a man with my husband's . . . oh, how do you say? This evening has addled my brain. I'm sorry. Fortitude! That's it. My husband is . . . was . . . a force of nature."

Stella nodded. "I understand. And we're sorry for your loss."

"Thank you, my dear. I appreciate it. I'm sure this all happening here will cause all manner of confusion. Do you know who I speak to about getting his . . . body . . . home?"

Stella consulted with the officers and then said, "They'll give you the name of the medical examination office."

Mrs. Lake paled. "He's going to have an autopsy? They're going to cut him open?"

"Likely so, yes. I'm so sorry. They need to establish the cause of death."

Mrs. Lake looked down at her lap for a moment before nodding. Softly she said, "Yes. Of course. I understand. But oh, how he would detest it."

At a prompt from Luca, Stella asked, "Did your husband have any chronic conditions? Heart problems, perhaps?"

"Not a one." Mrs. Lake shook her head. "Healthy as a horse. Prided himself on it. You'd never met a man as committed to his gym routine."

"You didn't hear him complaining of any odd symptoms recently?"

She shook her head. "Nothing. Though I'll be honest, our lives didn't intersect as much as it does for many couples. I'm afraid my condition meant him slowing down, which was not in his gift. I have the most energy in the mornings. So we would talk over breakfast, but I'm often asleep by the time he'd return in the evening. My son might know more."

Stella waited for Salvo to write, as she was sure he would, to circle back to Tripp about his father's health. Though the autopsy report would be the best historian of Mr. Lake's condition.

Stella hesitated. "Do you know if he packed his own charger?"

Mrs. Lake closed her eyes for a moment and Stella thought perhaps she'd fallen asleep. Just when Stella thought she might need to put her hand out to awaken the older woman, Mrs. Lake opened her eyes and said, "I'm sorry? You said something about a charger? What kind of charger?"

"For his iPhone, to charge it?"

"Oh, yes. I know what you mean. That thing that plugs into the wall."

"Exactly."

Mrs. Lake shook her head. "He packs for himself. I'm afraid I don't know. But I'm not sure why he'd bring his own. Chelsea always provides them. They think of everything."

Stella passed this information along and then asked, "And your husband … did he have any negative interactions with anyone at the party?"

"I'm sorry, dear. Will this be much longer? My head is killing me and it is long past my bedtime."

Stella consulted with the officers. "We're almost finished."

Nodding in gratitude, Mrs. Lake said, "I apologize for how little help I am. I wish I had the stamina I once did. Now, negative interactions? Is that what you asked about?"

Stella inclined her head.

"I didn't see anything myself, but I heard that there was a moment between him and Morton. That's not unusual, though. They haven't gotten along in years. They pretend to, for my and Claire's sake, but you know how men are. Blustering around like they own the world, but in reality, they're not much more than little boys who pout when someone takes their favorite toy."

Stella smiled. "I know what you mean."

Mrs. Lake patted Stella's hand. "I thought you might, dear."

At a nod from the officers, Stella rose. "Can we offer you help to get to your room?"

Luca moved to take her arm.

"If you could get my daughter, Gillian? I'll need help preparing … for …" She flushed faintly.

Stella understood. Of course, she didn't want to talk about changing in front of the strange Italian men. Luckily, Gillian was outside the door, speaking in low tones with Mrs. Durant. "Gillian, honey … can you help me?"

Gillian didn't seem to notice her mother's question.

"Gillian, darling?"

"What? Oh." Gillian looked up. She called over her shoulder, "Louisa. Mom needs help."

"Gillian, can't you …" Mrs. Lake pleaded.

"Mother, you know Louisa is better at this stuff than me. Louisa!" Gillian turned to call her sister-in-law again. She turned back to say, "I always rush and you stumble. It's a scene. Here's Louisa, she'll help."

Stella felt the crackle of irritation come off of Louisa. Gillian smiled broadly. "Mother needs to change for bed."

Stella didn't miss Mrs. Lake's flush of embarrassment. "I'm such a nuisance," she said in tones of mingled humiliation and annoyance.

Louisa said nothing, just offered her right arm, her lips set in a straight line.

"Not that arm, the other," Mrs. Lake snapped. "You know I can't lean that way."

Louisa opened her mouth to respond but then seemed to decide it more expedient to switch sides and offer her left arm, a grumble barely escaping her lips.

The two of them shuffled down the hallway.

"Don't mind my mother, " Gillian said. "She gets cranky when she's tired. And tonight has been a lot."

Gillian strode away but then stopped, stock still. She went completely white.

And screamed.

Stella wondered how often this woman screamed in her ordinary life.

Gillian pointed, gasping, at Mimmo standing at the open French door. "That's him! That's the vagrant who killed my father!"

Gritting her teeth, Stella fought the urge to bite back that Mimmo had a home, in disarray though it may be, and for all they knew, her father's death was an accident.

Stella strode up to Mimmo, who glared around the room but did not enter. "Mimmo? What are you doing here?"

"Why aren't all these people asleep? It's late."

"Yes, but why aren't you?" Stella asked.

He shrugged, his shirt coming loose from his pants at the motion. Stella realized to her chagrin that he not only wore the worst of his stained shirts but he'd forgotten to button the final four buttons. His tidiness hardly mattered on a regular day, but on a day when he was being accused of murder . . .

Stella said, "Mimmo. *What are you doing here?*"

"My dog. She ran off. I wanted to see if she came into the house."

"Why would she be here? We're a few kilometers from your house, at least." He didn't answer and Stella realized. "You weren't at your house, were you? You were here. In the woods."

Mimmo didn't answer. Instead, he looked over Stella's shoulder and whistled.

Gillian began shrieking. "It's him! Arrest that man!"

Luca stepped around her to join Stella at the door. "Mimmo. Your timing couldn't be worse."

Mimmo glared at Luca. "You don't choose when your dog runs off. She probably smelled something cooking over here and snuck in through this door. Why did they leave it open?"

Stella remembered Mimmo explaining that he, like other hunters, kept his dogs hungry to fuel their prey instinct. No wonder the dog took off at the scent of . . . Stella lifted her nose. Ah, yes, the chefs were reheating a porchetta-style pork loin. Stella appreciated the addition of fennel pollen to the roll of roasted pork, though the dog was probably in it for the pig.

Scowling, Luca said, "Why didn't you ring the bell like a normal person? Seriously, Mimmo. Your idiosyncrasies are growing pathological."

Mimmo blinked. "I'm a hunter. I can go where I want."

Stella looked from Mimmo to Luca. "Is that true?"

Luca nodded. "Yes, technically. In Italy, a hunter can cross property lines. For foraging too, mushrooms, or asparagus, or whatever."

Mimmo's face brightened. "That's right. I can go where I want. That's what I said."

Luca sighed. "But Mimmo. You aren't allowed this close to a house when you're hunting. You know that."

"Now it's a crime to come to people's door during a party?" scowled Mimmo.

Luca started to argue with Mimmo, but then seemed to think the better of it. Instead, he turned to the crowd and called out, "Anyone see a dog?"

The Italians craned their heads to peer around, some walking around corners to search. The Americans watched the Italians with barely concealed anxiety. What was happening? Stella saw the mayor explaining in a loud voice, though the Americans didn't look any more informed by his speeches.

Marta, in her purple gown, sans headdress, stepped out from the crowd. "Mimmo! Which dog?"

Mimmo grunted, "Valentina."

Valentina?

It seemed a romantic name for an animal Mimmo kept caged most of the time.

Marta pulled someone close. It took Stella a moment to recognize Leo, dressed in a gold-spangled tunic and enormous ram horns. Leo listened to Marta and then shouted in English above the crowd. "Anybody seen a long-hair pointer with brown and white markings?"

Half the Americans began chattering about why no one was arresting the murderer standing in plain sight while the other half joined the Italians in looking around the house.

Marta said to Mimmo. "I'm sure we'll find her. Don't worry."

"She's old," Mimmo said, his voice cracking.

Marta put a hand on his arm, studiously avoiding making eye contact with Stella.

Stella's heart clenched; she knew Marta would never forgive her for the imagined transgression. Unless Stella apologized, and how could she apologize for what Leo did to *her*? Just the thought turned her stomach. Everything suddenly felt too hot and too close and too loud. She felt like she might throw up. Turning away, she darted outside, hoping the cool air would clear the fingers of disgust from her ribcage.

Luca called after her, "Stella? Are you okay?"

Louisella, Stella's neighbor that she hadn't even noticed—probably because she wore a cream chiffon and gold dress with black ruffles rather than her usual vintage Chanel—piped up. "I saw a dog. By the pool."

Stella turned back to the party to see the mayor's wife, dressed in a cobalt blue velvet dress trimmed in sweeping peacock feathers, announcing to the person next to her, "She didn't see anything. Louisella always demands attention. She's still smarting that I got all the good movie roles." Veronica didn't seem to notice that her confidant was Mr. Durant, who understood not a word she said. Too bad, Stella thought. Perhaps he could have asked the right questions and finally resolved the mystery of how these two movie starlets wound up in Aramezzo. Nobody had ever given Stella a satisfying answer.

Mimmo grunted and then turned toward the pool. At the uproar from the Americans, Luca stopped him. He nodded to Salvo and said, "Get the dog."

Salvo said, "And if we find her? The Americans won't appreciate our bringing a hunting dog into the house, and if we let Mimmo leave with the dog, the Americans will lose their minds."

The two of them began discussing what to do and Marta, standing behind them, huffed before storming outside, hitching her dress up to step over the threshold, into the courtyard. Stella joined her, but Marta waved her hand dismissively. "I got it, Stella. The dog doesn't know you."

Stella hesitated but then fell back, listening to the officers debate.

A debate that ended with a pounding at the front door.

Luca exhaled in relief. "Finally. The captain is here."

Salvo rushed forward, but TC Durant beat him to the door and threw it open. Stella had only caught a fleeting glance at him before, but there was no doubt this was the new chief of police. This man had *captain* stamped across his broad bearing like a sign of oak and metal. He put his hat under his arm and waited for an invitation before being welcomed across the threshold. Following his host's direction, he made his way to the interview room. Stella noticed a mousy man with a comb-over drifting along in the Captain's wake.

Luca and Salvo followed. Stella didn't feel that she could leave without being dismissed. For all she knew, the timid-looking man was the Captain's butler. Not that police captains had butlers. But if any did, it would be this police captain.

The mayor rushed forward, his voice loud enough to carry to Stella. "It's unconscionable! I *told* the officers my wife needed to get home. She's of a delicate constitution, and this amount of tension is detrimental to her system." The captain's eyes widened almost imperceptibly. Stella thought she could read his sentiment, and she agreed—the mayor's wife fed on tension like Barbanera fed on beef tongue. There was no chance Veronica wasn't lapping this up.

Despite herself, Stella admired the new captain. The mayor kept up a constant stream of complaints. "I told them the man merely had a heart attack. Disappointing for the party, surely, but hardly cause to keep us hostage. But they refuse to do as I say!"

Captain Tribuzio pulled short. He stared at the mayor for a moment, his gaze unflinching. The mayor stammered. Before full words could form, the captain leaned down to speak in the mayor's ear. Stella couldn't hear the words, but given how the mayor paled, she figured the captain had asserted the chain of command. The mayor was not the officers' boss. That was Captain Tribuzio's position.

The mayor half-shrugged before fading back into the crowd. Stella watched him locate his wife and huddle with her for a few moments, their gazes sliding to the captain, who either didn't notice or didn't care as he continued to make his way to the interview room.

When the captain reached for the doorknob, Gillian brushed up against him to block his entrance. Was it Stella's imagination, or was Gillian purposely sticking out her chest to make her breasts heave? If it was intentional, the effort was wasted. Captain Tribuzio didn't look further south than her chin. Undaunted, Gillian's eyes welled with tears. She put a hand on the captain's arm. He stared at it until she removed it.

Yes, Stella very much liked the new captain. Much more authoritative and much more controlled than Captain Palmiro. The former captain was friendly enough nowadays, or what passed for friendly in his world, making snide remarks when they saw each other at the fruit market about Stella's tendency to get into trouble. But she couldn't like him and she'd never respected him.

Gillian let out a wail. "The killer is right here. Right *here*! And your police officers won't do a thing about it! They don't care that my father is d-d-dead! And *he* killed him!" She flung her arm out, trying to locate Mimmo.

Mimmo, who had caught sight of Marta returning with the hunting dog trotting at her heels, yelped and raced outside to scoop up Valentina. A roar went up from the crowd, voices accusing him of fleeing and resisting arrest.

Mimmo looked back at the crowd, confused. He shrugged and started away again when Leo jockeyed through the crowd to reach Mimmo and Marta. The three of them talked, their heads ducked together. Mimmo seemed to understand and glared at the captain, his chin up. However, he diminished the defiance of his expression by his scratching at his belly as if he had fleas.

The few Americans who had begun to close around him took an

instinctive step backward.

Stella waited for what appeared to be the translator to step in. But before he could, the captain said to Gillian in crisp, British-accented English, "Signorina. On behalf of the police department and indeed, on behalf of the town of Aramezzo, I am sorry for your loss. Rest assured, if the cause of death was not accidental, we will investigate … *all* … suspects." He looked at her significantly.

Gillian's mouth dropped open. "You can't possibly mean … he was my *father*! He was my *world*."

"If you'll excuse me, Signorina."

Stella wondered if he actually would add Gillian to the suspect list or if he simply wanted her to get away from the door. Wind sucked from her sails, Gillian moved to allow the captain and translator passage.

Luca pulled the captain aside and consulted with him for a few moments. By their eyes flicking to Stella, she assumed Luca was filling Captain Tribuzio in on the interviews. She held up a hand in a half-wave. The captain shook his head slightly and turned into the interview room. Luca paused at the closed door before striding toward Stella. Before he opened his mouth, she said lightly, as if it hardly mattered, "It seems my services are no longer required."

Luca nodded. "I'm sorry, Stella. Especially since I know this translator. Not well, but we crossed paths during my training."

"His English is terrible?" Stella asked hopefully.

"No," he smiled, reading her easily. "But he has all the subtlety of an ax. I wasn't a fan of your going off-script in there, but you got good information. This guy has none of your way with people."

She adjusted her bandana. "I was glad to help. Anyway, I'm surprised you'll need a translator. Captain Tribuzio's English is pitch perfect."

Luca smiled, his dimple winking. "Didn't I tell you? He is something. But in a case like this, we have to cover our bases and do everything we can to acquire a department-approved translator. If we couldn't locate one, then yes, he could have managed on his own. Or you could have continued."

As Luca turned away, she grabbed his arm. "Will you let me know? If anything comes up?"

Luca paused. "Stella. We can't pursue your phone charger theory unless we find out he was electrocuted. You understand that, right?"

Stella swiped at a curl that had gotten loose from her bandana. "But what if he was electrocuted and you wasted all this time when you could have been solving the case?"

Luca stepped close to her to tuck the escaped curl back behind her ear. "We're doing this by the book. But if he was electrocuted, then we'll look into it. Okay?"

She bit her lip, trying to control her breathing. She nodded.

He looked at her appraisingly before striding away.

Stella watched the graceful way he swiveled his hips to maneuver past the guests and slip into the interview room. She wondered who they would interview next. She also wondered if there was any way she could listen in. Wasn't there a nanny cam or something? After being part of it all for the last hour or two, she hated feeling shut out.

Salvo walked out of the room and made his way to Mimmo, still standing with Leo and Marta. "Mimmo? Captain Tribuzio needs to speak to you."

"No!" shouted Marta.

"I need to get my dog home," said Mimmo. "She's tired. This is too many people."

"C'mon, Salvo," Leo said. "You know Mimmo didn't do anything wrong."

Salvo looked from Marta to Leo as if he was undecided. Then he straightened with resolve. "He's here. On the premises. So he's a suspect like anyone else."

Marta clutched Salvo's arm. "Salvo! You know Mimmo. You know he couldn't have done anything."

Mimmo stared at Marta, who was furiously wiping away tears. "Marta?"

"I can't watch," moaned Marta.

Leo put his arm around Marta. "It'll be all right. They'll question him and let him go. You'll see."

Reaching out to touch her shoulder, Mimmo said, "It's all right, Marta. I'll be okay. Don't worry."

Marta opened her mouth to protest, but Mimmo had joined Salvo in his walk down the long parlor and didn't notice. In fact, he didn't seem to see much of anything, given how he crashed into Louisa Lake on his walk to the interview room. He must be less sanguine about this than he tried to convey to Marta.

Stella watched him go, wondering about the quasi-paternal relationship he had with Marta. What an odd sort Mimmo was. Just as likely to hunt out of season and lie about it as show up to help Marta with shearing her sheep.

She heard Marta, her voice quaking, "I know. I know they'll have to let him go. But I also know . . . they'll make him feel like a fool."

Stella turned to look at Marta. This effortless stroke of feeling and insight, it embodied what she loved about Marta. She wished she could go to her, join her. But at the sight of Marta and Leo wrapped together, his lips pressed against her forehead, Stella instead moved back inside the house.

Mrs. Stafford ran up to her. "Stella! Are we allowed to go now?"

Before Stella could answer, Mr. Stafford joined them. "This is unreasonable detainment! Why won't they let us leave? Question us in the morning."

Stella suddenly felt tired. So tired. "You have to understand. You all have passports and the means to take off in the night. They need to question you while they have you."

Mr. Stafford scowled and muttered, "This isn't right. We heard Hollis had a heart attack. Sad for his family maybe, but not a big shocker. All this questioning, it's convincing me this is bigger. And here we are, trapped in someone else's house in someone else's country. I won't stand to be a sitting duck. A man has a right to protect himself." He pulled out his phone and started typing madly.

Stella stared at him. She didn't want to imagine either of her guests as murderers. But this reaction to the inconvenience of a little waiting... was it possible Mr. Stafford had something to hide? She remembered, suddenly, the mysterious package from China.

Stella realized that the police hadn't yet interviewed these two. She couldn't question them officially, but why couldn't she see what they knew?

Her exhaustion evaporated as if she'd thrown back three espressos. She smiled at her guests and said, "You must be exhausted."

Mrs. Stafford's eyes welled with tears. "So exhausted. You have no idea."

Stella guessed, "Because of Judith."

Mrs. Stafford nodded, but Mr. Stafford grumbled, "She'll be better off if you ask me. Without all his games."

"Games?" Stella asked.

"Morton. Don't," cautioned Mrs. Stafford, her lips in a thin line. Was she trying to avoid her husband saying too much?

"What does it matter now, Claire?" he said. "The devil is dead. And I'm sure he was the one who turned their house into an uproar. I'm not buying that garbage about the immigrant housekeepers."

This amount of content sent Stella's brain swirling. "Come again?"

Mr. Stafford ignored his wife, clearly grateful for the chance to vent his ire. "We heard about it from Gillian. Of course, Judith would never complain. If someone took a necklace, she'd assume they needed it more than she did. But Gillian? No way."

At Stella's confused expression, Mrs. Stafford clarified, deciding this was safer territory than maligning the dead. "For the past … few months? I can't remember. Things kept disappearing. A wallet. Glasses. A phone. Jewelry. Tripp and Gillian blamed the new Mexican housekeepers." Stella instinctively winced at the assumption, which Mrs. Stafford must have noticed because she said, "I'm not racist, dear. Poor people feel they have something coming to them. If they were Polish, I'd say the same." Stella believed it, but it didn't assuage her discomfort with this conversation. Mrs. Stafford went on, "Besides, Louisa admitted the housekeepers might be at fault, too, and she sits on the board of Habitat for Humanity. So you see, it's not racist."

Stella fought down her irritation. She remembered something, a memory pushed its way into her consciousness. Right! During Tripp's interview, he said that when his father couldn't find his phone, he blamed it on the … the … what was the word? Ah, yes. "The gremlins."

Mr. Stafford nodded. "No surprise you've heard about it. Family lore at this point. Anyway, all the missing stuff eventually reappeared, so Hollis didn't punish his probably illegal staff." Stella winced again. "So the story goes. Claire never believed anyone was taking anything. That house is huge. Things were busy. They obviously kept misplacing things."

Mrs. Stafford added, "That's what Judith said, and it made sense to me. That everyone was too distracted. Then she went on a rant about Twitter destroying everyone's attention spans. But the family didn't pay her any mind. They've learned to tune that out." Mrs. Stafford sighed. "Anyway, Gillian insisted that the housekeepers had caught wind of getting found out, so they'd replaced everything they hadn't already fenced."

"Hogwash." Mr. Stafford intoned while typing on his phone.

"He never bought into any of it," Mrs. Stafford said, smiling indulgently at her husband like a boy who won the spelling bee.

"It had Hollis written all over it," he said without looking up.

The smile vanished from Mrs. Stafford's face. Her eyes darted to Stella as she said with the sunniness of a nursery school teacher, "Darling, one mustn't speak ill of the dead."

"You can if the dead guy is a jerk who delights in other people's misery. Look, Stella, don't get me wrong. I didn't like Hollis. We had our differences. But that doesn't change the fact that he loved pulling strings and watching everyone dance. It would be just like him to take a wallet left on the sideboard and then return it when he felt like it. A poor housekeeper could never feel as entitled as Hollis. He believed the world owed him everything."

"Even if he did play a prank," Mrs. Stafford added evenly. "It was only a little joke."

Stella wondered. She'd known men like that, who took what they didn't even want just to revel in their power. But if he did, why would he mention the gremlins when he couldn't find his phone? Perhaps to remind himself of the good joke he pulled on his family? Stella shook her head. Carefully, she said to Mr. Stafford, "Did you notice him pulling strings here tonight?"

Mr. Stafford said easily, "Believe me, I gave that man a wide berth. I have no idea who he might have ticked off, but I wouldn't be surprised if more than one person had reason to resent him tonight." He slipped his phone in his pocket. "There. Done."

Stella frowned. Why was Mr. Stafford lying about the argument? Or was Mrs. Durant lying? She'd said she didn't want to implicate Mr. Stafford, but perhaps she'd said that to throw the officers off her scent. Then again, what possible motive could Mrs. Durant have for wanting Mr. Lake dead? After all, she invited him to her home. She might not have liked his treatment of her childhood friend, but leaving Mrs. Lake a widow? Mr. Stafford might assume Judith Lake to be better off without her husband, but given her disability and relative isolation, Stella couldn't imagine the woman to be better off without her husband, overbearing though he was.

Mrs. Stafford clutched Stella's arm. "How much longer are they going to keep us?"

Shaking her head, Stella said, "I can't say. Ring me when they let you go. I'll have something ready for you to eat before you go to sleep, no matter the hour."

Mrs. Stafford put her hand on Stella's arm, peering into her eyes. "Oh, Stella. That is very dear, but they are feeding us plenty. And you look like you need sleep. A solid breakfast will be more than enough for us. We're easy."

Stella nodded, grateful. All she wanted was to curl up with Barbanera in her cozy bedroom with the worn bedspread and the lamp that cast a golden circle of light. Without the image of dangling phone cords and murderous plague doctors looming in her brain space.

"Oh," Mrs. Stafford said. "I like that jam pie you made! Can we have another?"

Mr. Stafford's phone dinged, and he took it from his pocket. "With a different jam."

"You didn't like the orange, darling? With that delightful hint of spice?"

"Let's try something new."

"Sure. Of course." Suddenly, Stella felt exhausted again. She ran through the jams in her larder. "How about plum?"

"Oh, glazie, Stella!" She probably should have corrected Mrs. Stafford's pronunciation long ago. Ah, well. Too late now.

"You have your key?"

Mr. Stafford nodded, before turning to talk to Gillian, who had come to complain about this abhorrent treatment she'd gotten from the police. Stella ducked away before anyone could see her smile.

She twisted her way to the front door, through the assembled guests, still in their costumes. She felt as if she was making her way through the contents of a fairytale toy box, covered in sparkles. Growing disoriented, she held a hand to her flushed cheek.

She heard Matteo's voice before she registered his presence. "Stella?

Are you okay?"

She offered a wan smile. "I meant to tell you, I like your costume."

"This old thing?" he looked down at his dark blue suit and neon bow tie. Stella smiled again. She always enjoyed hearing what she thought were English expressions, but in Italian. "You didn't answer my question."

"I'm tired."

He grinned. "And I figured getting to be this close to a murder investigation would be better than caffeine for you."

"How do you know it's murder?" Had someone dropped something while they milled around, picking at the plates of food the chefs brought out?

"Why else would the police be interviewing everyone?"

"Oh. That's just a precaution. But there's no real evidence."

"Is there unreal evidence?"

Stella's mind returned to that charger. Also, the image of all the guests on the lawn, taking selfies . . . something about that stuck with her. Something seemed wrong. She couldn't figure out what it was. "No, not exactly. But something smells off."

"It's not the pork."

She smiled. "No, the pork smells amazing. Those chefs know what they're doing."

He walked her to the door and said, "How are you getting home?"

She stopped walking. "The car. *Cavolo*, I forgot, I need to get someone to—"

"Luca did that," Matteo cut in. "It's been towed. He called Domenica."

"Right, right," Stella said. "I guess I'm walking."

"No way." Matteo darted a look around the room. "I'll drive you."

"No! You have to stay here."

"I'm not letting you walk alone. At night. Especially now."

"Matteo. I promise not to play with any outlets—no matter how beguiling they are—on the entire walk home."

"Outlets? What are you talking about?" Matteo ran his hand down his long face. He sighed and said firmly, "I'm not having this argument with you. I'm driving you home."

"The police won't let you leave."

"Well, I'm not letting you walk."

"Well, I guess I'm staying, then." She turned and flopped dramatically onto the sofa, bouncing the mayor's wife, who shot her a look of death.

Stella closed her eyes and leaned back. Maybe she would fall asleep right here.

"Come, Stella. I'm taking you home."

She opened her eyes to find Giancarlo sitting on the arm of the blue sofa.

She looked from Giancarlo to Matteo, with their identical looks of determination. "But—"

"No one stays angry at a soccer star." Matteo shook his head. "They can get away with," Matteo stopped himself before saying, *murder,* "anything."

Stella's gaze drifted back to Giancarlo. Could this be true?

He shrugged. "Membership has its privileges," he said in English.

Despite herself, Stella burst out laughing and had to clap her hand over her mouth as incredulous stares met her from around the room.

She rose, as Matteo said, "I don't get the joke. What did you say? Stella, what did he say?"

She shook her head. "Hard to explain. But you'll get your way. Giancarlo. I accept that ride."

He nodded and took her by the elbow, steering her out of the room.

Stella was not a woman who enjoyed being steered, but she leaned into Giancarlo's strength with mingled curiosity and relief.

"Cosimo, you would not have believed it."

The antiquarian looked up from his plate of leftover orange *crostata*. "I imagine that's true, considering I haven't paid attention to a word you've said. How do you get your pastry so light?"

"Ice packs on the counter to chill it before rolling," Stella said instinctively before she realized what he'd said. "Hey! I tell you the whole story of my evening with the Americans and you didn't listen at all?"

He smiled, the sunlight streaming through the window illuminating his eyes. They glowed, one blue, one green. Stella no longer startled at the discontinuity in Cosimo's eye color, but the light made the difference starker. "I'm teasing you, Stella. It sounds like quite a debacle."

"You're lucky you missed it." In thought, Stella added, "You know, I'm surprised they didn't invite you. You're such a fixture of Aramezzo."

"Be no longer surprised. They did invite me. They do every year. And I always abstain."

"Really? But you love a good party."

"Which is why I abstain. I went to a party at the villa years ago. They'd come in here to purchase vintage decor for the villa and must have decided my historical acumen lent me a degree of old-world charm. I went that year, not wanting to insult them and cut myself off from their custom."

"And?"

He chewed slowly. "What is there to say? The event could not have been more boring. Every year, the family gets more elaborate with their theme, I believe to obfuscate the very ordinariness of the conversation."

"The food is good, though. At least it was last night."

"Indeed. They hire well, I will say that for them. If they could only hire partygoers with interesting lives, we'd be discussing another matter." He pointed at the *crostata* with his fork. "Speaking of good food, I hope your guests were pleased with this. It's a triumph. You've nailed the balance of spice to fruit."

Stella shrugged. "Mrs. Stafford picked at the filling and ignored the crust. I have no idea why she asked me to make another this morning."

"I suppose if you'll be eating only three bites to open your day, you want those bites to be sublime."

Stella thought about it. That could be true. Anyway, it soothed some of the morning's irritation at watching Mrs. Stafford nibble like a mouse at the breakfast Stella had baked while they slept. As for Mr. Stafford, he took one bite and put down his phone to concentrate on finishing his slice. Something about that niggled at Stella, though she couldn't think what. She sighed. "Well, I suppose your not going to the party worked out for the best."

He nodded, distracted by the pastry. Then looked up. "I heard Giancarlo gave you a ride home."

Stella hated the instant blush rising up her neck. "How did you hear that?"

As much as an old man with candy-floss hair could mug at a pretend camera, he mugged.

Stella had forgotten Cosimo's love of gossip. For a man who seemed to have no romance in his life, he sure fed on it. She cleared her throat to buy her a second to even her voice into one of nonchalance. "Matteo didn't want me walking. And I didn't want him getting into trouble by driving me."

"Brilliant plan. Get a lift from the unimpeachable soccer star. The *handsome* unimpeachable soccer star."

"Is he handsome?" Stella said airily. "I hadn't noticed."

"Don't be coy," Cosimo said, pointing at her with his fork. "It doesn't suit you."

Stella smiled and said nothing.

"Did he make a move?"

"Cosimo!"

He grinned. "Thought if I took you unawares, I might surprise you into truth."

She grinned back. "He was a perfect gentleman."

"He kept his hands to himself?"

"Totally. And he waited until I was inside and turned the lights on before returning to Villa delle Acque." She had seen him still in the street when she'd peeked out the curtain a few moments after going inside.

"Ah, well, that's unfortunate."

"Is it?"

"One likes a little more assertiveness. But perhaps he held back out of respect for the night's events. With time, I predict you'll prance off into the sunset together."

"But if I prance off into the sunset, I won't be here to bring you *crostata*," Stella smiled, putting a hand on his gnarled one. A flash crossed Cosimo's face and did Stella imagine him wince? Stella's heart turned over. He must not want her to leave and was preparing for it by sketching out this fantasy. No need to remind him her leaving was predestined. One more good season and she'd be ready to sell the bed-and-breakfast.

Cosimo swallowed. "You won't leave suddenly, like your mother, will you?"

"Was it sudden?" Stella asked. "Isn't the story that she met my father and they fell in love so she moved to the States? I never got the sense that it was a quick decision."

"You're no doubt correct. You get to be my age, and timelines become relative."

Stella frowned. "Actually, I feel like I've heard this before. About my mom. But she never mentioned anything."

Nodding, Cosimo said, "Then again, she didn't talk much about Aramezzo at all, did she?"

"She didn't." Stella paused. "And when she did talk about her life here, it was with bitterness. I admit, I expected to find Aramezzo a bit of a wasteland. It's such a mystery to me, why she made her hometown out to be so awful."

With a shrug, Cosimo said, "Some people revile that which they must leave. It makes it easier."

"I suppose."

"Now. About you and the handsome Giancarlo. You wouldn't deny an old man the joy of watching young love in bloom, would you?"

Thrown by the abrupt reversal of topic, Stella was surprised into saying, "Luckily, you have Marta and Leo."

"Ah," he waved his hand. "That one has grown stale. Besides, I don't consider this romance as advantageous for Leonardo's personality as other people do." He gave her a knowing look.

Stella didn't know what to think. Did someone tell him? Maybe someone in the bar had noticed Leo's hand on her after all? "What . . . what do you mean?"

He watched her evenly, his eyes shining bright in his softly wrinkled face.

"Well. Well." Stella shifted uncomfortably. "I should probably take this to Domenica." She lifted a plate of *crostata*.

Turning back to his plate, he said, "I'm rather surprised you didn't stop in there first."

"I did," Stella smiled sheepishly. "The shop was closed tight."

"And Matteo? He doesn't get a portion?"

"He swung by this morning."

"I guess I should be glad I'm in the rotation." Did Stella mistake the hurt in his voice? "I suppose none of the Americans can leave Aramezzo?"

She shook her head. "Not for another few days at least."

"Do you have to juggle the Staffords with new guests arriving?"

"No, thank goodness. My next ones aren't until the end of the month."

"American?" he asked.

"French."

He smiled. "You must be delighted."

"You have no idea." She laughed and hopped off the stool. "Okay, I better get moving."

He waved her off, "Go, go. Be off with you." He smiled to soften the bluntness of the words. "And Stella?"

She turned back.

"Be careful."

"Of what?"

He paused as if debating what to say. "You know. Dangerous things." His eyes moved to her pendant pointedly.

She touched it and cocked her head before waving once more and closing the door behind her.

The sudden brightness blinded her momentarily. Even with the sun filtering across Cosimo's shop, refracting off the crystal chandeliers and glowing through the antique lampshades, she always emerged as if from a deep and rocky cave. She shook her head and balanced the plate.

As she made her way to Domenica's, she waved to neighbors but kept on striding past, pretending she didn't see them opening their mouths to pull her in for conversation. Maybe that conversation would be of the normal variety—if she'd had luck finding wild asparagus, what she was cooking, what she'd made Barbanera for dinner—but she suspected she'd be pulled into conversations about last night.

Stella looked forward to unpacking it with Domenica, but that was it. She would have loved to talk to Matteo, but he had only enough time to bolt down the coffee and pastry before heading out to make the rounds, his broom slung across his uniformed shoulder. She'd barely been able to ask about Giancarlo, only enough to prod the door open by asking if he'd safely returned to the party last night. Matteo had yawned and said archly, "Yeah, safe enough." Before rubbing his eyes. "I can't believe I couldn't get the morning off."

"The trials of a garbage man."

"I know you're trying to be ironic, but it's factually true. Especially a garbage man held hostage at a masquerade ball he never wanted to go to in the first place."

"Plus the dead body," Stella added.

"Plus the dead body," Matteo said.

And that had been it.

Anyway, she didn't know how to have a casual conversation with people about last night. The other times she'd been on a murder scene, she'd been so on the outskirts of village life, it had been fairly easy to keep to the margins. Now, though, after celebrating Christmas, New Year, Easter, and particularly the wild asparagus harvest, she felt connected to her neighbors in a way she hadn't realized until she found herself tucking her chin down and barreling past them.

She felt their eyes follow her down the road.

The feeling lingered until she walked into Domenica's bookshop. Domenica looked up from pouring a cup of coffee. "What's going on?" She peered earnestly at Stella. Not for the first time, Stella wondered how this woman could see through her. "Aside from the obvious. Which I will need a full report about, not the wild ravings I heard at Bar Cappellina."

"Oh. Yes. I'll tell you."

"But first. What else? Something is pulling you." Domenica held up an empty cup and Stella nodded, dropping the plate on the desk and flopping into the waiting armchair.

"It's just . . . I've worked to convince people I'm a decent person, and yet I blew past people on the way here, without stopping to even say hello." She exhaled slowly. "I am such a brat."

Domenica placed the warm mug into Stella's outstretched hand. Softly, she said, "Stella, eventually you'll learn that we may live in your mother's village, but that doesn't mean we see you as she did."

Something moved within Stella's chest, a shade of unlocking or unfreezing. She shook her head. "It's silly. Of course, it's fine. I'm sure everyone is allotted their share of bad days."

Domenica sat in her chair and adjusted her scarves, keeping her eyes on Stella.

After taking a noisy sip of her coffee, Stella asked, "Any news of your car?"

"Oh, yes! Stella, I about died when Luca called. I can't believe you were stranded on a dark road."

"I wasn't stranded long." Stella lifted her hand with the coffee cup out of the way to allow Ravioli to leap into her lap. She petted the calico with her free hand as she said, "So you got the rundown about last night."

Domenica nodded and settled herself into her seat, blowing across the surface of her coffee and lifting the foil from the plate. Her eyes widened at the sight of the *crostata*, today's plum, rather than yesterday's orange, since she'd given Domenica orange the day before on the way to the vet. "At least they didn't ask for *rocciata*."

"Counting my blessings. And this one came out better, so I'm declaring it a win. Note to self: a little lemon zest in the crust." Stella chuckled.

"They better leave you an excellent review."

"With a death as part of their visit to Aramezzo? I'll be lucky if my cooking sweetens their memory even a tiny bit." Stella smiled, tiredly. "Speaking of. Tell me: What have you heard?"

Domenica reached for a fork, saying, "Not a lot. Mostly speculation.

Signor Lake died. Which happens. But the police questioned everybody so now rumors are flying about whether it's a murder investigation. Especially since no one can leave until at least after the autopsy."

"You'll be glad to know the rumor mill is intact and working fine."

"I also heard you had a steamy moment with Giancarlo."

Stella looked up from her coffee. "And there's where it breaks down."

"I took a shot." Domenica took a bite of the *crostata*.

Stella raised her eyebrows.

"Rest easy, *cara*. Matteo mentioned he'd convinced you to let Giancarlo take you home. And hinted that he'd like it if something happened with the two of you. I wanted to see if it had."

"Well played." Stella rolled her eyes. "Anyone speculating when the autopsy will happen?"

Domenica's eyes flicked to the grandfather clock. "I think it happened already."

"Already!"

"Sure. You hold this many rich Americans until an autopsy, you move that autopsy to the front of the line."

Stella's mind raced.

"*Cara?*"

"So I have this theory. About what happened."

Domenica's fork stalled on its way to her mouth. "Already? Go on."

"Well, it looks like a natural death, like you said. No wounds, no nothing. But something felt off to me. The biggest sign was Signor Lake's hand still holding his phone. Like a vise."

Domenica sat back. "Okay."

"There was glitter, just a touch, but definitely there, on the phone and in an outline around where the phone must have been sitting on the nightstand."

"That doesn't sound very—"

"Signor Lake's costume had no glitter."

"Ah." Domenica nodded. "I see. So someone was in his room."

"Someone had his *phone*."

"The same phone he was holding when he died."

"Gripping is more like it."

"Noted. What else?" asked Domenica.

"Okay, this is going to sound weird."

Domenica's eyes widened.

Stella laughed. "Okay, maybe it won't sound weird to someone who has seen everything."

"Not everything, but I get your point."

"Thing one. There was this odd smell in the room."

"Odd how?"

"Well, it was acrid. Like something burning. But kind of sweet." Stella shrugged. "I thought of a rubber spatula melting over a gas flame. Salvo said a flame thrower at a lamb cook-out, I don't know what he's talking about but got the idea. Luca said it smelled like country train tracks in summer."

"Did he?" Domenica's eyebrows went up. "I've always liked that boy."

"Yes, yes. He's very poetic." Stella took another sip of coffee.

"So you're thinking electrocution?"

Stella looked up from her mug. "How did you know?"

"The hand. The smell."

"It's not enough for the police to go on."

Domenica straightened her headband. "I would imagine not. But once the autopsy result comes back. If it's electrocution…"

Stella said nothing.

"Stella? What else?"

"Well. This is going to sound farfetched. But," Stella said carefully, "Assuming he was electrocuted, I don't think it was a house wiring issue."

"Of course not."

"Of course not?"

"You said he was charging his phone?"

"Yes. By all appearances."

"That house wiring is all new. And I'm guessing top-tier, if the house, and the amount they threw around during the renovation, is any indication. It's way more likely to be a faulty charger."

Stella's mouth dropped open.

Domenica took another bite of *crostata*. "What?"

"Nothing. Only you weren't even there."

"If I told you my bread didn't rise, could you tell me why?"

"Probably." Stella frowned.

"Even if you weren't there?"

"Probably." Stella's expression lightened as she understood.

"There you go."

Stella nodded thoughtfully, running her hand over Ravioli's patchwork coat. "Okay, Signorina Expert. Can you tell me more about this faulty charger thing? I remembered how my friend Grant who worked at an Apple store told me that if I didn't get a charger from Apple, too much power could enter the phone and it could send an electric shock into a person. But some of it was hazy. You know how I tune out people talking about technology."

"Your most egregious personality flaw," Domenica said fondly, before leaning forward with bright eyes. "Let's begin the lesson. You probably already know that a charger works by providing a phone's battery with a low-level voltage and current. Now, you understand the concept of a power supply unit, don't you?"

"Domenica."

"What?"

"Dumb it down."

"Okay, okay." Domenica chuckled. "I won't get out my graph paper. The most basic way to say it is that a charger adapts the current of the fixed wiring system, like of the house, and reduces it, to meet the specific demands of the device's battery."

"Oh! Is that why it's sometimes called an adapter? Because it adapts a charge?"

"*Brava*. Which is, of course, confusing, given that we also have adapters that adapt outlets for the variations in plug shapes between countries. Now, a charger is a more sensitive instrument than you'd imagine, given how cavalierly people pop them into sockets. Knockoffs are made as cheaply as possible, without the safety testing used by legitimate outlets, of which Apple is just one, by the way. Not every non-Apple charger is a bomb in disguise, no matter what your friend says."

"Grant is prone to exaggeration. It's why I would have gotten a cheap one if he hadn't put a factory one in my hands."

"Well, he didn't exaggerate the dangers. About 98% of knockoff chargers fail basic mechanical and electrical tests."

"That many! Whoa."

"Right. Whoa. You can see why they'd be hazardous. If chargers don't successfully dampen the voltage, they risk the device overheating, catching fire, or delivering an electric shock strong enough to electrocute a person. "

Stella turned this information over in her mind. "Could you tell the difference between a factory charger and a knockoff? Signor Lake's looked different from the ones Signora Stafford provided. But I can't tell if it's a meaningful difference."

"You have photos?"

"Getting there," Stella said, scrolling through her phone.

Domenica put down her coffee. "Let me see."

"Here it is." Stella rested her coffee on the floor to hand the phone to Domenica. Ravioli rode the wave of Stella's movements and then stretched out again across her lap.

"It's a fake."

"You're sure? That quickly?" Stella took the phone back to peer at it, scanning for obvious clues. It looked like a charger. "Don't you need to see the photos of the others?"

"Why? This one is definitely fake. Look—trustworthy chargers are made from a single piece of plastic, smooth. This one is rounded, like a factory-made charger, so it's a high-quality fake, but it's a fake, as evidenced by the fact that it's made from different pieces of plastic. Moving on, the interlocks on the shell of a well-made charger are regularly spaced and trapezoidal. This one has right-angle interlocks and they're inconsistent."

"What happened to dumbing it down?"

Domenica ignored her. "Plus, look at the pins. Don't worry, this part is about color, not shape, low-attention-span girl."

"Hey! I pay endless attention when—"

"Yes, when an explanation involves food. But stay with me. What do you see here?"

"Well, the pins are bent from when his falling body knocked it from the wall."

"That's irrelevant." Domenica pointed at the screen. "Legitimate chargers' pins are matte, fakes are glossy."

Stella squinted. "Umm . . . sure. If you say so."

Domenica harrumphed. "And if all that wasn't enough, see this sticker?"

"Yes. It says 'Designed by Apple in California.' Seems legit."

"You see the logo."

"What are you getting at? It's the Apple logo. Which doesn't prove your point."

"Look again, *cara*."

"I ask for your help and instead I get a pop quiz," Stella muttered. But she enlarged the photo and her mouth dropped open. "There's no bite out of the apple."

"*Esatto*."

"Oh . . . wow." Stella sat up straighter. "You need to look at the other chargers. The ones Signora Durant provided her guests."

"Why? What did I just tell you? This one is a counterfeit charger. Prone to exploding. Not typically like this, I grant you. But deaths have certainly been reported. In Argentina. In Japan. In—"

"But, Domenica, maybe they are *all* fake. The ones Signora Durant showed us looked different than this, that I know, but if they are all fake and sloppily constructed, then maybe Hollis Lake drew the short straw, so to speak. But if the others are authentic, it suggests that maybe somebody switched his charger to a knockoff."

Domenica nodded slowly. "Show me."

Stella flipped ahead and enlarged the photo of the chargers on the coffee table. She held her breath as Domenica studied the photo. She enlarged it, moved the image around methodically.

Finally, Domenica placed the phone on the desk. "All legit. All from Apple."

"You're sure?"

"*Cara*, don't insult me. From their shape to their pins to their stickers to their roughly sequential serial numbers. A recognized factory made these, with all the regulations to assure safe chargers."

Stella nodded, scratching Ravioli between the ears. "So then the question becomes, did he bring his own charger? And unwittingly brought a weapon?"

"He seems like a guy who has his secretary buy his chargers."

"Would she have known to only buy from a certified vendor?" Stella shook her head. "Anyway, I'm still stuck on this: Even if Signor Lake was murdered by a faulty charger, how in the world would a killer know the charger was this level of faulty? As a murder weapon, a knockoff charger seems deeply unreliable."

"Well."

Stella waited.

And waited.

"Domenica? Did your brain short circuit?" Stella winced at her words.

"I'm not sure how to explain." Domenica took a noisy sip of coffee and then leaned toward Stella. "Remember how I said that certified third-party vendors sell chargers made from multiple components?"

Stella nodded, confused about where this was going.

"Well, a charger that's made from multiple pieces is easier to tamper with."

Realization dawned. "So a killer could use the inherent weakness in a knockoff charger to weaponize it."

Domenica nodded, and Stella leaned back, her eyes closed in thought. She imagined Mr. Lake waiting for the party to start and reaching for his phone. He laughs, not finding it. Wonders if it's stuck in a hidden pocket. Stella cycled on this image for a moment. She decided to move on. Then, later, Mr. Lake scans the downstairs surfaces before deciding he left his phone upstairs. He pushes the door of his room open and spies the phone on the bedside table. Stella paused—why wouldn't he have slipped the phone in his pocket and returned to the party? He must have registered that it was out of battery. Mr. Lake huffs impatiently and plugs the cord into the phone, connecting it with the dangerous charger that, unbeknownst to him, is lying in wait. Before he can form thought, he's fallen to the floor, the electrical current running through his body, stopping his heart. His phone lies beside him.

His phone lies beside him.

Stella opened her eyes. "The sides of the phone were scuffed. Can you think of any reason for that?"

"Wear and tear. It happens." Domenica gestured to Stella's phone on the desk, littered with scratches.

"My phone is a zillion years old."

"No more than four. But carry on."

"His is the newest model. I remembered from your ranting. And, unlike me, a fancy rich guy is hardly going to throw his phone on the counter while he whips up a batter for *strufoli*. Then clean off the dried batter with any available cloth."

"I hate that you do that, *cara*. Though I did love those *strufoli*."

Stella continued as if Domenica hadn't spoken. "And anyway, his scuffing is all around the sides of the phone. Not the back. Why would a phone have scuffing and scratches around the edges?"

"I can't think of any everyday reason," Domenica considered. "But opening the phone would ding the sides."

"Why would anyone do that?"

"Most wouldn't. A phone's motherboard is a zoo under the hood."

"That's most people. Why would *you* open a phone?"

"To fix a problem. Change the battery when it's not holding a charge anymore. That kind of thing."

"But he probably wouldn't do it himself."

"I should think not. He'd have to know what he was doing. Most people buy a new phone when their battery stops holding a charge. It's usually time for an upgrade by then, anyway."

"We know he charged his phone, which suggests his phone's battery was drained. Maybe it was often drained, so he'd watched YouTube videos to figure out how to change the battery?" Stella frowned. "But no, if he'd changed it, the battery *would* hold a charge. It wouldn't have been empty. If, that is, he had remembered to charge it the night before like most people."

"Lots of ifs in that statement."

"I have to think about it for a moment." Stroking Ravioli, Stella considered the life of a battery, all those photos taken, recipes looked up, apps used. Stocks checked. There it was. Stella leaned back, struck. "Wait. Not related. But I realized something. These money guys, they are never ever without their phones. It's like an appendage."

Domenica nodded. "It's true. People make fun of adolescent girls on social media, but full-grown men checking their stock portfolios? They're equally addicted to their phones."

"Even when the markets are closed, Signor Stafford is on Twitter trying to read tea leaves about the next day."

"But what does that have to do with Hollis Lake?"

"Domenica, there's no way he *accidentally* left his phone upstairs. Even with the hubbub of a party starting. He would have noticed he didn't have it as soon as he walked out of the room. I've seen Signor Stafford on his phone walking down the stairs—these guys have to fill every available moment with content. Someone *took* Signor Lake's phone. And did something to the battery so he'd have to charge it. Then moved the phone upstairs, next to a faulty charger. A *purposely* faulty charger."

Domenica paled. "Someone swapped the battery with a drained one. Hence the scratches."

"Which means it was murder."

Silence sank into the bookstore.

Domenica said, "Stella?"

Stella nodded. "I guess it's time to meet the new captain."

"You don't want to run it by Luca first?"

She shook her head. "I don't know how long they can keep the Americans here if there is no cause. If it looks like an accident. I can't count on the time it takes for the word to drift upward."

"Stella!" Domenica called. "It will only take an additional few minutes to contact—"

But the door had already closed.

On Stella's walk to the station, Domenica's words lingered.

She stopped in the street, thinking. Domenica was right—she needed to start with Luca. He'd be miffed if she went above his head. Justifiably.

Also, she knew for sure he'd listen to her, would value her input. She couldn't say that for anyone else in the police department. With some measure of surprise at her sudden ability to temper an impulse with reason, Stella strode to the station.

Only to learn that Luca wasn't in.

The waggle of Salvo's eyebrows as he said that Luca had called in "sick" suggested Luca was making the most of Liliana's time in Aramezzo. "After all, he needs to … *recover* … from last night." Right. A death cut their date short.

Feeling suddenly disoriented, Stella leaned on the doorjamb. She hated this feeling, like ice and fire roiling in her belly. She hated it so much, she needed to divert attention—

Captain Tribuzio strode through the office, a cup of strong coffee in his hands. French press, rather than made in a moka, if Stella's nose was to be trusted. A smell she rarely smelled in Aramezzo where if caffeine wasn't pumped through an espresso machine, it was made on the stovetop in a silver moka, with the shapely figure of a 50s starlet.

The smell made her feel a little reckless.

"Captain Tribuzio!" she called.

His steps slowed, and he turned. He said nothing as he regarded her levelly, like a lion in the zoo stares down children pretending to roar in front of the enclosure.

Stella stammered, "I—I'm Stella. Buchanan. I own Casale Mazzoli … that way." Here she gestured to the west side of town, only belatedly realizing she lived on the east side. Her voice came out strangled and she coughed as he continued staring at her. "I've got some information. That might be useful for you."

He stood straight as a lamppost in daylight, giving as little.

"About the case?" she added hopefully. "At the villa? Last night?"

After another beat, he said, "The Staffords. Yes, come in."

She didn't know what he meant but allowed herself to be led into his office. After so little time in this department, she would have expected boxes or some amount of disarray. But the office had not one book, not one paper out of place. She noticed with some surprise it also had no framed photographs. No spouse or children or even siblings or parents to smile fondly upon from time to time. Perhaps the captain never felt fond.

Stella dropped into the open seat but at a look from the captain instantly realized she should have waited for an invitation. Or at least until he himself sat down. She was going about this all wrong.

Finally, he sank into his chair and said, "Fire away."

Stella exhaled. "Last night. Before you arrived. I was helping with translation."

He inclined his head. Not news to him.

She went on. "I noticed something. The charger in Signor Lake's room was not the same as the others, the ones Signora Durant provided."

Captain Tribuzio frowned. "So he brought his own."

"That seems doubtful. And even if he did, it's unlikely that he purchased a knockoff charger."

With his thumb, Captain Tribuzio flicked each of his fingers in turn, as if managing mounting annoyance.

Stella rushed on. "Here's the thing. The sides of Signor Lake's phone, they were scuffed. I saw."

"Scuffed?" His eyebrows rose.

"Yes." She wondered if maybe she was using the wrong word. But Domenica had seemed to understand her. "I think someone took Signor Lake's phone and replaced it with drained batteries, which explains the scratches along the edge of the phone. Then that person moved the phone upstairs. Signor Lake noticed the phone had no charge, plugged it in, and got electrocuted. By the fake charger. That could easily have been tampered with to deliver a full charge. Electrocuting him. You see, the hand. The hand seemed like electrocution. But maybe you know that already."

She wondered if she'd made any sense at all. It felt like she'd left out a vital piece of the puzzle.

Captain Tribuzio listened to her, hands steepled under his chin. "You've finished?"

She looked down at her hands, clasped on her lap. "Yes."

He rose and moved a paper from one side of his clean desk to the other. "It was good of you to stop by."

"That's it?"

He looked up. "Should there be more?"

"It doesn't look like you are taking this seriously." Stella paused. "At all."

"Ah. I can imagine it does look that way." He nodded. "Because it's true."

"How can you ignore what I'm telling you?"

"Signora Buchanan—"

"I'm not married."

He blinked. "Signorina Buchanan. I'm not in the habit of taking direction from civilian women other than my wife and my mother. They have proven themselves. You have yet to do so."

Stella felt her mouth gawping like a landed fish. Had he not heard about the last two murder cases in Aramezzo? And his last statement, did he hit the word *civilian* or *women* harder? "You don't listen to your female officers? Your superiors?"

"I have no female superiors." Stella could easily believe it. "As for my officers. No. Neither the women nor the men have yet to earn my consideration. But I am paid by this department to accept their information; I'm afraid that courtesy doesn't extend to you. Now, if you don't mind, I have a case that requires my attention, so you best return to your kitchen."

The words flew out before Stella could stop them. "Because that's where women belong, I suppose. In the kitchen."

He stared at her levelly. "Women who are paid to cook, I would imagine."

Oh, right. There was that. Seething, she turned to go. She should have started with Luca. Never mind that he was in a bed somewhere with his girlfriend with perfect hair.

Stella pressed a hand against the red rising in her cheeks and stumbled out of his office. To her retreating back, Captain Tribuzio said, "And the Staffords?"

She turned, slowly. "What about them?"

"Anything to add?"

She considered. "Like what?"

"Ah," he said. "You don't know. Well, you will soon enough."

Gritting her teeth, she said, "Why all the riddles? Have they done something wrong?"

Captain Tribuzio checked his watch. "That remains to be seen."

Her mouth dropped open. "Are . . . are you bringing them in?"

"That will be all." He looked down at his desk.

Salvo stuck his head in the room. "They found a gun, Captain. I guess that anonymous tip was pretty useful!" He glanced at Stella. "What are you still doing here?"

"The Staffords?" Stella gulped. "A gun? You found a gun? At my bed-and-breakfast?"

Salvo grinned. "I sure hope it's not yours, Stella."

"What! You know I don't have a gun." He had to be teasing.

Salvo chuckled before saying to the Captain, "They should be here any moment."

Stella turned to the captain. "I don't know anything about a gun!"

He stared at her and then glanced over her shoulder as a commotion came bustling through the front door of the station. Stella heard Mr. Stafford shout, "Don't make me repeat myself! Get your hands off her! Why can't any of you speak *English*?"

Stella rushed from the captain's office. "Mr. Stafford! Mrs. Stafford!"

"Stella!" Mrs. Stafford fell into her arms. "I don't know what's going on! These officers knocked on the door and we were having breakfast, and they saw a gun and assumed it was ours!"

Stella's eyes slid to Captain Tribuzio, watching so carefully she wondered if he'd somehow engineered this encounter. "You brought a gun into my home?"

Mrs. Stafford said, "I never said it was our gun," just as Mr. Stafford said, "You can't keep it! It's private property! It's an antique!"

Mrs. Stafford groaned.

Stella said, "But how did you get a gun into Italy?"

"We have rights, you know!" shouted Mr. Stafford. "The second amendment! Citizens have the right to keep and bear arms."

"Those rights end at the water's edge," intoned Captain Tribuzio. Mr. and Mrs. Stafford stilled at the booming baritone of his voice. Stella hated herself for noting once again that his English really was impeccable.

Stella broke in, "There's no way you could have gotten it through security. And you wouldn't have put it in your checked baggage, you have to know if you got caught with it, there'd be hell to pay." She had a thought, "Oh."

Everyone stared at Stella.

"Oh," she said again. "That's what you had mailed to my house. A gun." She had another realization. This must be the anonymous tip. Someone at the post office was suspicious of a package arriving from China for people blowing into town to attend a party where someone wound up dead.

Captain Tribuzio's lack of expression when she mentioned the package convinced her she was right.

Mrs. Stafford whined, "I told you the package was, well, it's nothing important. Nothing *relevant*."

Stella turned to Captain Tribuzio. "Signor Lake wasn't shot. I get that the gun is bad and there will be consequences, but it cannot relate to Signor Lake, can it?"

"That's what we're going to find out, *signorina*." Was it her imagination or was there a mocking note at the *signorina*? "If you'll excuse me. Salvo, will you show our young friend out?"

The captain ushered Stella's guests into what looked like an interview room as Mr. Stafford shouted, "I want a lawyer! I know my rights!"

Salvo took Stella's elbow and walked her to the door. She wrestled her arm free. "Salvo, you have to listen to me. That charger, I was right, there's something wrong with it. It's a knockoff, a fake, which can cause electrocution. Worse, they can be tampered with to make them deadly. I suspect the murderer counted on everyone considering the death as a heart attack or at most electrocution due to faulty wiring or a freak accident. But you've seen these finance guys with their phones. How in the world could Signor Lake not have it charged and on him? Doesn't that strike you as strange that it was neither?"

Emboldened by Salvo's slowing steps, Stella continued. "I think someone switched the battery to a drained one so Signor Lake would have to charge his phone. On his own, with no one around. That person tampered with the charger and left it where he'd find his phone. It's too much coincidence otherwise, don't you see?"

Salvo pitched his voice low, "The Staffords?"

"I don't think so. But maybe, I don't know. I suppose it could have been a charger in that package, not a gun." Stella stopped walking. "Wait. If someone switched out the charger ... where did the original one go? You need to check everywhere—"

Salvo shook his head. "We searched the entire premises for anything remotely strange. Every bush, every flowerbed, every cupboard."

"For the charger? But you didn't know how to tell a knockoff from—"

"If we'd found a charger—any charger—in the flowerbed, don't you think it would be in the report?"

"No," Stella shook her head. "This killer is too clever. No way he'd toss the charger in a flowerbed. Too lazy."

Salvo nodded, slowly. "I see what you mean. But, Stella…where are we supposed to look?"

Closing her eyes, Stella played it out. Someone snuck into Mr. Lake's room and swapped out the original charger, the one borrowed from Mrs. Durant. Where would he put it? Her eyes opened. Suddenly, it seemed so simple. Exactly how the murderer approached this mission. Economy of motion, bare shades of subtlety. "That basket of chargers. Remember? The one Mrs. Durant showed us? Have you counted them again? Maybe now there's one extra. You can check them for fingerprints."

"I'll have someone do it," Salvo said, his lips thin below his mustache. "But only if it turns out that the cause of death is electrocution."

"Thank you," Stella breathed, tamping down her impatience. This was the best she could ask for. "When are you supposed to know? About the autopsy?"

Salvo glanced at the clock on the wall and frowned. "It should have been an hour ago. I don't know what's taking so long."

Stella debated extracting some kind of promise from Salvo to let her know the results, but feeling they were finally on the same team, she couldn't push it. Suddenly, she remembered. "Wait. I don't understand. If you're assuming a natural death, why is the captain interviewing the Staffords?"

Stella expected him not to answer, to shove her off. But he shrugged. "The tip. Officers went to ask them about the package and saw Mr. Stafford holding a gun. A gun he has no permit for."

"Any chance he *does* have a permit?" Stella hoped.

Salvo snorted in laughter. "Are you kidding? Do you know how hard it is to get a permit to carry a gun in Italy? The number of lessons and the number of exams, both written and practical? And that's just to carry one specific firearm in one specific shooting range. Carrying a gun across regional borders? That's serious work. Most people don't pass. You think your guest could have done that in less than a week?"

She hung her head. "I guess not."

"I should think not." He shook his head. "Here, people can't just pick up a gun and start toting it around like John Wayne."

"A fan of Westerns, are you?"

"Luca is not the only one who has layers."

Stella looked up with a start. Was he mocking her? Coming onto her? No, he simply looked pleased. Maybe he was congratulating himself for the banter, which had been pretty nice. Perhaps there was more to Salvo than she'd previously assumed.

Still smiling, he said, "Go on, I have to get back to work."

"Will you let me know what happens?"

"No," he smiled. "But I'm sure Luca will."

"Isn't he too busy with Liliana?"

He shrugged. "Much like you're too busy with Giancarlo."

"For a police officer, you sure are pretty distracted by budding love stories. Reading romances as well as Westerns, nowadays?"

"I leave that to Luca." He grinned broadly and turned on his heel, hurrying deeper into the station.

Hurrying out of the station, Stella ran headlong into Matteo. "Stella! You've got to look where you're going." He grabbed her shoulders. "I stopped in to see Domenica, and she told me you were here. But then I saw the Staffords marched down the street, police on either side. What is happening?"

Stella had never been so happy to see her friend. She held onto the front of his shirt as she shook her head. "They think the Staffords are in on it. That one of them killed Signor Lake."

"Because of their fight at the party?"

"You heard about it?"

"Hard not to." Matteo smiled. "If you ask me, it's bad form to dredge up old grievances over cocktails."

"Please don't judge all Americans by these people. Their whole lives have been easy. They assume the rest of the world is here to meet their every whim."

"I would never judge you," Matteo smiled and tucked a lock of Stella's hair back under the bandana where it had come loose.

She smiled back. Then she remembered, and the smile fell from her face. Her voice lowered, she said, "The Staffords. They brought a gun. To my *casale*."

"*What?*" Matteo's voice came out strangled. "They wouldn't!"

"They did," Stella said grimly. "And seemed unrepentant when the police found it."

Matteo paused, staring down the road in thought. "But Signor Lake wasn't shot."

"Right. I imagine the police are using this opportunity to get information from them. Anyway, there will be some consequences for them bringing a gun into Italy without a license." She paused. "Last night, Signor Stafford said something about protecting himself. I wonder if he somehow ordered a gun. Which means that's not the secret package."

"Money really can buy anything," Matteo said. "But into your home? I can't believe it."

"Imagine if Barbanera had startled them in the night or something."

"If you don't mind, I will not be imagining that." He shuddered. "I guess with the commotion around the Staffords being brought in, you didn't get to talk to the police about the charger?"

"Domenica filled you in?" Stella wasn't surprised.

"She did. And I can tell you I'm going home and checking all my chargers."

"The new captain, it seems, doesn't share your caution."

Matteo frowned. "What do you mean?"

"Apparently, because I am a woman, I am not worth listening to."

"Did he *say* that?"

"Not in so many words. But his meaning was unmistakable."

"What did he say? Exactly?"

She rolled her eyes. "Some nonsense of not listening to civilian women who aren't his wife or mother. Then he told me to get back to the kitchen."

"Stella."

"Matteo."

Matteo took a beat. "You are a chef."

"Whatever." Stella's brow furrowed. "I know what I know."

"C'mon, Stella. You read misogyny into any episode of *Friends*."

"Because there *is* misogyny in any episode of *Friends*!" She set her jaw. "It's also pretty homophobic, in case that escaped your notice."

He rolled his eyes. "How could it escape my notice when, every time we watch it, you point out how they use homosexuality as a punchline?"

"Watched it. We haven't done that in ages."

"And now you know why." He smiled. "I get it, Stella. I do. You've had to struggle everywhere to prove yourself. To prove your worth. So you're struggling even now."

"He is a misogynist."

"Maybe we all are." He shrugged. "One thing is for sure, I'm sorry he didn't listen to you. It took Domenica a few tries to walk me through it, but it sounds plausible. And now I can't think of another way for this to go down."

"You don't think it could be an accident?"

"Not if someone replaced the charger. That's intentional. But," he frowned. "How to prove it?"

"I suggested to Salvo that they check the chargers in the basket for prints. I figure that's the most logical place for the killer to put the original charger, the one Signor Lake had been using before it got switched."

He nodded, slowly. "Right. Someone clever enough to know how to tamper with a charger so that it delivers a deadly shock seems smart enough to know you can't just put that original charger in the trash."

"Exactly!"

"I hope Salvo listened to you." Matteo smiled fondly at her before his face stilled. "But...do you think it was one of the Staffords?"

"Not with a gun. But could they have switched the chargers? I don't know. I mean, it comes down to who had a motive, right? Who would want Signor Lake dead? Who stood to gain? I don't see Signora Stafford doing it. Signor Stafford certainly had a grudge. But..."

"Stella? Tell me what you're thinking."

"I can't. It's all half-cooked in my head. But I know there's someone who makes sense."

Matteo chuckled. "I'll make sure I skip lunch today. And I'll tell Giancarlo to do the same."

She looked at him, puzzled.

"Sounds like you're going to bake something."

She grinned. "You know me too well."

He cupped her face and leaned his forehead against her own. "I'd say just well enough."

As she waved goodbye to Matteo, Stella wondered what to make. What flavors had she enjoyed recently? She stopped in the street, remembering the trip to Spoleto she'd taken with Matteo and Domenica back in April. She'd fallen in love with the colorful city, which seemed to have had its heyday in a later period than other Umbrian towns. It appeared more Renaissance than medieval. Aramezzo and Assisi and Gubbio and Spello—they had the stony, squat nature of towns built in architecture's early days. Spoleto, like Perugia, felt airier, grander, lighter.

She closed her eyes to better remember Spoleto, not noticing the bemused looks of neighbors passing her in the street. That pistachio gelato. She'd never had anything like it—so nutty it veered into floral, with a grounded earthiness that balanced out the sweetness. The awards listed on the outside of the gelateria were well-deserved.

But she couldn't make gelato without an ice cream maker.

What else from Spoleto? There was that legume stew with local farro, but she couldn't make it without picking up farro from a shop around Spoleto. She'd loved the antipasto of local cured meats. Salumi platters across Umbria might look the same, but they tasted different thanks to the differences in animal diet and curing traditions. Delightful, but not a source of today's culinary inspiration. Ah, yes, there was that satisfying plate of *strangozzi alla spoletina*, the irregularly-shaped handmade pasta in a slightly spicy tomato sauce. Wonderful, though it didn't demand the intense cooking process she required.

Then she remembered dessert. Stella opened her eyes. Yes! Perfect. The *crescionda*. At the first bite of the chocolate cake, so soft it was almost a pudding, she knew she had to make it. But that intention had gotten lost in a slew of guests followed by Aramezzo's festival.

Stella stayed still, considering. Did she have the ingredients for Spoleto's famed chocolate cake? She closed her eyes again to allow her palate to remember the flavors. Eggs, sugar, flour, lemon zest, milk, dark chocolate. She remembered the anise lilt to the cake. She still had the sambuca she'd found in her cabinet when hunting for anise-flavored liquor for the *strufoli* she'd made around Carnevale.

But there was one other ingredient.

She thought back, imagining the cake, and trying to fit it with the memory of the list of ingredients. Something almondy. The image of little cookies exploded into her mind like almond fireworks. Amaretti biscuits! Crushed amaretti biscuits!

Stella veered into the little market, waving at Cristiana, the owner of the *alimentari*, and made a direct line toward the cookies. She loved how any little shop in Italy, no matter what quality of goods they sold, always had amaretti biscuits. So good on their own with a little coffee or an after-dinner digestif, but also excellent crushed in baked goods.

Remembering she'd used the last of the lemons for zest in the *crostata* crust, she picked up a few of those as well. As she placed the items on the counter, she remembered she hadn't eaten yet today. Which explained her lightheadedness. She added a can of tuna to the pile.

"Hope these don't all go together in one dish," Cristiana said good-naturedly as Stella handed over a five euro bill, plus thirty euro cents so that the change would be a one euro coin. Umbrian shopkeepers loathed handing over small change.

Stella laughed. "I'm not that into experimentation."

As Cristiana gave her the coin, she said, "I heard about the death. At the villa. Are you okay?"

Seeing the worry in Cristiana's eyes, Stella's heart twisted. How could there be so much care in such a little village? "Didn't get much sleep, but other than that..."

"I saw some of the Americans at Bar Cappellina this morning. They didn't get much sleep either."

"You could tell by looking at them?" Stella was surprised. She didn't picture them ever leaving the house without being effortlessly smooth and glossy.

Cristina laughed. "Are you kidding? Not an eye bag among them. They were talking about it. Leo filled me in after they left." She lowered her voice, her eyes scanning the shop toward the elderly women in blue dresses arguing next to the pasta section about which shape went better with greens picked on Monte Subasio. "They sound pretty sure Mimmo had something to do with it. But I don't think that can be true, do you?"

Stella thought of Mimmo's calloused fingers. "He hasn't made friends with them, that's for sure."

Cristiana's laughter filled the store. "No, making friends isn't Mimmo's thing. But he has spent the last few years complaining about the Americans to anyone who will listen."

"I wish he hadn't been hanging around their property last night."

"That's not illegal, though. All land is available for hunting."

"From foraging asparagus and mushrooms to hunting birds and *cinghiale*. I know. It's a great thing about Italy, but it does mean he was in the wrong place at the wrong time."

"I guess," Cristiana said. She stacked Stella's items in a bag and turned the handles toward her. "Big baking plans today?"

"I'm making *crescionda*."

"*Crescionda*? Oh! Spoleto's cake! It's not the right time, though. Long past Carnevale."

Stella picked up the bag with a smile. "There's no bad season for good cake."

Cristiana laughed and waved goodbye.

When Stella got home, she listened for a moment before remembering the Staffords were at the police station. She wondered how long they'd be there. Her thoughts turned to the gun. *In her house*. She hoped the police took it with them.

Barbanera wound around her legs and Stella picked him up. He rarely consented to a cuddle in arms, but he let his head lean against her chest, his eyes lingering on hers for a moment before he remembered his refusal to be domesticated. He scrambled to get down, sitting at the door of the refrigerator and yelling for his lunch.

Chuckling, Stella said, "I'm not sure if your expectation of being fed brands you as more or less domesticated."

He stopped yelling and stared at her, his single ear flat back. Stella felt a hook in the middle of her stomach. Poor little cat. Then again, "little" was entirely the wrong word for a cat the size of a small dog. She opened the fridge and Barbanera ran to his usual spot, waiting. He took a cursory sniff at the plate before burying his chin into the food on the vintage saucer, this one Delft blue and white. Stella scratched the top of his head, delighting in the low purr rumbling from this beast of a cat.

She rose and opened her can of tuna, scarfing it down as she watched Barbanera do the same. Thoughts swirled through her brain—motive, method, and opportunity. Who had them all?

Partway through her "meal," she grew impatient. She stuck the half-eaten can in the fridge and slipped on her chef's coat before pulling out the cookbook, thumbing through it as she returned to the kitchen. She set out eggs, flour, sugar, lemon, milk, dark chocolate, and the sambuca from the liquor cabinet.

The swirl of her thoughts slowed as she crushed the amaretti biscuits. Motive. Motive was first.

She considered Mr. Lake. He certainly didn't seem a fan favorite of anyone at the party, save his family. But who particularly seemed to rankle at his existence?

Mr. Stafford seemed the most obvious suspect. They had a history that could amount to a motive. But did Morton Stafford have the means? The opportunity?

Stella's hands stalled as she separated egg yolks from their whites. The gun . . . did he bring it with him or have it sent from China?

The package. It didn't seem heavy enough to hold a gun. Not even a small one. But . . . maybe . . . a charger?

Her hands paused as they whisked sugar into the egg yolks.

If the police found the Staffords suspicious, they'd likely return to search the house. They wouldn't look for a charger, either Mr. Lake's original charger or evidence that they'd brought a rigged one. At least not until, or if, they declared electrocution the cause of death.

She grated the chocolate and listened. Quiet, other than Barbanera's chewing. She checked the time. Would the Staffords be coming back soon? She rinsed her hands, thinking. She'd tiptoe upstairs and have a brief look around. With two of them, she'd definitely hear them coming before they could sneak up on her.

Stella rounded the staircase and took them two at a time. Now that she decided to look for... evidence, she supposed... she felt a press of hurry at her back. She had to be out and done before they returned. If they returned. For all she knew, her guests could be spending the night in some Italian jail for having an unregistered handgun.

She paused as she crested the stairs. Shouldn't she be careful of fingerprints? She opened the bathroom cabinet and took out the cleaning gloves. Bulky, but at least they'd protect her. Her fingerprints would be expected on surfaces, but not on any questionable items the Staffords might own.

First, the bathroom. Remembering how Mrs. Stafford had suggested the package from China contained something medical, Stella opened the cabinet, looking for anything remotely foreign or odd. Nothing remarkable—a container of Advil and an incredible array of Sisley-Paris skincare products. No wonder Mrs. Stafford looked so good.

Based on the contents of the cabinet, it did not seem like the package contained medicine. Which Stella had doubted from the beginning, given how cagey they'd been about it.

Stella crept out of the bathroom, grabbing a trash bag on the way. If the Staffords arrived home, she'd say she was cleaning up. Perfectly reasonable. Her eyes scanned the surfaces of the bedroom. The Staffords were tidy, she could say that for them.

Listening out one final moment, Stella strode to the nightstand— empty, save a fashion magazine and a tube of hand cream, this one from La Mer. Stella opened the drawers and carefully, so when they returned they wouldn't notice any shifts, rifled through the clothes. Where where *where*? And what was she looking for? A charger? What would that even mean? Wouldn't the Staffords themselves require a charger? Her eyes flew to the wall next to the nightstand. Two chargers. Could one of them have been taken from the Durant's villa? She hurried to them, hunched, and ripped them from the wall. Her eyes scanning the surface, she forgot to listen out until the door slammed behind her.

She bolted to standing, her mind racing.

Two chargers clutched in her hands clad in yellow cleaning-up gloves. How in the world could she explain—

The unformed words died in her mouth.

Only Barbanera stood before her. In front of the door he must have slammed. Unless a breeze from the opened window helped.

"Barbanera!" she said, the word choking her. "It's you, only you?"

His tail whisked from side to side, as if to say, "Perhaps you expected otherwise?"

Stella worked to still her galloping heart. She opened the bedroom door and listened. Not a sound. "You stay put," she told the one-eared cat.

He narrowed his eyes and looked away.

She remembered the chargers in her hand and checked them. They were both made by Apple, as far as she could tell from Domenica's lesson. How could she tell if one had been taken from the villa?

Serial numbers!

Stella checked these serial numbers. They were in the same ballpark as each other. She took out her phone but couldn't open the screen with the gloves, so she used her teeth to rip off the right one. She found the photo of the chargers in the basket. These two serial numbers weren't even close.

She slipped the glove back on and returned the chargers to their outlets, tensing for a moment. Would she ever be able to plug in a charger again without fearing death? Domenica's voice came into her head, reminding her that only plugging the end of the cord into a device would draw a charge. She couldn't help her sweaty palms. Wouldn't water and electricity also be deadly? Maybe the gloves would protect her from that, too.

Chargers successfully reinstalled, Stella paused. She'd found nothing. What a waste.

She closed her eyes. Where else might someone keep a contraband or suspicious item? Suitcases! She found them in the corner. Focusing on stilling her shaking hands, Stella unwound the zipper to open each case. Nothing. Not even a loose piece of paper.

Loose paper . . . perhaps the trash?

She jogged back to the bathroom and, blessing her covered hands, rooted through the garbage which amounted to an empty lipstick, makeup remover wipes, used threads of floss, and wadded-up toilet paper that Stella tried not to think too much about.

In her mystery books, she had never gotten the impression that so much of sleuthing amounted to sifting through trash.

Her eyes snagged on the lipstick. Empty . . . but Mrs. Stafford had to have more. In fact, she would require an entire make-up kit, probably with tiers and a variety of brushes. Where could that be?

Her purse!

But wouldn't she have her purse with her?

Stella frowned in thought. Not if she'd been so rattled by the police that she forgot it. After all, a trip to the police station, flanked by *carabinieri*, was hardly an occasion to get gussied up. Stella tried to remember what Salvo had told her about when the police arrived. The Staffords had been downstairs. Could Mrs. Stafford have left her purse in the living room or the breakfast area?

Stella hurried downstairs, her eyes scanning the room. There! On the couch! Mrs. Stafford's purse. She felt like a prize idiot for not noticing it earlier, resting against the couch cushions.

A glance over her shoulder and she snatched up the purse. No charger. Yes, a bag of makeup, though relatively small. A clear vial of pills, which, given the lack of label, didn't look like prescription medicine. Unless it was now *de riguer* to transfer meds from ghastly orange plastic to fine glass bottles. Kind of like putting mouthwash in glass flasks as if one lived in an apothecary.

Or maybe they were vitamins?

Stella removed the top of the glass bottle and inhaled. Her eyes watered and she gasped for air. This did not smell like anything a doctor had ever prescribed her, which only ever varied from smelling like a lab floor to smelling like a bitter lab floor. The smell reminded her of something, though. She stood for a moment, lost in thought. A dim room. With the smell of books and antiseptic and herbs, but like no herbs Stella had ever smelled before. Not cooking herbs. So it wasn't a spice store, though there was a scent like valerian root, which she'd used before to make bitters. So not herbs, really, more twisty roots.

Dang.

She couldn't think of it.

The sound of the wind tossing tree boughs against her window reminded her that she probably shouldn't be standing in the living room, elbow-deep in her guest's pocketbook. Hurriedly, she put everything back in the purse and then rested it against the cushions. She stepped back and eyed it afresh. She adjusted the purse to center it, and then drew off the gloves, and returned to the kitchen.

If only she could remember where she'd smelled something like what was in that bottle. It felt tantalizingly out of her grip. Well, if the autopsy showed Mr. Lake had been poisoned, she'd think harder about it.

She had to admit, the sleuthing had been a bust. She hadn't found anything that exonerated the Staffords from the killing of Mr. Lake. Then again, she thought as she whipped the egg whites, she hadn't found anything that suggested they did it either. No charger. No manual about changing batteries or tampering with chargers. No smoking gun, as it were.

She realized she felt some measure of relief. The Staffords could be demanding and inconsiderate, but it seemed a childlike kind of self-involvement. When they came out of it, she delighted in the glee they found in flavors or a view. And their love of each other seemed real and uncomplicated. Their adoration of Judith, too.

Egg whites in peaks, she picked up the lemon to zest the peel.

Who else could have killed Mr. Lake?

Stella rejected Mimmo hopefully as easily as the police did. Perhaps he did hate the Americans, but if he wanted to kill some of them, the owners of the villa were more obvious targets. Besides, finagling a charger to deliver a killing blow did not seem in his wheelhouse. If the villa had gone up in flames, perhaps, she could more easily believe him the culprit.

She shivered as she tipped the lemon zest into the bowl of flour.

Besides Mimmo, besides the Staffords. Who else?

The Durants seemed out. Why invite him to their home to kill him? Unless the whole point was to lure him to foreign ground where they thought they could get away with something? Stella shook her head as she poured milk into a bowl. They didn't seem to love Mr. Lake, but they didn't seem to hate him either. And they seemed distressed by his death.

Who else, she wondered, as she added a splash of sambuca to the batter.

In mysteries, the killer was often a family member—which implicated Judith, Tripp, and Gillian. And, she supposed, Louisa. Louisa seemed unhappy enough with her situation to want to change her fortune. Then again, her resentment seemed aimed at her forced role as her mother-in-law's handler. Wouldn't that role only become more intense without Mr. Lake to shoulder at least some of the burden? If Louisa was going to kill anyone, it would be Judith Lake.

How about Tripp? Stella paused in stirring the batter, remembering the glimpse of him at Domenica's. He clearly resented his salary. Enough that he would kill his father, though? Yes, it happened in books, but this was real life. People didn't kill their father for an inheritance, did they? Plus, he hadn't seemed to leave his father's side all night. She'd put a question mark next to his name.

Gillian. Mr. Lake's daughter made no sense as a suspect. Her father was her golden goose. Why would she jeopardize her cash flow? Unless he'd threatened to cut her off? Stella frowned as she poured the batter into the greased cake pan. She'd heard nothing suggesting Mr. Lake's intention to remove financial backing. But she supposed it was possible. He certainly seemed to delight in sowing chaos.

Then there was Mrs. Lake. Stella imagined that if she were married to Mr. Lake she might want to murder him, but Judith seemed to accept her lot with a kind of sanguine compliance. Probably secondary to her accident. Even if she detested the man she married, why now? Wouldn't it make her already challenging life more challenging? Stella shook her head. Anyway, even if Mrs. Lake had a motive, she had no means. With her traumatic brain injury, she couldn't go two rounds with a gnat, let alone bring down her husband.

This was getting her nowhere, Stella thought as she set the pan into the oven. Everyone potentially had a motive.

How about the weapon? How about opportunity?

As far as she could tell, not one of the family members had gone upstairs the whole evening. She supposed they could have replaced the charger earlier in the day, but somehow someone got the phone resting next to the charger. How would they have gotten it off Mr. Lake without him noticing? How could they have swapped the charger with no one noticing?

It seemed they all had eyes on each other the whole night. Mostly warily, but they did.

Beyond that, none of them seemed technologically-minded enough to mess with a charger. Then again, how could she know? It's not like anyone walked around with a book of electrical principles tucked under his arm. She paused. Maybe someone had bought one at Domenica's? No, no way. No killer smart enough to rewire a charger and replace a battery would be stupid enough to buy a book on the subject where the murder happened.

Any other suspects? None of the Italians, she decided. None could have a motive to kill the guest of a sometimes resident of their village. Not even Mimmo.

So as of now, her best bet seemed to be Morton Stafford or Tripp Lake. As she washed the dishes, she wondered how to find out how much they knew about electricity.

She wondered if Luca might have information, like something a guest said after she left. Or maybe Matteo could help. After all, milling about the party might be even better than an interview room for gathering information. Rumors, most likely, little barbs of hidden resentments. But those could be purer than the canned responses they got in the interview room.

Blessing the *crescionda*'s short bake time, Stella drew it from the oven and wiped her hands on her chef's coat. Picking up her phone, she dialed and said, "Matteo? Where are you? We need to talk."

Stella paused as she passed the police station. Should she pop in to see how the Staffords were faring? Not yet, she needed to get to Matteo, sweeping the streets outside Aramezzo's church.

She jogged up the final set of stairs, arriving at the top level of Aramezzo, which held only the church and its gardens and lawn. Her feet slowed when she noticed Don Arrigo, the village priest, clipping stalks of lavender. He removed an earbud from his ear and called, "Stella! Can you believe what happened?"

She could smell the lavender scent as he waved the drying blossoms. She shook her head. "It was a scene. Like, out of a movie."

He thought for a moment and smiled. "The costumes."

"The costumes, the intrigue. All of it." She'd been so caught up trying to figure out how the murder happened and who the murderer was, she'd hardly processed the dramatic backdrop of the night before. She blinked and slid her eyes to the view of olive trees rolling into the distance until they met the mountains swooping up to the navy-tinged horizon.

Don Arrigo drew closer, meeting her eyes. His normally animated face grew still. "Come for a glass of port tonight, you can tell me all about it."

"There's not much to tell."

He smiled and put a hand on her shoulder. Stella inhaled the scent of lavender clinging to his hands as he said, "I find that hard to believe."

"Do you know them? The American family or their guests?"

He shook his head. "They told me they're not Catholic."

Stella shrugged. "Neither am I. But you welcome me."

"God welcomes all, *cara*," Don Arrigo said, warmth threading his words.

"Then why—"

"They choose not to associate with me."

Stella frowned in thought. "I guess that makes sense. Vacation and religion don't mix."

"One day I'll tell you about my vacation to an ashram."

"Ashram? Aren't those Hindu?"

"Wisdom is everywhere." He smiled and tucked a few blossoms of lavender into Stella's shirt pocket. "For later."

She breathed in the scent, her brain flooding with the sunny, purple smell.

"Now, Stella. Please tell me you're keeping clear of this one. You've had enough excitement these last months. Let's leave this one to the professionals."

She shrugged.

"Stella."

"Something about this case. It's important. I have to figure it out."

He smiled at her affectionately. "Oh, Stella."

"What?"

Don Arrigo shook his head. "Is it so hard to understand?"

Unsure, she said, "I mean, I love mysteries. And I don't want my guests arrested. Or Mimmo. Not if I can help it."

"Stella. Don't you think at some level you are always searching for the mystery driver who took your father and sister away?"

"No," Stella said flatly. Then added, "Have you and Domenica been talking?"

A smile tugged one side of Don Arrigo's too-full-for-priesthood lips. "She says the same, then?'

"Something like that." She shook her head. "But that's not it."

"Isn't it?"

"No!" Her feelings tangled—this seemed presumptuous. He didn't know her all that well, did he? Did she walk around with her emotions streaked across her person like bread dough and cocoa powder? At the same time, the scrabbling beast in her heart quieted at his words. Something akin to comfort settled over her, even while she continued scowling.

"Just a thought." He popped his Bluetooth headphones back into his ear. Stella knew he had hip-hop music cued up while he gardened. "Come anytime, Stella. To talk about this. To talk about anything."

She nodded, suddenly uncertain. Not wanting to leave the priest's sunlit presence.

"You looking for Matteo?" At her nodding again, he pointed around the bend in the path.

Stella nodded her thanks and followed the path until she arrived at Matteo, sweeping cigarette butts into a pile. "Strange place for smoking," she said, to announce her presence.

He turned and smiled at the sight of her. "Took you long enough."

"Don Arrigo."

"Ah," Matteo said. He pointed at the butts with the top of his broom. "Bunch of hooligans. Why they suddenly decided this was the place to smoke, I do not know."

Stella hunched next to the pile, scanning the refuse with her eyes before rising. "American teen girls. Probably getting out from under their parents' collective thumbs."

He frowned, glaring at the butts as if accusing them of sharing a secret with Stella rather than himself. "How do you figure?"

"I can tell they're menthol from the smell. But it also says Newport right there close to the filter. They're popular with Americans, but aren't sold much abroad."

"Which you know how? You're not a smoker."

"Of course, I'm not. It ruins the palate. But you'd be surprised how many restaurant workers don't seem to care about that. Whenever I came to Italy for an apprenticeship, invariably someone asked me to bring a pack or a carton. A request which I would promptly forget." She grinned. "I'll enable no one to destroy taste sensitivity."

"Okay. Fine. Americans. But why teens?"

"The lipstick color. No adult would wear cotton-candy pink."

Matteo's belly laugh filled the spring air.

"The good news is, these must be from the American teens here for the party. Once they're released, they'll leave our streets in peace."

"If the police let them all go." This reminded Matteo. "What did you want to talk about?"

"The party. I need more details. Anything you can tell me?"

He leaned on the broom. "Like what?"

"Signor Lake went upstairs between the grilled shrimp and the gorgonzola puffs course. Did you notice anything happening around then?"

"Well, we got there late. The gorgonzola puffs went out soon after we arrived."

"Were you there for the flare of temper between Signor Stafford and Signor Lake?"

"Not for the original burst, but for the fallout."

"Where was the family during that time? Signor Lake's family?"

Matteo's gaze drifted over the valley as he thought. "Tripp wasn't there. Oh, right, we passed him going to the bathroom when we arrived."

"The bathroom? Are you sure?" Stella remembered she'd asked Tripp specifically if he'd gone to the bathroom and he'd said no.

"That's what he said. I don't know what he did, it could have been a few lines."

Which could explain why he didn't think of it as going to the bathroom. Or why he didn't mention it at all.

"How long was he gone?"

Matteo frowned in thought. "I don't know."

Stella furrowed her brow.

"Don't look at me like that! I can't help it, it was a party. Not only that, it was a costume party. Can you blame me for not logging every move made by people I don't know?"

"Fair enough." Stella sighed. Then she startled. "Oh, get this. When I asked Tripp Lake about the confrontation between his father and Signor Stafford, he said he hadn't heard anything. Now that makes sense. He was gone. But still...the fact that he didn't tell me he left the party for any length of time is suspicious."

"I suppose so," said Matteo, thoughtfully.

"How about Gillian?"

"Gillian...I know I saw her." Matteo frowned. "I remember! She was placing an empty spritz glass on the tray when I was getting one. I remember because it made me realize how late we were. The Americans were already on round two."

"What do you remember about her when you saw her?"

"Her costume stuck with me. Mermaids seem to be making a

comeback. Not much other than that. It was only for a moment. I heard her tell Louisa to check on Signora Lake. Louisa sniped about it, but Gillian said that she was helping entertain, so couldn't possibly leave her duties to tend to the infirm. And then she went to stand with Signora Durant."

"Wait, you understood all that?"

He grinned. "No chance. Giancarlo told me."

Stella thought. "Did you see anyone going upstairs? Or even inside?"

"I didn't, though I wasn't paying careful attention. I did see Louisa check on Signora Lake when Gillian ordered her to."

"How long was she gone?"

"Couldn't have been more than half a minute. When I passed, Signora Lake looked asleep, not much to check."

"And did you get any sense that any of the Italians had a problem with Signor Lake?"

Matteo stabbed at a cigarette butt stuck in the stones of the path. "Veronica, the mayor's wife, she made a cutting remark when Signor Lake told Louisella she hadn't aged a day since when she'd made *Il Rocco*."

"What is it about those two?"

"For that, you'll need to ask someone dustier than I," Matteo grinned. "Any other questions?"

"No, I don't—wait! Yes, did you hear Tripp mentioning anything about money?"

"I didn't. But shouldn't you ask someone who speaks English? Giancarlo, perhaps?" He added with a sly smile that lit his long face.

"I never figured you for playing matchmaker," Stella said, adjusting her bandana while avoiding the threadbare patch.

"Are you kidding? I've already named your babies."

"What! Matteo!" Stella hated the flush heating her cheeks.

"I'm kidding, Stella. Relax." He grinned. "I've only named the first one. Matteo, of course."

"I'm leaving," Stella turned on her heel.

"But Stella!" Matteo called to her retreating back. "Maybe I have more *information*."

"Text it to me."

Matteo jogged to catch up. "Hold up. I wasn't kidding about Giancarlo. He talked to everyone at the party. I've never seen anyone work a room like that. He'll for sure have picked up on more among the Americans than I would have."

She thought for a moment. "I gotta say, I'm having trouble with the visual. Giancarlo doesn't say a lot, does he?"

"He was 'on'," Matteo shrugged. "They must teach it in soccer school, along with dribbling and shooting. Need to woo donors."

"Any donors at the party?"

Matteo laughed. "You wouldn't think so, but yes! Signor Lake!"

Stella's face stilled. "Say again?"

"Yes!" Matteo continued laughing. "He was investing in Giancarlo's team's rival! So they can buy that great player out of Portugal, I can't ever remember his name. But it's the one Giancarlo's team wanted to sign. Can you believe it?" He shook his head, chuckling now. "Such a small world."

"Matteo . . . do you hear what you're telling me?"

"What? No . . ." He continued chuckling and then the smile froze on his face. "*Cavolo.* Stella. You can't be thinking—"

"If Signor Lake was about to invest money in a team that would make it harder for Giancarlo's team to succeed . . ."

"Forget what I said! I wasn't supposed to know any of it, anyway. All that soccer contract stuff is super secret."

"Matteo . . . you need to tell me. Was Giancarlo right beside you all night?"

"Yes!" Matteo said without thinking. Then he paled.

"Matteo?"

"Okay, he went to the bathroom. One time! For like, a minute! Two at the most!"

Stella frowned, trying to imagine how long it would take for someone to run up those three flights of stairs, replace the charger, then run back. "When?"

"I don't know! I can't remember!" He paused. "Signora Lake!"

"What about her?"

"I bet you can ask her. She was in that room right off from the party. Ask her if she saw Giancarlo go to the bathroom on the first floor or head up the stairs."

Stella shook her head. Could Giancarlo have a hand in this? Either way, Matteo had given her an idea. She needed to talk to Signora Lake. By all accounts, she was lodged on a chair all night. If anybody knew who had sneaked upstairs, it would be her. Provided, of course, she'd been awake.

Stella paused outside the police station. Little as she wanted to return to the place from which she'd been so summarily dismissed, the image of the Staffords, cowed and alone, wouldn't leave her mind. And she no longer had the excuse that someone was waiting for her.

She inhaled slowly and then pushed open the glass door. Salvo looked up from his desk, gave her a tight nod, and then turned away. She wondered if he'd taken her idea to the Captain and been roundly mocked for it. She hesitated for a moment and then approached him.

He kept his eyes on his papers, though he must have heard her. As Stella's long-ago ballet teacher had noted, she might be small, but she moved with the grace of an escaping elephant.

Stella cleared her throat.

Salvo checked his phone.

Finally, she said, "Can you tell me what's happening with my guests?"

"Oh!" Salvo said, tension draining from his posture. "Your guests. Sure, sure. Happy to. I think they're wrapping up. Why don't you wait for them in the piazza?"

"Wrapping up?"

"They got a lawyer from Assisi here about an hour ago. Must have had him on speed dial or something. They've accepted the fine for possession of an unregistered firearm, and the lawyer won't let them answer any questions about the party. Luca is processing the paperwork and they'll be out. But like I said, there's a lot going on, so if you could wait—"

"Is that all?"

Salvo cleared his throat. "All?"

Was it her imagination or did his voice sound higher? "Yes. The results of the autopsy?" She smiled to appear full of friendly curiosity rather than overbearingly pushy.

"Right, right. Electrocution."

The blood drained from Stella's face; hearing it aloud felt like a hammer blow. "Are they sure? It couldn't be like poison or something?" Her mind darted to the strange pills, and Mrs. Stafford's caginess around them.

Salvo nodded, appearing cheerier. "Definitely sure. There was damage to the heart consistent with a massive electrical shock. On its own, that wouldn't be enough to rule out some other causes of death, but there's also some burns on the hand where he'd gripped the phone."

"But then why didn't we notice—Oh. We did notice."

"Yes. The smell. The phone hid the blisters from our sightline." Salvo seemed to recover himself and began picking up papers, "So, anyway, I'm pretty busy here, Stella, so I'll catch you later."

"But—"

"Oh, look! Here come the Staffords," Salvo grinned broadly. "Just in time."

Mrs. Stafford fell into Stella's arms with such force, she was knocked a pace backward. "Stella, you won't believe what's been going on! Please, take us home."

Mr. Stafford nodded at her. "Stella. Good of you to pick us up."

"Oh, well, I didn't exactly know—" Stella remembered that a little bit of clairvoyance was never bad in a host. "It's my pleasure. You're allowed to leave then?" She glanced at Salvo.

He looked away. "See you later, Stella. Keep your guests in line now, okay? Out of the armory." His jovial tone didn't match his refusal to meet her eyes.

Mrs. Stafford pulled Stella out of the station. As they walked, Mr. Stafford muttered, "We should have gone to Fiji."

Mrs. Stafford snapped, "Don't you even start. This is your fault, having a gun messengered over. I told you it was a bad idea."

Mr. Stafford stiffened, but then sagged, reaching for his wife's hand. "I know. It was a mistake. I couldn't stand the thought of being vulnerable while so far from home. If anything happened to you—"

They leaned into each other for the rest of the walk.

Opening the door of the house, Stella tensed, watching Mrs. Stafford go directly to her purse. Would she register that it had been moved or rifled through? She didn't seem to, as she sagged onto the couch beside it and reached in for a lipstick.

Stella closed the door. "I'm so sorry about all of this. What do you need? I made a chocolate cake. Or if—"

Mrs. Stafford said, "Honestly, I want to go to sleep. But I need to check on Judith. I can't imagine what she's going through. Especially if she heard we were taken in for questioning."

Mr. Stafford said, "Call her."

"But, Morton, you know she's terrible on the phone. I want to see her."

"We'd only be in the way."

"You just don't want to drive me."

"You're the one who refuses to get an international driving permit."

"*You* said you didn't want me behind the wheel with all these crazy Italian drivers!"

He sighed. "Claire. I have to work. You know this, I've wasted the whole morning and who knows how long I'll be trapped here. Call her. I'll take you later if you want." He turned and went upstairs.

"It's *Saturday*!" Mrs. Stafford called to his retreating back. She sighed and then took her phone from her purse and dialed. Stella hung close, an idea forming in her mind. When she heard Mrs. Stafford sigh again, Stella said, "She didn't answer?"

"No. I'm not surprised. She doesn't use her phone much. Her hands get pretty shaky, which was hard enough when phones had buttons. With a touch screen, it can be overwhelming."

Stella nodded in what she hoped was a sympathetic fashion. "I'm happy to take you, if that would help."

"Oh, Stella," Mrs. Stafford said, her eyes filling with tears. "Would you?"

"Sure," Stella tried to tamp down the excitement from her voice. "Only, I'd need to use your car."

"That's okay! Let me get the keys."

Mrs. Stafford hurried upstairs. Stella heard the couple arguing in hushed voices. Finally, Mrs. Stafford appeared, jingling the keys. "Are you sure you don't mind, Stella?"

Stella shrugged. "Not at all."

Without speaking, they made their way to the parking lot.

Stella tried to project an air of general competence while hiding her surprise at the responsiveness of the Audi, especially compared to Domenica's Fiat Panda, which was all she'd driven in months.

She couldn't believe she was going to have the chance to talk to Mrs. Lake. Stella tried to figure out how to work questions into casual conversation.

The Audi purred into the parking circle and Mrs. Stafford dashed out of the car. In haste, Stella stumbled out of the car and ran to catch up. Mrs. Stafford regarded her with surprise. "You're not going to wait in the car?"

Before Stella could answer the question, Louisa met them in the driveway with a basket of cut roses. "Claire. Everyone will be so glad to see you. As you can imagine, they're all in an uproar." She glanced at Stella. "Hey, Stella right? Nice of you to give Claire a ride."

Mrs. Stafford said, "Is everyone home?"

"Most people are napping or have gone for walks. These Italian police are not to be trifled with," Louisa said, her voice dark. At Mrs. Stafford's confused look, Louisa clarified. "Oh, did you not hear? The police came about a half hour ago. They took the phone chargers and told us we needed to stay close to the villa for follow-up questions. We all need to catch flights, so we're being as available as possible. The sooner this is sorted, the sooner we'll get home."

It took a beat for Stella to realize what Louisa had said. "The phone chargers. They took the phone chargers? Which ones?"

Louisa shrugged and rearranged the roses in her basket. "Beats me. The ones in Chelsea's basket."

"Did . . . did they say why?"

"Who would bother telling me?" Louisa asked dryly.

This explained Salvo's weird behavior. He had told the captain Stella's idea. They must not have found anything, and Salvo didn't want to explain all that with the Staffords about to exit. Dang, it had seemed such a good idea. Then again, there were woods all around, many places for someone to dump a charger. She hoped the police wouldn't default to blaming bad house wiring just because the basket of chargers didn't pan out.

Mrs. Stafford murmured vague words of comfort and they followed Louisa into the house. The house did not look like there'd been a party the night before, let alone a murder. Without the decorations and crowds of costumed people, she was better able to take in the rosy stone floors that if she hadn't known better she would have assumed were marble, but she'd learned came from Monte Subasio. All of the villages on this side of the valley had this pinkish hue, unlike the houses across the valley, where the stones trended toward cream and beige or even brown.

Tripp and Gillian sat on the blue chaise, deep in conversation. "Thank goodness you're here, Louisa," Tripp said when Louisa walked in. "Mom needs her medication and Gillian says she doesn't know which ones."

"It's not like you know, either," Gillian spat.

Stella began to wonder if perhaps it wasn't that these kids didn't want to take care of their mother so much as they wanted to win some long-standing power struggle.

Louisa sighed. "She's up then? Already?"

Gillian stared at her phone and didn't answer. Tripp said defensively, "Just for a minute or two."

Louisa dropped the basket of flowers in exasperation and spun around toward Mrs. Lake's room. Claire left Stella's side to approach the siblings, "How are you? How's your mom?"

Gillian shrugged. "Like crap. It's all crap. I can't believe any of this is happening."

Tripp added, "Have you heard? The police think it's murder. By electrocution."

Mrs. Stafford gasped. "How do they know it wasn't an accident of some kind?"

Gillian waved her hand to dismiss Mrs. Stafford's words. "My brother, as usual, is leaping to conclusions. Based on facts the rest of us can't see. One wonders how he can be so sure."

Tripp flamed red. "You were here. You saw them collect the chargers. Why would they do that if they didn't suspect foul play?"

Gillian stared at her brother and then swiveled her head to say to Mrs. Stafford. "So you see."

Mrs. Stafford shook her head in bewilderment. "But who could do such a thing?"

Gillian and Tripp exchanged knowing glances.

Stella wondered if their squabbling was so normal to them, they didn't bother hanging onto resentment and suddenly felt unified in their suspicion of Mrs. Stafford's husband.

The flush creeping up Mrs. Stafford's cheeks suggested she knew exactly what they weren't saying. Stella wondered if word of the gun had yet reached the villa. Rumors and gossip traveled through Aramezzo as quickly as a torch crisped the top of a brûlée, but how much reached the villa?

A handful of teenagers came tumbling from the room that had been the interview space, giggling. They looked like they were going to the kitchen, but then turned right at the end of the hall into what Stella thought, given what she could see across the courtyard, was a sunroom. Stella considered telling them to please find a different spot to smoke, but remembered her job. Fly on the wall and see if she could talk to Mrs. Lake.

As if summoned by Stella's thoughts, Louisa brought a shuffling Mrs. Lake down the hallway. Stella could hear their bitten-off comments to each other, "If you wouldn't rush me, Louisa! I'm going to fall and then what? It will hardly make you get anywhere faster."

"If I'm doing it all wrong, why not ask one of your children to help you instead? Oh, that's right. They shove it all on me."

Mrs. Stafford ran to her friend. "Judith! How are you?" she took her arm from Louisa, "I've got her." They settled into a set of chairs.

Mrs. Lake sighed and gathered her wooly vest around her chest. "Oh, Claire. It's been such a trial. I can't believe Hollis is...gone. Can you? I mean...you know what I mean."

"I do," Mrs. Stafford assured her friend. "Louisa, I'm sure Judith is hungry after her nap. Can you get her something?"

Mrs. Lake shook her head, and in a low voice, said, "No, not again,

I'm fine—"

Louisa gritted her teeth and made a low growling sound. "Tripp? Gillian? Either of you want to help your mother out?"

Gillian kept her eyes glued to her phone. "I'd only mess it up. You know what she likes."

With another look shot at Tripp, likewise scrolling through his phone, Louisa stormed into the kitchen.

Mrs. Lake said, "That girl has no gratitude. We bring her to Italy, encourage her to leave her children with their other grandparents, and she fusses at every little thing."

Mrs. Stafford lowered her voice and Stella hung along the side of the wall to lean closer. "She's not wrong, though, Judith. Why can't your children help?"

Mrs. Lake sighed and muttered about being a burden.

"If you ask me, I think Gillian and Tripp see taking care of you as some sort of war. The one who helps you loses."

A-ha! thought Stella.

"Oh, Claire. They've been in this war for a decade. It's hardly new. Or even noteworthy." Stella's feeling of triumph evaporated. "I can't help getting testy with Louisa, but I know it's not pleasant, being stuck with me. And . . . well. I'm afraid the situation will deteriorate with Hollis's passing."

"Morton and I were talking about that on the way home last night. I know you hate the idea, but perhaps it's time to hire someone to help you. So you aren't reliant on . . . anyone," Mrs. Stafford ventured.

Mrs. Lake was saved answering by Louisa arriving with a plate of cookies. Before Stella saw them she smelled the nutty, fruity poppy seeds.

Mrs. Lake held out her hands to accept the plate. "Poppy seeds?" she said faintly.

Gillian looked up from her phone. "Louisa. You know mom can't eat poppy seeds. They interfere with her medication."

Louisa shrugged, unconcerned. "That's all I could find."

Gillian shoved her brother. "Can't you get your wife to do one thing right? She spent the whole morning unable to turn the flashlight off her phone and now she can't find a snack for Mom that won't make her sick?"

"What?" Tripp looked up, his eyes glassy. "What are you talking about?"

Gillian rolled her eyes. "You know very well what I'm talking about. Your wife. Totally inept. As usual. No wonder she had to delete her Instagram account. Probably couldn't figure out hashtags."

Mrs. Stafford said to Louisa, "You deleted your account? Is that why I haven't seen photos of the children lately?" Stella didn't understand why Mrs. Stafford looked so troubled but then decided that perhaps, with this set, not being on social media was tantamount to opting for living in a cave.

Louisa's face stiffened as she reached for a Travel + Leisure magazine on the side table. "Why is everyone suddenly so concerned with my digital footprint?"

Laughing, Gillian said, "Don't trouble yourself, Louisa. We don't mind at all. In fact, maybe we should all get off our phones more often. Starting with my dear brother here."

Tripp scowled. "Do you mind? I'm working. Someone has to keep the business afloat."

With a sneer, Gillian said, "Quite a power trip you got there, brother. You don't even know if you have a job when we get back."

Stella startled at this. Could it be true? Or another arrow in the sibling war?

She couldn't tell because Tripp ignored the insult to find his own. "You're the one without a job. Make yourself useful for a change."

Gillian's laugh tinkled harshly. "You number types have zero perspective. Without my art, this world you finance would be empty."

Snorting, Tripp said, "I'm pretty sure I could get along fine without your red circles."

Mrs. Lake put a hand out. "Please. Stop bickering."

"But he—" overlaid with "but she!"

Closing her eyes, Mrs. Lake said, "Both of you."

Mrs. Stafford clasped Mrs. Lake's hand, and Mrs. Lake's eyes briefly opened as she smiled in return.

The only sound in the room was Louisa flipping magazine pages.

Gillian seemed to remember Stella's presence. "Did you need something?"

Her eyes still closed, Mrs. Lake said, "Don't be rude, Gillian."

"Mom!"

Mrs. Lake said nothing.

Dark pink spots appeared on Gillian's cheeks. She looked away, muttering, "If Dad were here…"

She didn't finish the sentence and nobody seemed to notice.

Mrs. Lake's eyes fluttered. "Stella. Tell me. How much of a ruckus has our situation caused your little town?"

Stella impulsively said, "Oh, we're used to it."

All eyes turned to her, including Mrs. Lake. Stella could kick herself. Her and her impetuous tongue. Dragging her hand across her forehead, Mrs. Stafford said, "Are you saying this has happened before?"

Mrs. Lake shivered.

Stella rushed to assure them, "Oh, sorry, that's not what I meant. I…" what a time for her mind to go blank! "Small towns. Much more action than you'd think. There's always something going on. Plus, all the history. Wars on home soil and all that."

Mrs. Stafford kept her eyes on her but everyone else nodded and went back to what they'd been doing.

"I do have a question though," Stella ventured. She wondered if her working with the police might lend her an authoritative air such that no one would question why she was asking. "Mrs. Lake, you were here all last night? In this chair?"

Mrs. Stafford dragged her hand again over her forehead. "Stella.

Judith is hardly in a position to—"

"No, it's fine, Claire." Mrs. Lake patted her friend's hand, still in her lap. She turned to Stella. "Doing a bit of sleuthing?"

Stella tried for a noncommittal shrug. "There are a lot of unanswered questions. If we can turn some variables into constants, it would help. And I know you all want to get home."

"We do. Though I can hardly stomach the tasks that await us when we land," Mrs. Lake said. "As for last night. After all the excitement of getting dressed and taking photos on the lawn, my head started pounding. I needed my medicine, which drains me. So yes, I was here the rest of the night."

"And did," Stella's eyes slid around the room, wishing everyone would find some reason to leave. "Did you see anyone go upstairs?"

"I didn't," Mrs. Lake said quickly, her gaze fluttering to the side where her children seemed to be bickering again. Did Stella imagine the hooded look in her eyes? "I'm sorry."

Stella had a thought. "Not even your husband?"

"Oh!" Mrs. Lake realized. "I suppose he must have gone upstairs, mustn't he? I don't know why—"

"You were asleep," Louisa grumbled, angrily flipping a page of her magazine. "Remember? I kept telling you you'd be more comfortable in bed, but you refused to leave the party."

"It's my one outing all year, is it any wonder?" Mrs. Lake said, irritation sparking in her words.

"That's hardly my fault!" Louisa said, her voice pitching up.

"And it's not mine! You think I asked for this!" Mrs. Lake gestured to her thin legs.

At a glare from Gillian, Tripp rose and stood behind his wife, stroking her shoulder. "Hey, come on."

Louisa's eyes filled with tears. "Sure. You step in when she snaps at me, but where are you when she needs to know which meds she can't have with grapefruit?"

He silently rubbed her back.

Mrs. Lake inhaled, slowly. "Much as I hate to admit it, Stella, Louisa has a point. I did nod off—"

A "ha!" exploded from Louisa.

"I didn't see Hollis go upstairs." Her eyes dropped to her hands worrying over each other. "I couldn't do a thing to save him."

Mrs. Stafford grabbed her friend's hand again. "Stella, that's enough third degree. Judith is tired. And you two," she looked from Tripp to Gillian. "This childish game of hide-and-seek has got to stop. She's your *mother*."

Gillian said nothing but rose and left the room.

Tripp murmured, "Sorry, Mom. Louisa. I'll do better."

Louisa leaned against Tripp and said nothing, relief etched in her features.

Eyes fluttering closed, Mrs. Lake slumped back against the seat. "My head. It's throbbing again."

Mrs. Stafford leaned forward and spoke in hushed tones. "I wish you'd try my acupuncturist. He worked wonders on my hot flashes. Modern medicine has nothing on the ancient wisdom of the Chinese when it comes to menopause."

Something niggled in Stella's memory.

"It's persistent post-concussion syndrome, love, not menopause," sighed Mrs. Lake.

"I know, but your migraines have been so awful and seem to be getting worse. Maybe..."

With effort, Mrs. Lake shook her head. "I'll consider it. But it didn't work for the fatigue. I can't imagine it will work for the headaches. And the teas they make you drink! The one thing I have going for me is I can still taste my food. Why ruin even that?"

"Oh, Judith. That was a decade ago! Only basic acupuncturists use teas nowadays. Now they—" Mrs. Stafford stopped herself and looked around, whispering in her friend's ear.

"That's it!" Stella said.

All eyes turned to her. "Oh, er…Umm…finally got this piece of batter off my shirt." She scratched at her T-shirt, which, for once in her life did not bear streaks of cooking matter, but she hoped the Americans were too far away to notice. Luckily for her, they simply didn't care. Which left Stella alone with her realization—those pills in Mrs. Stafford's purse. Stella finally remembered what they smelled like.

An acupuncturist's office.

Two years ago, her friend Martin had dragged her to one when she'd developed tendonitis after a week of whipping meringues by hand thanks to a restaurant's mixer dying in the middle of service.

She'd never been sure if it was the needles or the passage of time, but she recovered quickly. Mr. Chang had not given her any teas, but she'd asked about them. She'd had to, with all those roots and herbs and mysterious ingredients stored in a wooden hutch that looked like it belonged in an ancient apothecary. The scent had been overwhelming, which is when Mr. Chang said that certain ailments required brewing up a special tonic from his collection, most of which he ordered from a Chinese supplier.

No doubt Mr. Chang was a "basic" acupuncturist, considering his address in the blurry area between the Lower East Side and Chinatown. Mrs. Stafford's high-end acupuncturist probably worked out of a spa-like location in the toniest part of Boston and wouldn't dare deign to sully his floral and incense-scented rooms with a hodgepodge of gnarled roots, but rather sent away for magical elixirs in sanitary pill form. Most likely in designer glass bottles.

So Mrs. Stafford's package from China was medicine, as she said. Then why did she look so flustered when Stella asked about it?

The answer fell into her brain fully formed. Of course. *Prohibitions.* Chinese medicine included all kinds of ingredients from endangered

plants and animals like tiger bones and bear-bile powder from threatened populations. This tracked. Mrs. Stafford had enough awareness of
her privilege to know that others might well deride her for participating
in the destruction of endangered wildlife. Though not enough to find an
alternative, and wildlife-preserving, option.

"I'll send you my guy's contact info. You come to Boston and we'll
make a weekend of it." Mrs. Stafford patted her friend's hand and then
said to Louisa. "Did she take her headache meds? Is that why she's slower
than usual?"

"Is it any wonder? She barely got any sleep last night."

Mrs. Stafford regarded her friend. "Well, I guess she'll be out for a
while. Can you help her call me when she's awake? I didn't get to ask if
she needed anything."

Tripp looked at his wife and she glared at him. He nodded. "Yes. Okay.
But Gillian—"

"Just do it," Mrs. Stafford sighed. "Let's go, Stella. I'm not sure why
we came."

Stella wondered—Mrs. Lake's caginess when asked if she'd seen
anybody go upstairs, the sudden evidence that Mrs. Stafford likely did
receive medication from China in that package, the fact that she and the
police finally seemed to be working off the same recipe, and the hint that
Tripp might find himself without work, which decreased his motive. It all
seemed a pretty lucrative visit to her.

Stella and Mrs. Stafford didn't speak on the drive back to Aramezzo.
Mrs. Stafford kept her arms crossed over her chest, glaring at the road as
if resentful of it rising to meet her. Once they pulled into the parking lot,
Mrs. Stafford hopped out of the car, slamming the door. Was she angry at
Stella for not waiting in the car at the villa? Or angry at everyone at the

villa for not valuing Judith Lake?

She ventured, "Shall I make you dinner tonight?"

Mrs. Stafford grumbled about eating in the piazza, but then changed her mind."That would be fine."

Stella nodded, mentally going through the contents of her pantry and freezer to think of what to make. All she wanted was to cook through the swirl of her brain to some sort of clarity. With the guests in the house, that wasn't a viable option. Barring that, she needed Domenica to help sift through the clutter. Dinner was the last thing on her mind.

As they reached the house, Mrs. Stafford put a hand on Stella's arm. "It's best if you don't tell Mr. Stafford what you heard at the villa."

Stella's mind darted, drops of water hitting a hot pan. What had she heard?

"It would only upset him. I need him to walk a straight line from here on out. No more mistakes. Like that gun," Mrs. Stafford said, grimly.

Stella ran through the conversation at the villa. It all seemed routine. Well, routine for these people. A lot of hemming about who deserved more privilege.

Unsure, Stella said, "I heard nothing worth repeating."

Mrs. Stafford patted her arm. "Thank you, Stella. As for dinner, something light if you don't mind. It's been a day."

Stella regarded the older woman, her foundation had rubbed off where she'd run her hand over her forehead repeatedly and the skin below seemed thin and fragile. Her eyes drooped, or maybe the bags below them made them seem so. Stella couldn't help but feel for her. "Of course." She had a thought. Light to her, and to much of Aramezzo, meant pasta. But Mrs. Stafford seemed to have a love-hate relationship with Italy's contribution to the carbohydrate scene. "Perhaps grilled chicken and a salad?"

Mrs. Stafford closed her eyes in relief. "Yes, that would be perfect."

She impulsively decided she'd put out the *crescionda* tonight. Even if Mrs. Stafford only nibbled a crumb, Mr. Stafford would no doubt cheer at the chocolate cake with its unusual, subtle flavor combination. She'd bring the leftovers to her friends later. "Why don't you rest, Mrs. Stafford. I'll get ingredients for supper. Anything I can bring you?"

"How about a time machine? I wish we'd never come." Her eyes widened. "Oh, I didn't mean anything by that, Stella. Your town is lovely. This has all been . . . too much."

"Please don't give it another thought. I understand," said Stella.

Mrs. Stafford headed up the stairs. "Thanks for the ride, Stella. Dinner at 5:30?"

"Absolutely." Stella waved goodbye as she ran through what she needed to do before this absurdly early dinner: A trip to the butcher shop for chicken—hopefully Bruno had some. Stella remembered it was Saturday, Bruno's chicken sausage day. They'd likely accept chicken sausage in lieu of chicken, once they believed her. Bruno's chicken sausage tasted nothing like the pallid versions Stella had tried back in the States. Probably because he used dark meat.

After the *macelleria*, where Bruno was thankfully not in one of his rare talkative moods, Stella stopped by the *fruttivendolo* to pick up salad greens and a head of radicchio that resembled an ocean creature. The Staffords might find it intriguing. She checked her watch as she jogged home with chicken sausage and vegetables. Yes, enough time to put together dinner.

She half expected the scent of wafting sausage to lure her guests downstairs while she was cooking—they must be starving—but they hadn't arrived by 5:30. She listened, wondering. They hadn't left, had they? Inhaling, she wished she had thought to pick up some sausage for herself. All she'd had all day was a half can of tuna. Did they need three sausages each? Mrs. Stafford wasn't likely to eat more than a half.

Stella decided she needed to get out of the house before she scarfed one down.

After setting out the *crescionda* and dessert plates, Stella sent a message to the Staffords, letting them know dinner was on the table when they were ready. She hoped that would be soon. She found delight in a cold sausage, but she suspected they might be more fussy.

Even though she needed to get to Domenica's, she couldn't help aiming her steps toward Bar Cappellina. On the walk, she dialed Domenica's to make sure she'd be there in a half hour. As entrenched in technology as Domenica was, she still turned it all off when she finished work for the day to retire to her apartment above the shop. Domenica didn't answer, but she almost always checked her messages before turning the phone off for the evening.

The bar was busy, so Stella could only gesture for a glass of hot milk. At this hour, she shouldn't have been surprised that the display case stood empty of offerings. Her stomach growled. Her face must have registered disappointment because Romina dropped off a bowl of peanuts with her cocoa-dusted milk. Stella could have kissed her, but Romina scurried off to deliver coffee to a group of officers. They cheered at the coffee's arrival and clinked their cups merrily as if they were glasses of champagne.

With her hunger pangs blunted, Stella turned to the officers. She didn't know any of them enough to do more than nod in recognition. So she listened. Her eyes widened until they felt at risk of popping out of her head as she heard one officer with curling blond hair say to the others, "I know. I felt bad for Luca when he got saddled with him as a partner. Salvo is good at putting one foot in front of the other, and he's nice enough, but . . . not exactly the brightest bulb in the lamp."

A tall, reedy officer said, "Goes to show you. First impressions aren't always accurate. Like the captain says."

"What first impression? I thought that last week, when Salvo left his gun in the bathroom."

Stella filled her mouth with peanuts to avoid the temptation of horning into their conversation. She'd learned her lesson, Italian cops did not like feeling managed. Probably no cops did, frankly.

Romina's eyes darted between Stella, eyes agog with a mouth full of peanuts, and the officers, sipping their espresso. She smiled and flicked her towel over her shoulder. She said to the men with a smile, "Are we celebrating?"

"Not yet. But soon," the blond officer said. "And then we'll have bubbly, instead of coffee, right, *ragazzi*?"

The men laughed and clinked their espresso cups again.

Romina said, "Well, don't leave me in suspense."

The curly-haired officer peered around and Stella stared at her milk, as if so captivated by the foam bubbles, she couldn't possibly be interested in their dull chatter. They lowered their voices and ducked closer to tell Romina, "Salvo. He nailed it. Figured out what the killer would have done with Signor Lake's original charger once he replaced it with the faulty one. We collected the basket of chargers from the villa, and sure enough. There was one extra. Scrubbed of prints."

"Which means," the thin officer dropped his voice so low, Stella practically had to rest her head on his shoulder to listen, "It was murder."

Romina stepped back with a chuckle. "Why the secrecy? Salvo's grandmother was in here an hour ago, crowing about her son cracking the case."

Scowling, the third officer said, "It's an open investigation. We're not supposed to talk about it."

"*Boh.*" Romina shrugged and started stacking glasses into the dishwasher. She must have noticed Stella's ashen face because she gave a questioning thumbs up.

Stella nodded slowly and tried to look chipper as she offered a thumbs up in return. Her mind raced as she trudged to the register to hand over a euro coin for her milk. Her eyes flicked toward the officers, deep now in speculating which American killed Signor Lake. Stella supposed they decided an Italian couldn't have done it.

Which reminded Stella of Giancarlo. She'd hoped that Mrs. Lake would report that Giancarlo hadn't gone upstairs, but since she'd dozed off, her report was useless. Stella focused on one foot in front of the other the whole way to Domenica's, thinking through Giancarlo as a suspect.

It felt easier, somehow, than contemplating Salvo's betrayal. She needed this whole affair over. The longer the Staffords were forced to stay against their will, the worse her rating would be. Not that they would blame her, but wouldn't being held hostage in another country mar one's memories of immaculate linens and attentive service?

Stella finally arrived at Domenica's. With mingled joy and relief, she saw the lights on against the darkness descending over Aramezzo. Pushing the door open, she called, "Domenica!"

Domenica appeared from behind the stacks, her arm filled with books. "There you are. I'd about given up hope."

Stella collapsed into the armchair. She looked for a cat to swoop up.

"The cats are at dinner. I'm sure Attila will make an appearance soon."

Stella leaned back, her eyes closed. "Did you hear?"

"That they've established the cause of death as electrocution now and are on the charger trail? Yes. What a delightful change. A captain who listens to you."

Stella opened one eye.

"No?"

"No," Stella said, closing her eyes once again and leaning back. Her head was pounding. Did Mrs. Lake feel this way all the time? Stella couldn't imagine.

"Then what—"

"It's too long a story," Stella said. At an impatient noise from Domenica, she said, "Salvo told the captain the theory about the chargers as if it was his idea." She opened her eyes. "Okay, it wasn't that long a story."

Domenica sat in her chair, but then spun around when the door opened. Stella smiled at Matteo striding into the bookshop. "Give me one of those," he gestured to the chairs.

Domenica clucked, "What? No pleasantries? No gentle words?"

"Please," said Matteo, with a glimmer of a smile. He took the folding chair from Domenica and opened it next to Stella. "What a day."

"Tell me about it," Stella said. Casually, she said, "Where's Giancarlo?"

"Why? You still think he did it?" Matteo bit off.

Domenica looked from Stella to Matteo. "Now, now, kids."

"Sorry, Domenica," they both said. After a few moments of quiet, Stella said, "You know I don't think he did it. But we have to turn over every stone."

He shook his head angrily. "I don't get you, Stella. One minute you're criticizing the captain for doing everything by the book, and then here you are. Maybe you and Tribuzio are more alike than you know."

"*Cavolo*, I hope not," said Stella.

Another few moments of quiet. Stella willed a cat to appear, but they stayed stubbornly away, and the bookstore felt empty without them.

Finally, Domenica said, "Anybody want to tell me what's going on?"

Matteo swept his hand as if ushering Stella onto a red carpet. "Go right ahead. I'm only surprised you didn't come running over here with your suspicions about my oldest friend."

"Matteo, if you must know, I've been dealing with my guests who are actual suspects in this investigation. Then I spent the last hour at the villa, playing what feels like mental tennis with experts at the game. I hardly know if I'm coming or going." She pointedly turned to Domenica. "It turns out Giancarlo has himself a bit of a motive. Not that he killed Signor Lake—I'm not saying that!" Her voice rose as she warded off Matteo's protestations.

He closed his mouth and turned away.

Stella went on. "But he does profit from Signor Lake's death. Without Signor Lake's funding a rival team, Giancarlo's soccer club is more likely to be able to afford to sign some hotshot player out of Brazil."

"Portugal," corrected Matteo, with a smile that looked like a grimace.

"Whatever."

"You are hopeless about soccer," Matteo complained.

"Anyway," Stella continued. "If Matteo would let me get a word in edgewise, I'd explain why Giancarlo *couldn't* have killed Signor Lake."

Matteo sat back.

Stella went on, "Signor Lake couldn't find his phone when the guests were taking selfies. So someone would have lifted it before then. Which means it couldn't be any of the Italians. They hadn't arrived yet."

"That's too bad. I had my money on the mayor," Domenica chimed in. All eyes turned to her, including the cats who had crept in, settling on the floor for postprandial cleaning sessions. "What? You don't get a vibe from that man?"

Matteo shrugged, and Stella raised her hand. "I know I do. But no. I figure it's got to be an American."

"You could have told me this earlier," Matteo grumbled.

"I only realized while I was walking here."

"Well, okay then." But he smiled. For real this time.

Domenica nodded. "Makes sense. Why not the Staffords?"

"A hunch. But I wonder if you can confirm it."

"Ah," Domenica said. "Time for some hacking?"

"If you don't mind."

"Get the door, would you, Matteo? Marta is supposed to drop by for a book of maps, and I'm not sure how kindly she'd take to my . . . er . . . unsavory hobby." She removed the blankets and scarves draped over the computer.

"Unsavory?" Matteo said, as he leapt up to lock the door and turn off the outside light. "But it's for a good cause!"

Light from the computer switching on reflected in Domenica's glasses as she muttered, "You'd be surprised how many bad deeds have been done for a so-called good cause. Stella? What do you need?"

"It's this. I know Signor Stafford didn't like Signor Lake for a lot of reasons."

Matteo nodded and listed on his fingers, "The philandering. The rudeness. The—"

"The what?" Stella turned to him.

"The rudeness."

"No. Before that."

"Before that? Oh. The philandering." He paused, noting her stunned expression. "You know about that."

She thought. "Am I suddenly immune to men's lechery?"

Matteo said, "Giancarlo just told me that when Signor Lake was looking to invest in Giancarlo's team some years ago, the manager told everyone to 'hide their wives.'"

Domenica piped up. "When I walked into the pharmacy a few days ago, he was standing way too close to Orietta. He left, staring at me like something gross on the bottom of his shoe. Orietta had never been happier to see me, said he'd started with being charming, complimenting her English, but then started lifting his shirt."

Stella's voice scaled up. "Lifting his shirt!"

Nodding, Domenica said, "He said to show her a scar, but then he tried to lift her shirt to see if she had any scars."

Stella shook her head. "I can't believe this."

Matteo pulled his long face. "How can this be a surprise? You know about—"

"Claire Stafford!" Stella interjected. "I bet Signor Lake hit on her at some point. Maybe that's why Signor Stafford can't forgive him. "

Matteo said, "So you think Signor Stafford killed Signor Lake? And they got the gun as a backup plan?"

Stella thought. "No, something about that doesn't ring right."

Domenica nodded. "The electrocution plan. It's elegant."

"And a gun is not. It's hackneyed. It's trite. Too on-the-nose." Stella agreed.

Matteo looked from Domenica to Stella. "You two are making no sense."

Domenica raised her eyebrows. "Maybe if you read more, you'd be able to parse symbolism and tropes."

"I read!" Matteo said.

"I don't mean spy thrillers."

"I thought you didn't judge reading material," Matteo muttered, resigned. It was an old argument.

"I don't," Domenica explained. "But you won't develop your eye for literary rhetoric through trade paperbacks." It was an old rejoinder.

Matteo sat up straighter. "Stella reads mysteries! I don't see you—"

Domenica cut in, "Not only mysteries. She's branched out."

He stared at Stella, his brow furrowed.

She raised her hands in mute acceptance. "I have a lot of time on my hands. When I'm not dealing with a killer on the loose. Which, if we can get back to the point…"

"Okay, okay," Matteo said. "So a gun doesn't jibe with the killer's modus operandi, so to speak."

"Exactly," said Domenica.

As she opened her mouth to go on, Matteo cut in, "I get no credit for a musical allusion with a smattering of Latin, no less?"

"Matteo!" wailed Domenica and Stella in unison.

"Okay, okay," Matteo said. "Pray, continue."

Stella waited to make sure Matteo had nothing else to say. But he only muttered, "Don't know why I bother. I have nothing to contribute here."

Domenica and Stella exchanged glances and seemed to decide not to pursue the lament. Stella said, "The only other thing the police have on the Staffords—I mean, no fingerprints, no one saw either of them go upstairs—is that package they got in the mail. From China."

Matteo said, "That's where a lot of faulty chargers are from."

Domenica countered, "Factories make faulty chargers everywhere.

Anyway, this wasn't just a faulty charger, this was a manipulated charger."

"A manipulated knockoff charger," Stella amended.

"Right," said Domenica. "Because a knockoff charger is easier to tamper with. You can pry the case open."

Matteo turned to Stella. "Can you look through their things? See if you find anything sent from China?"

"I did," Stella said. Domenica and Matteo burst out laughing. "What? I don't make a habit of going through my guests' belongings."

Domenica adjusted her glasses. "I think we can agree that when there is a mystery to solve, you are less scrupulous about privacy."

Stella grumbled.

Matteo said, "And? What did you find?"

"A vial of something."

'Could you tell what it was by the smell?" asked Matteo.

"Unfortunately, I failed the drug-sniffing dog exam," Stella said. "That said, I think it's a kind of Eastern medicine—possibly violating restrictions on harvesting ingredients from endangered populations. Morally questionable, but not related to Signor Lake's death."

"Nothing charger-related," confirmed Matteo.

"Right. So where we stand—the gun doesn't implicate them. Neither does the mysterious package. All we've got left is the possibility that Signor Lake cornered Signora Stafford."

"We don't know that," cautioned Domenica.

"Correct. And, now that I'm thinking of it, it seems unlikely that Signor Lake, no matter how horrible a person he was, would make a move for someone in their social circle, whose husband already hates him. So perhaps that's not a motive. But we know that Signor Lake screwed Signor Stafford in a business deal. A long-ago grudge to the tune of millions of dollars lost."

Matteo whistled through his teeth. "That's a motive."

"That's what I thought. But then at the villa, it occurred to me how much money these people swim in. So much, I can't make sense of it. For you or me, a few million dollars would be life-changing. For them? I think it's a rounding error."

Matteo's large eyes widened as Domenica nodded and said, "Agreed. But I never thought it was about the money. I figured Signor Stafford's resentment didn't come from monetary loss so much as loss of face."

Stella, pulling Attila onto her lap, said, "That too. The whiplash that comes from lost deals…isn't that, too, par for the course? Part of the game? That's what I want to check."

"Ummm…how?" Matteo asked, even as Domenica whirled around, typing in quick staccato.

Stella drew out her phone, saying, "We need to access Signor Stafford's bank account. If there are ups and downs with regularity, I think we can say that it's unlikely that Signor Stafford was out for vengeance. Because wins and losses, they're part of the game."

Domenica turned to Stella, but before she could ask the question, Stella told her the bank information from the wire transfer that paid for their stay.

"What is happening?" Matteo looked from Domenica to Stella before muttering, "I'm only slowing you down. Why keep me around?"

Stella, her eyes on Domenica's screen that swept and changed from blue to black and back to blue as she established the bank information and wormed her way into the account, said nothing. She did, though, transfer Attila to Matteo's lap.

Domenica mumbled, "That's a joint account. Not business."

Stella made a noncommittal noise and then said, "Can you—"

"Just give me a minute." After a few minutes when only Domenica's furious typing filled the bookstore, Domenica spun to face them. "Hunch confirmed. Enormous amounts of money coming and going into Signor Stafford's business account. A couple of million dollars is not just a rounding error. It's a predictable rounding error."

Stella nodded. "If Signor Stafford was going to fly into a murderous rage about it, sounds like he would be in a murderous rage with pretty much everybody pretty much all the time. There'd be a trail of bodies on Wall Street."

"*Esatto.*"

"I get it!" Matteo said. "So why was he so angry at Hollis Lake?"

Stella shrugged. "I don't know. Maybe he resents being forced to socialize with him, to pretend they like each other, just because their wives are childhood friends."

Matteo said, "Huh. It's not only the wives who are friends. Signor Stafford, he seems to like Signora Lake. Brought her water during the party. Brought her an onion tartlet. I saw them chatting for a bit."

Stella nodded slowly. "Right. Signor Stafford despised Signor Lake not for any specific circumstance. He simply didn't like or respect him. Hardly a motive to kill him."

Matteo said, "Will you tell the police this to exonerate the Staffords?"

"Why? They'll blow me off again," Stella said. "Maybe for good reason. This is conjecture based on human nature. Plus the hacking that I can't exactly tell them about."

"Too right," Domenica said. "Signora Lake...how about her as a suspect?"

Stella said, "Her life is about to get much harder without her husband. Besides, him not being much of a charmer isn't a motive, as we just decided."

Matteo said, "The philandering?"

Stella said, "Based on what Giancarlo told you, it sounds like that's been going on for years." When Matteo nodded uncertainly, Stella added, "Anyway, she was asleep for much of the party. People were in and out of the room, including the kitchen staff. She was always there."

Domenica added, "Plus, have you seen that woman climb stairs? You said Signor Lake's room was on the third floor. It would take her at least a half hour to get up there and back."

Stella nodded. "Not to mention how in the world she'd get the phone off her husband. He's hardly ever in her orbit and when he is, he stays more than an arm's length away."

Matteo said, "Who then?"

Slowly, Stella said, "Right now, my money is on Tripp Lake."

Matteo frowned. "He didn't seem to have a problem with his father. Followed him around like a puppy."

Stella shrugged. "You push a puppy hard enough, it'll bite."

Domenica counted on her fingers. "He hated how much his father gave his sister. I heard him grumbling more than once about how his father spoiled her. His father kept him on a short leash—leash!" Domenica shook her head, laughing at her unwitting connection to the puppy metaphor. "And, who knows? Maybe he didn't like his father hitting on anything that moved."

Matteo frowned. "Does he seem the type that would care?"

Stella said, "Good question. I figure men in that echelon count notches on their bedpost as a kind of badge of honor."

Domenica said, "But wouldn't he feel the affront to his mother? You know men and their mothers."

Stella wondered, "You're thinking of Italian men and their mothers. But I sort of think promiscuity, even at the expense of fidelity, is baked into an entitled American man's psychology."

Matteo said, "But he has the most to gain, financially speaking, right? The inheritance, plus he works for his father. Won't he inherit the business?"

Domenica said, "That's true. Still. Patricide. Kind of a big move. Would a guy like Tripp Lake have the stones?"

Stella wondered aloud, "Plus, his sister made a remark that makes me wonder if he's next in line for his father's throne. Without a financial incentive, I can't think of what motive he'd have. Domenica, is there any way you can check how much money Tripp stands to gain from his father's death?"

"I'm a hacker, not a magician," Domenica reminded Stella in a tired voice.

At a knock on the door, they all jumped. Domenica shot a look at Matteo. "I thought you locked the door."

He said, "I didn't exactly put a force field around it."

Stella breathed, "It's Marta."

Domenica whispered, "I love Marta, but her timing couldn't be worse."

Matteo shot a look at Stella. "I'll let her in."

Stella sighed. "You have Attila. It's fine. We have to learn to coexist." She rose slowly, giving Domenica time to cover the computer with shawls and scarves.

Marta smiled as the door opened, but the smile vanished at the sight of Stella. "Oh. Stella. I didn't know you were here."

Stella paused, regarding Marta, who usually dressed in loose clothes, appropriate for mucking stalls, but today wore a tight pink dress. Realizing she was staring, Stella said, "Come on in. Domenica's expecting you."

"Then why was the door locked?"

Not having an answer, Stella said, "How's Ascanio?"

"Hiding," said Marta, entering the bookshop. "If you must know."

"He's still scared about—"

"No, he's scared because he heard Leo and me arguing."

Stella's eyes slid to the side. "Arguing? I'm sorry to hear—"

"No, you're not, sorry, Stella. You're looking pretty smug."

Stella's mouth dropped open, and she heard from behind her, "Marta!"

"Well, I'm sorry, Domenica, but it's true." Marta's eyes welled with tears and her chin shook.

Stella reached out a hand but dropped it when Marta moved away. "The book, Domenica. The one with all the maps. I promised Ascanio."

Domenica shot a look at Stella, who nodded. Domenica scooted back her chair and disappeared into the back.

Marta noticed Matteo. "Looks like you're having a cozy time."

Matteo looked helplessly at Marta and then lifted Attila. "Did you want to pet him?"

Marta choked on her laugh. "No."

Matteo, sensing a foot in the door, said, "You sure? He's pretty soft."

Marta shook her head, her curls coming loose from the braids wound around her head.

Domenica appeared with the book, an atlas by the look of it. "This is the one. It has maps that fold out."

Snatching the book up, Marta searched in her pocket. Domenica put a hand on her arm to stay her. "I told you. Even trade. For the cheese."

"I don't want to owe anyone anything," Marta said, wiping her eyes while pretending she wasn't wiping her eyes but merely using her forehead to gather her sleeve up to her elbow.

Domenica shot a look at Stella, who shrugged. Domenica pitched her normal rough voice to a velvety softness she usually reserved for her cats. "*Cara.* I told you. That cheese, with those lavender blossoms, a total winner. If anything, I owe you."

Marta glared at Domenica for a moment to see if she was joking. When she saw only kindness radiating from behind the older woman's glasses, Marta nodded and spun to leave.

Domenica mouthed to Stella, "Go."

Stella followed Marta into the street. "Marta, wait!"

Marta continued walking, if anything, faster.

Stella hesitated. If Marta didn't want her company...Stella stood, undecided. A movement from the top window caught her eye. Stella lifted her hand to wave at the woman, hanging laundry on the line that stretched from one window, along the wall, to the other window. The woman inclined her head to acknowledge Stella, but then turned away.

Silence, all around.

A silence suddenly rent by a piercing scream.

Stella followed the sound, echoing against the ancient stone walls. The taut noise propelled her feet until she ran, racing through the tunnel to Bar Cappellina. There, in the piazza, Stella saw Louisa, her mouth still open in a choking sob, pointing at Mimmo.

Stella sighed. When would these Americans realize Mimmo was harmless? Well, essentially harmless. Certainly nothing to scream over.

Mimmo looked around, wondering what the loony American was making such a fuss over.

Uniformed *carabinieri* pounded into the piazza.

"Thank God you're here!" Louisa shouted. "That man! That man has the watch! My father-in-law's watch!"

Almost afraid to look, Stella's gaze shot to Mimmo's wrist. Covered with a heavy, silver watch. "Please," she prayed to herself, "please let it be a cheap one from the market."

She wondered if the police would understand Louisa's accusation, but with a double take, she saw one of the officers was Luca. The other was, blessedly, not Salvo.

"Mimmo," Luca said. "We need to see that watch you're wearing."

"No," Mimmo said, holding his hands behind his back. "It's mine."

Luca took another step. "Don't make this harder than it needs to be, Mimmo. Come on."

Louisa practically shouted. "I can tell from here. It's an Omega. Hollis Lake's Omega!"

A flash of understanding crossed Luca's face. He might not know what an Omega watch was, but he remembered how Gillian had said it was missing from her father's wrist.

Mimmo glanced over his shoulder, as if contemplating bolting. "Try it, and we'll have to arrest you, Mimmo," the other officer said. Stella recognized his curly hair from earlier at Bar Cappellina. He must have gone back to work.

Out of the corner of her eye, Stella noticed Marta hurrying into the piazza, her gait awkward from the tight dress. In a voice pitched soft, Stella said, "Please, Mimmo. You can do this the hard way or the easy way. The easy way is to listen to Luca."

Mimmo made a noise like a firecracker. "Trust an officer with all their rules about permits and regulations? 'Do *this* Mimmo, not *that*, Mimmo.' No, thank you."

Stella said, "Trust *me* then, Mimmo."

Mimmo regarded her for a moment, staring into her eyes as if evaluating a beast in the forest. He scratched his cheek and then held the watch out to the officers in an abrupt gesture. Marta yelled, "No, Mimmo!"

Luca turned his head to see the face of the watch, his lips moving as he read, "Omega."

"I didn't take it, you idiot," Mimmo said.

In a steady, casual voice, as if to not spook Mimmo, Luca said, "Then where did you get it?"

"I found it." Mimmo crossed his arms over his chest, satisfied. "In my pocket."

The officers looked at each other. Marta rushed up to them, saying, "Mimmo didn't kill anyone."

Luca gestured toward Mimmo with his chin. "He's wearing the victim's watch. The one that went missing the night of the murder."

Marta shook her head. "You don't know it was murder. It could have been an accident—"

"No," Luca said, his eyes sliding to Stella as if apologizing for not keeping her in the loop. "When we found an extra charger, swiped clean of prints, we had someone examine the one in Signor Lake's room. It wasn't faulty. It showed signs of being manipulated."

"But, but, how would Mimmo know how to do that?" Marta said as Louisa strode up and said, "I take it you'll be arresting this man."

Luca glanced at Marta, "I'm sorry, Marta. But we have to." To Louisa, he said in halting English. "We will take him to the station now to ask questions."

"Wait, does this mean we're sprung free?" Louisa said.

Luca looked at Stella, confused.

Stella steadied her breath. "She wants to know if they're free to go. They have plane tickets."

Nodding, Luca said to Louisa, "We will let you know. Soon."

Marta yelled again, "No!"

Luca regarded her sadly. "I'm sorry, Marta. I am. I hate it, I don't want to think he did it, but—"

"I didn't do nothing," Mimmo said flatly. "I told you. I found the watch in my pocket. Why would I kill that guy?"

The curly-haired officer said, "Because you hated him being on land you want for hunting. You made it very clear how much you resented them."

"Not *them*," Mimmo said. "Just them."

Everyone looked at each other.

Mimmo sighed. "Who cares about the dead guy? I don't. My problem is with those stupid people who have ruined the land I used to hunt on."

"Right!" Marta said, "You see? It doesn't even make sense. Besides, how could he even know how to turn a charger into a weapon?"

Luca shrugged. "I hate to say it, but he could pay someone to do it. Same as the next guy." Marta opened her mouth, and Luca held out his hand and said, "And I'm sure someone could make a case that he tried to kill Signor Durant but wound up killing Signor Lake. That once he sneaked inside, he got turned around. Mixed up."

"This man can find his way through a forest at night," Marta protested.

"For some, a villa is more complicated," said Luca.

Marta moaned as Luca and the other officer flanked Mimmo and walked him toward the steps down to the police station. Mimmo threw Stella an accusatory look over his shoulder.

In her state of confusion, Stella didn't know what to do or what comfort she could offer. Even though she knew that the officers would have gotten hold of the watch without her convincing Mimmo, she couldn't help feeling like she'd sent this baffling man to his doom.

Spinning on her heel, Marta confronted Stella. "I hope you're happy now."

Stella stared at Marta. "Why in the world would this make me happy?"

"You hold a grudge against him because he cheated you out of a little money before he even knew you! Like a few euros is worth a man's life."

Stella said nothing.

Louisa observed the officers hauling Mimmo away before hurrying away herself. No doubt to Villa delle Acque. Where the Americans would hail her as a hero, that was for sure—finding the watch, cracking the case, allowing them all to go home.

Finally, with no idea of what to say to Marta, Stella let the words unspool. "Marta, you have lost the plot. I wonder if you even know yourself anymore."

Gawping for a moment, Marta said nothing. Then she rushed away as fast as she could manage, the dress binding her legs together.

Alone in the piazza, Stella wondered if she would ever forgive herself. She knew Marta wouldn't.

Stella stood for a moment longer, her gaze fixed at some distant point in the mountains. Finally, she gathered her strength and returned to the bookstore.

Domenica said, "Did you catch her?"

Stella shook her head and filled them in on what happened in the piazza.

Matteo let out a breath. "Mimmo? Do you think it could be?"

"I'd say not in a zillion years, but how did he get that watch?"

Domenica offered, "Maybe he found it? Like the killer stole it but then deemed possessing it too dangerous and discarded it somewhere?"

"Then why wouldn't Mimmo say that? It sounds way less suspicious than finding it in his pocket." Stella said. "All I know is, this is one sticky question I don't think I can bake my way out of."

"I don't know," grinned Matteo. "How about another *crescionda*?"

Domenica pushed her glasses higher on her nose. "I didn't get that!"

"No one did except the Staffords." Stella petted Ravioli, standing on Domenica's desk. "I'll bring some by tomorrow." She checked her phone. No word from her guests. Though maybe they didn't think her message needed a response. Perhaps they sat at her table right now, wondering why the chicken sausages tasted so decadent.

Still, she had a weird feeling. Like a wall was rushing at her, a crash looming.

Stella dropped a kiss on Ravioli's head and said goodbye to her friends.

Matteo said, "Wait, Stella! I'll come with you."

Stella smiled to cover her frisson of irritation. With so little time to think about this murder, with so many loose ends tickling her brain, she'd counted on a quiet walk.

At her expression, Matteo stopped. "Unless you'd rather—"

"Oh, no, I welcome the company." Stella lied. Or not exactly lied. She loved his company, just needed to catch her hurtling thoughts. "But aren't you seeing Giancarlo?"

"For dinner." Matteo checked his watch. "And since Italians eat dinner at dinnertime and not at *aperitivo* time, I've got plenty of time."

"Great!" Stella summoned enthusiasm. She'd have to wait to figure out the missing piece. Maybe after dinner, she'd bake something. *Brutti ma buoni*? No, too easy now, she couldn't find the zone she needed to focus. Another *crescionda*? Maybe. Though she was out of chocolate.

Matteo fell in step beside her.

More to make conversation than anything else, Stella told him about the visit to the villa, ending with, "I've never seen siblings as competitive as Gillian and Tripp. They're like some weird version of Tom and Jerry cartoons."

"How old are you?" Matteo's laugh carried down the cobblestone street. A head poked out from an upper window, and a white-haired man called, "I thought I heard you, Matteo! Ha ha!"

Matteo grinned and waved, saying to Stella out of the corner of his mouth. "Wave. That's Niccolo. Have you met him?"

She shook her head but waved.

"Terrible gossip. Best avoid."

Stella chuckled and wound her arm through his. "So, are you like cartoon enemies with your sisters? Modern cartoons or vintage, I'll accept either."

At the word "sisters," Matteo gripped her arm a little tighter, containing Stella's pain. Then he said, "Normal childhood stuff. Being the youngest and the only boy, they treated me like a pet. I hated it. But I always knew they had my back. They're the ones who told my parents I was gay."

"I thought you said your parents always assumed. That it wasn't a big deal."

"It wasn't a deal at all, but my sisters couldn't have known that."

Stella's turn to grip Matteo's arm. She leaned against him, breathing in the air, threaded with the scent of browning onions and rosemary. "I guess I should feel lucky. I didn't have Grazie in my life for long, but when

I did, she added joy and color. Not aggravation."

Matteo nodded and said nothing.

Stella sighed. "Anyway. The whole dynamic is weird. Especially when Louisa became part of the power struggle."

Matteo nodded again. "I know, right? You'd think they'd be empathetic toward her, considering."

Stella nodded, listening to their footsteps against the cobblestones before she realized. "Wait. Considering what?"

"Signor Lake. Hitting on Louisa. Why, what are you talking about?"

She stopped walking.

The sudden ceasing of movement jerked Matteo back, and he said, "What? What's going on?"

"Signor Lake hit on Louisa?"

He shrugged. "Sure. Isn't that what you were talking about?"

"No! I was talking about how Gillian and Tripp treat Louisa like an unpaid nurse for their mother!" She frowned. "How do you know this?"

"How do you not?" He adjusted her bandana, loosed by the sudden stop in the street. "It was pretty obvious."

"Obvious?"

"Obvious. What else do you call him chasing her down the street, saying if she didn't have sex with him, he'd demote her husband?"

"WHAT?"

"And that he was finished being patient with her puritanical streak. He'd waited months, and it was time."

"WHAT?"

Matteo grimaced. "I know. Gross, right?"

"He said all that? Out loud? Where people could hear him?"

"Not people. A trash collector."

Her brow furrowed, she said, "Are you telling me that people say and do anything they want around trash collectors because they don't see them as *people*?"

Matteo shrugged again.

"Not people in Aramezzo, surely."

"No, not locals. To them, I'm the Matteo, who always had holes in his pants and now wears a city uniform with no holes in his pants. But you'd be surprised how many foreigners assume I'm deaf, dumb, and blind. That I can't understand anything. Especially if they're speaking English."

Stella thought for a moment. Had she considered trash men in New York part of the street scene? Maybe. Quite possibly. Goodness, she wasn't any better than these Americans. She sighed. And then had a thought. "Wait. How *did* you understand them? You couldn't get through *Love, Actually* without subtitles."

"I didn't want to miss anything." He shrugged. "Anyway. Leo came out from Marta's right as the two of them passed. So he heard the tail end and filled in the words I hadn't caught. Though, honestly, Stella, some things can be in Greek or code or an alien language and you'll still understand. A human exerting power over another human? Unmistakable."

Stella processed this information. Or tried to. It kept bumping up against the swirl in her brain. "When did this happen?"

"The day before the party, I think. Or maybe the day before that? Louisa needed to come into town to pick up something for Signora Lake. From the pharmacy. Some sort of cream? I didn't catch that part. Signor Lake drove her. *Voila.*"

"But Matteo," Stella said, still reeling, "How could you not tell me?"

"I thought you knew."

In a small voice, Stella said, "How would I know if you didn't tell me?"

"When you came to the house and mentioned that Leo had said something weird and put his hand on your leg... I don't know. I guess I assumed he'd told you, and that was the weird thing. But to be honest, his hand on your leg seemed so much bigger," the corner of his mouth twisted down, "I guess I got fixated on that and didn't check in that you knew what went down."

"Yes. I can see that." Stella considered for a moment before grinning. "Matteo. Do you see? This changes everything."

Matteo grinned. "I guess garbage men can be useful for some things."

Stella wrapped her arm around his waist and pulled him close. "For all the things."

They continued walking and Matteo said, "So you think it was Louisa, then?"

"Louisa, why Louisa?"

"To avoid her father-in-law's advances." Matteo frowned, as if this was obvious.

Stella nodded. "Maybe. But I think that's unlikely."

"What do you mean?"

"This is going to sound terrible," Stella ventured.

"Ooh, I'm all ears." Matteo looked down into Stella's face as they walked. "Do go on."

"I don't think she's . . . well . . . smart enough. Technologically."

It was Matteo's turn to stop in the street.

Stella rushed forward, "I know what that sounds like—"

"Stella! Don't tell me you think a woman isn't smart enough to pull off a murder."

"You know darn well I couldn't possibly think women aren't capable of murder."

His brow furrowed, and he said nothing.

She sighed. "I could see a woman like Signora Lake, or even maybe Signora Stafford having the know-how. Or at least being able to figure it out. And I'm not saying Louisa isn't smart in other ways—"

"Just that technology is man's work."

"Matteo! How could anyone who knows Domenica think that?" She pointed down the road as if to remind him of the conversation only a few moments ago.

His attempt at a smile couldn't move his stiff cheeks. "I don't know,

Stella. It sounds like you think women's technological skills are the exception rather than the rule."

"Matteo. Listen to me. I've seen Louisa with her phone. It's a family joke. She barely knows which end is up."

Matteo thought for a moment.

"Anyway, there's the timing. Louisa was seen checking on Signora Lake when ordered, always in full view of everyone. Someone is always telling Louisa to do something, there's no way she went upstairs without someone noting her absence and making a stink about it."

Matteo nodded slowly. "Okay. Yes. I'm with you."

"How could you think I'd be anti-woman here?"

He mugged sheepishly, "Maybe you're rubbing off on me? I guess I'm seeing misogyny everywhere."

"Except in the police captain."

"You got me there," Matteo said. "But I've been thinking about it. I think maybe you're a little right. Only he doesn't know it. Does that make sense?"

"Does institutionalized misogyny make sense? Umm....Yes. Yes, I think it does."

He chuckled. "Anyway. I guess you saying that about Louisa seemed like a big assumption, when she's the most obvious candidate."

"Motive-wise."

"Yes, right. Motive-wise."

"But means and opportunity, she comes up dry." Stella closed her eyes.

"Stella?"

Her eyes still closed, she said, "*Aspetta*, wait. I'm thinking." She ran through the scene, cataloging. The charger, knocked out of the outlet. The phone in his hand with scratches along the side. Scratches.... Scratches. That reminded her of something, but she couldn't think of what. She moved on...The stone floor, with no trace of footprints. The body, wrapped in a cloak with golden gears coiling along the edges. The nightstand with the fall of glitter.

With glitter.

"With glitter!" Her eyes flew open.

"Glitter? What glitter?" Matteo frowned. "We need to get you to a kitchen. I think you may be malfunctioning."

Stella was so busy pulling his arm she didn't hear his words. "Glitter! I'd forgotten about the glitter! There was glitter on the phone. But there was no glitter on Signor Lake's costume."

Matteo shook his head. "Stella, you're ranting."

"The photo!" Stella crowed. She pulled out her phone and opened the messages until she found the most recent photo from Coralina, the catering chef. She opened it and zoomed in on Mr. Lake. "Look! Signor Lake. No glitter. Not a bit."

"I don't know, Stella. It's a little hard to tell—"

"Look!" Stella had scanned and zoomed on Tripp. "Glitter! On his mask, on his hat."

"What kind of hat is that?"

"A magician's hat, remember?"

"Oh, right. The kind American magicians pull rabbits out of."

She stopped. "What do Italian magicians pull out of a hat, cannoli?" Matteo opened his mouth, but Stella cut him off. "We don't have time for banter and costume dissection! The point is this—*glitter*. The glitter I saw on the nightstand, someone was in Signor Lake's room. Someone with glitter."

Her face paled. "I thought Tripp losing his job with his father's murder made him less of a suspect. But if he knew about his father pursuing his wife. That changes everything."

"Are you sure, Stella?"

She frowned. "Not totally sure, no. He might not have been the only one with glitter on his costume. And maybe I've overlooked another motive." She quickly scanned the photo again. "Okay, the girls, those

Durant kids, they have glitter on their costumes, but it's pink. What I saw was gold. And look, I think everyone else who has gold on their costume, the gold comes from sequins. For obvious reasons. Glitter gets everywhere. No wonder my mother never let anything with glitter into the house."

"You'd think someone smart enough to swap out a phone battery and manipulate a charger would be smart enough to not leave a trail of their costume next to the body."

"There wasn't a lot of it. The killer either cleaned up most of it, or only a tiny amount fell, too little for a rushed assassin to notice." Stella thought aloud. "Anyway. When the police picked up Mimmo, they said that maybe he hired somebody to manipulate the charger. So maybe the killer doesn't have to be technologically genius-level, just comfortable around wiring."

"But the phone battery?"

"True. That takes some skill to change. But maybe if someone practices a few times, it's not so hard."

Matteo nodded. "So we're no longer looking for an evil genius."

"Or any genius. Just someone with glitter on their costume, who wanted Signor Lake dead, who lifted the phone before the party and changed the battery in a jiffy, before racing upstairs to place the phone and charger into position." She stopped, realizing.

"Stella?"

"Oh, dang," Stella said. "Tripp only works if he knew about his father preying on his wife."

Matteo started walking again. "How in the world can you find *that* out?"

Stella thought about Mr. Stafford. Maybe he knew more than he said. Maybe what Mrs. Stafford didn't want Stella to mention to her husband was Louisa. Because he might spill some beans about what Tripp knew. "If the way to a man's heart is through his stomach, let's hope the way to his truth is there as well."

Matteo shot her a confused look.

"Don't eat breakfast tomorrow," Stella warned. "I'll be baking."

SUNDAY:

TWO DAYS AFTER THE MASQUERAVE

Luckily, the *alimentari* had been open for Stella to pick up a can of chickpeas for her dinner and a sackful of ingredients. Entering the house, she'd held her breath . . . if the Staffords hadn't eaten dinner, she'd have to knock on their door to check if they'd overslept from a nap or . . . taken off.

She'd returned to find her house dark and quiet.

One plate was cleaned of food, the other looked untouched. She had stood staring at the table, wondering what it meant. Had Mrs. Stafford slept through dinner?

Finally, Stella had decided to make *maritozzi*, the Roman brioche buns filled with whipped cream. Prepping the dough tonight and making the buns tomorrow would soothe her fractious brain. She had to figure out if Tripp Lake knew his father had been pursuing his wife. And she had to figure it out before the police let the Americans go, thinking they had the killer behind bars.

Mimmo.

She also had to free this man. He wasn't her friend, not at all. But he was connected to her. And connected to Marta, who—however Stella felt about her now—didn't deserve the pain of having Mimmo in jail.

Mixing the flour, sugar, salt, eggs, and water did nothing to quell her darting thoughts. Nor did the ten minutes of kneading the dough. The whole time, something had bothered at her about the costumes, but she couldn't corral her brain to behave.

She kneaded butter into the dough, then put the dough in the refrigerator to rise and slowly ferment for a more complicated flavor profile. Exhausted, she'd finally gone to bed.

But she'd hardly slept. Every time she closed her eyes, images of Tripp Lake jumped out at her. Or no, someone wearing a mask with Tripp Lake's face, glitter pouring through the eyeholes. Whenever she nodded off, a sound like lightning and a flash of neon awoke her with a gasp. Each time she sat up, the covers clutched to her chest. Barbanera, though initially annoyed at her restlessness, as evidenced by his baleful looks and stalking to quieter parts of the bed, eventually stretched out against Stella, one paw over her arm. Their breathing synchronized, Stella fell into a dreamless sleep. For a little while, at least. At the darkness filtering in from around the shutters, Stella thought it was still the middle of the night. But her clock said otherwise. Five in the morning. As her eyes adjusted, she noted the blue tinge to the darkness. Sunrise was coming.

She threw off the covers.

Tripp Lake.

He killed his father. Even if his father's death didn't enrich his own coffers, learning his father had been pursuing his wife—people had killed for less. There was a whole category of murders labeled "crimes of passion."

But how to prove it?

As she rolled the dough out and divided it into individual pieces, rolling them smooth, she considered. Maybe the hitch she had was that this didn't feel like a crime of passion. It was methodical, deliberate, exacting. Which didn't smack of an impulse gone haywire. How could Tripp learn of his father's lechery and instantly hatch this plan? No, he would have had to arrive in Italy with the steps laid out. Which seemed strange. If Tripp wanted his father gone, wouldn't it have been easier to hire a hitman to mow him down in the street? Or orchestrate a drive-by shooting?

She shook her head as she covered the array of what would soon be buns with plastic wrap for one more rise. Nonetheless. It had to be Tripp. He had the motive, a far better motive than Mr. Stafford, if Tripp knew his father had been lusting after his wife. He had the means, if one could imagine him hiring someone to tamper with the charger. From the charger, Stella thought of the phone with its depleted battery.

Fetching the whipping cream from the refrigerator, Stella considered the details that kept sticking in her mind. Opportunity. He hadn't had much opportunity. The glitter suggested he'd been there, but how to execute this plan with no one noticing his absence?

Realization shook her so thoroughly, she practically spilled the cream as she poured it into a bowl. She had been assuming that Tripp Lake hadn't gone upstairs because nobody saw him. But Matteo had seen him on the way to the bathroom, a detour Tripp denied he'd taken. Plus, if he'd been present the whole time, how had he missed the altercation between his father and Mr. Stafford?

Stella began whisking the cream. How long had he been gone? Enough time to swap out a phone battery and leave it beside a faulty charger?

The only person watching the whole affair was Mrs. Lake. Perhaps Mrs. Lake had, in fact, seen her son creep upstairs. Perhaps he'd been gone for plenty of time to change the phone battery and the charger. Perhaps Mrs. Lake understood all of this but also understood that if she admitted as much, it would implicate her son in his father's murder. Which is why she'd looked uncomfortably at her children when asked if she'd seen anyone go upstairs. Mrs. Lake was covering for her son.

Stella had to find out how long he'd been gone. Would Matteo know? She picked up the phone to call him, but then noticed the time. Far too early.

It wasn't too early, however, to call the police. Which she should do right away. Call the police. Right now.

Stella's hand on the phone didn't move to dial.

What did she have, really? Gut instinct, observation, and a fall of glitter. Not even Luca would buy her story. She heard his voice in her head, "But Stella, it was a costume party. Lots of people had glitter on their masks or costumes."

She needed a little more evidence. A little more evidence and they'd have to believe her, she thought as she rested her whisking arm by pre-heating the oven.

Under the return of her rapid whisking, the cream thickened, ballooning with her thoughts. She added powdered sugar and continued whisking. Just as it reached the perfect stage for filling *maritozzi*, Stella felt a click in her brain so forceful, she almost dropped the whisk.

Gillian.

If there was one person who would be tuned into how long Tripp had been gone, it would be Gillian. Their competitive energy made them constantly aware of what the other was doing and how much favor they were currying.

A knock on the door sounded as Stella put the finished cream into the fridge. So faint, Stella wondered if she'd imagined it until she saw Barbanera leap off the back of the chair and was now stalking to the door. Stella stopped and listened. Nothing. But Barbanera glared at the door, like one of Mimmo's dogs at the scent of a black truffle.

Before she could stop herself, Stella strode to the door and threw it open. At first, she assumed whoever had been there—if anyone—had left. Then she noticed a shadow on the bottom step. A shadow that turned at the sound of the door opening.

"Marta?"

"Ciao, Stella."

"What are you doing here so early?"

"Is it early? I saw your light on."

The answer didn't fit. Stella sank on the step above Marta's, noticing that Marta was in her old overalls and soft jersey shirt.

After a moment, Marta leaned her head on Stella's knee.

Stella raised her hand and gently put it on Marta's curls, escaping from her braids like a flock of sheep storming away from a shepherd. At the touch, Marta sniffed. "Can you forgive me?"

Stella kept stroking her curls. "Forgive you?"

Marta sat up, looking Stella in the eye. "At the beginning, it was so good. When everything started changing, I guess I tried to change with it. To make things how they'd been."

"Because nothing feels better than standing in that ring of sunshine."

"Not many things, no. But some things do." No doubt she was thinking of Ascanio.

Stella considered the ring of sunshine in her own life. The way ingredients tasted when they came together in a singular balance. Laughing with Matteo as she overlooked yet another asparagus spear, but knew more opportunities lay ahead. Talking about books with Domenica, a cat on each of their laps. Spooning the food she made Barbanera onto an antique saucer. "Agreed. There are a few things."

Marta nodded contemplatively.

Stella inhaled and asked, "So what changed? After last night—"

"Last night," Marta huffed with derision. "I can hardly think of it."

"Marta . . . go easy."

"If it makes you feel any better, I stopped trusting me, too."

"Surprisingly, that makes me feel not at all better," Stella said.

Marta looked up and smiled wanly.

"So. Marta?"

"Oh, right. What happened." Marta shrugged. "Things have been rough since the ball. That night, before the party went off the rails, it seemed Leo was more interested in the American women than me. He said he hasn't let go of the dream of that media opportunity, but I couldn't help how I felt. Like I was in the way. After Mimmo got taken away last night, I lost it. I tried to track Leo down and couldn't. When he finally came over, he seemed uncomfortable. I mean, he tried to be sympathetic, but I could tell he was distracted. When I pointed it out, he grew impatient. We got into it. Worse than before. In the heat of it, I accused him of hitting on you and he was so mad, I guess he wanted to make me mad, too. So he admitted it."

Stella came down to Marta's step and wound her arms around her. "I'm so sorry."

"You didn't do anything," Marta said.

"Not on purpose. But playing any role in this…"

Marta leaned against Stella again. "Once the clouds parted and I could see things clearly, I realized of course you didn't mean to implicate Mimmo."

"I know he didn't do it."

"I know," Marta sighed. "I don't want to believe it either."

"That's not what I mean," Stella said. "I think I know who did it."

"You do?" Marta breathed. "Who?"

"It's too soon to tell." She had a thought. "But the night of the party, did you notice anyone, Tripp Lake or anyone, disappear into the house?"

"No. But I wasn't paying attention. Too busy watching my boyfriend."

"Did you notice any tension between the Americans?"

Marta shook her head. "I'm sorry. Now I wish I'd paid closer attention."

"I get it. It's okay."

Marta nodded. They stayed still for a few moments, watching the sky lighten on the sliver of the horizon visible between Aramezzo's stone walls. Barbanera came through the open door and sat on the step above them. As the clouds turned pink, Stella said, "Well, I have to get these *maritozzi* into the oven. I'm sorry though. About you and Leo. I wanted it to work for you guys."

Marta's eyes widened. "No need to be sorry. Now that we talked it through, and I understand that the intensity of our connection scared him into doing what he did, we're stronger than ever."

Stella could hardly believe her ears. "You...you mean you didn't break up?"

Marta smiled. "I guess I didn't explain it well. It's so fresh. He wants me to tell you that he's sorry he made you uncomfortable."

Stella frowned. She did not care for this kind of apology. As if her feeling bad were the problem. If he were sorry, he'd apologize for crossing a line, for betraying his girlfriend, for acting inappropriately and then lying about it.

This was no apology.

At her silence, Marta went on, "I hope you won't hold it against him. I want us all to be friends."

Stella patted Marta's knees. "As long as you feel you can trust him—"

"Oh, I do!" gushed Marta.

Pretending a satisfaction she didn't feel, she said, "Well, then. That's great." Stella winced at the flatness of the words.

Marta was rising and didn't seem to notice. "I'm so glad. I hated being at odds with you, Stella. I hated myself, I hated the tension, and I hated not feeling like I could change anything. I should have trusted you—you've never given me any reason not to—and I certainly shouldn't have blamed you. I'm sorry."

Stella rose as well. At least she'd gotten an actual apology from one of them. "It's all good." Was it though? How could she maintain a friendship with Marta while muting her contempt of Marta's boyfriend? Well, maybe she was wrong. Maybe Leo had gotten scared, and maybe he was different now.

Sure, and maybe adding salt to a sauce would sweeten it.

Once back in the house, Stella popped the *maritozzi* into the oven, listening out for sounds upstairs. Nothing. She couldn't worry about that now. Instead, she texted Matteo to see if he was awake yet.

He Facetimed her in response. She noticed he was in the piazza. "I'm getting a coffee. What's up?"

"I need to get to the villa this morning. I'd walk, but I'll have a tray of *maritozzi*."

"*Maritozzi*?" Matteo chuckled. "Sounds like you did bake last night."

"I did. And I realized something."

"Of course you did."

Removing the *maritozzi* from the oven, Stella didn't answer.

"Where'd you go?"

"Oh, sorry," Stella said.

"So, what did you realize?"

"Two things. One, I think Signora Lake saw her son go upstairs, and she's protecting him by denying it."

"Makes sense. What else?"

"I'll tell you if you let me borrow your car."

Silence.

"Matteo?"

"Stella, please don't tell me you're going to do something stupid."

"Me? Never."

"Why do I not believe you?"

"I have no idea. I'm the very picture of restraint."

Matteo guffawed. "I can't lend you my car, anyway. It's my father's birthday and I'm headed to pick up flowers in Assisi for us to take to the cemetery."

"You didn't get flowers from Flavia? She'll be furious."

"It's her closed day."

"Right," Stella remembered. She'd yet to learn to keep track of all the shops' different closed days. "Can you drop me off at Villa delle Acque on your way to Assisi?"

"I don't like the sound of this."

"Well, if you want to talk me out of it, you'll need to drive me.

Otherwise, I'm borrowing someone's car."

"Not Domenica's. It's still in the shop."

"You think you two are my only friends?" Stella scoffed. Though really, who else did she know well enough to borrow a car? Luca, maybe? But no way would he agree to take her to the villa. Marta?

"Okay, fine. Be ready in a half hour."

Stella made a gesture of wild celebration.

"You know I can see you, right? This isn't a phone call."

"Ha ha, I'll meet you in the parking lot."

The *maritozzi* didn't wind up looking as nice as she hoped, what with the rolls still being warm when she filled them. It broke her heart to see the cream leaking out of the corners. She had to hope that what she saw as a bit of a mess, the Americans would still consider impressive, or at least satisfactory.

She left two on the table for the Staffords, along with a thermos of coffee and a note. Where could they be? Perhaps sleeping in after their ordeals? Hopefully, they'd be up and feeling good from breakfast when she returned. If she hadn't gotten what she needed from Gillian, Mr. Stafford could be her backup.

Matteo was leaning against his car when she ran down the steps, staggering under the weight of the huge tray. "One of those better be for me," he cautioned.

Stella popped a napkin-wrapped *maritozzi* into his hand. "But I suggest you save it for the walk to the florist. One shouldn't *maritozzi* and drive."

Once they'd settled into the car, Matteo with his *maritozzi* propped on the dashboard and Stella with her tray across her lap, Matteo said, "Spill it."

"Gillian is the key. If anyone knows whether Tripp went upstairs, it'll be her."

"You don't think she'd protect her brother?"

"I don't see her able to hold that stance. Their relationship is so brittle, I think she'll crack or at least contradict herself."

Matteo said nothing on the drive, deep in thought as he took the turns up the mountain. "So you think Tripp murdered his father in a rage?"

"Well, that's the part that I struggle with. This was not a reaction, this was planned. I need to get more of a sense of Tripp to be sure. But look, the glitter at the crime scene was the same as what he had on his costume. I'm pretty sure he went upstairs for some length of time. He was there when the phone went missing. And he has a motive."

"If he knew about Louisa."

"Right. Or if he stood to gain financially from his father's death. His job might be in jeopardy with his father gone, but he must stand to inherit millions. Enough to buy the Italian villa he has his eye on."

"That's a lot of information you're after."

"I have a feeling. I'm on the edge of something here."

Matteo pulled into the driveway and killed the engine. "I'm coming with you."

"Your family is waiting. And anyway, nothing is going to happen in a crowded house. Look," she pointed to the parking lot, filled with cars. "They're all here."

Matteo frowned uncertainly. "I don't like this. It's like I'm abandoning you to the lion's den."

"I've got teeth."

"You've got pastries."

"It amounts to the same thing." Stella grinned tenuously. "Listen, I'll call you when I'm leaving."

"Or if you're in trouble."

"Or if I'm in trouble." Stella nodded and opened the car door.

"Wait! How will you get home?"

"I'll walk." To his running his hand down his face, Stella added, "The tray will be empty. It's downhill."

"But Stella!" Matteo leaned over the passenger seat to stare up at her. "What are you going to say?"

"I'll wing it."

The last thing Stella expected was for Tripp himself to open the door. She felt the blood drain from her face and she stammered uselessly. Mrs. Durant came from behind Tripp and said, "Tripp? Thanks for getting the door, who is—Oh. Hello again, Stella."

Stella gathered her nerve. "Ummm. I made these for Mr. and Mrs. Stafford. Then realized you may all be hungry. I know you didn't expect to be here this long." Did they? She didn't know. The guests had likely planned to leave already, but didn't the Durants stay a month or more? No matter, she had to press on. "So perhaps you might be short on provisions."

Mrs. Durant smiled faintly and stepped back to allow Stella entrance into the house. A passel of teens hunched over their phones in the seating area that once held the dance floor. From the other side of the room, one called, "Was it the delivery service? I'm waiting on that travel pillow. I can't believe the first-class seats are booked solid tomorrow and Tuesday."

One of the other teens kept her eyes on her phone while saying sympathetically, "I know, right? I told Dad we should stay until we can get the big seats. But he droned on and on about getting back to work."

The older Durant girl looked up. "At least you get to leave. It's gonna be so *boring* with you all gone."

Mrs. Durant called out, "Hey, kids. Here is some of that famous Italian hospitality you've heard about. Stella—you remember her? The American who lives in town—brought us," Mrs. Durant turned to Stella. "What was it again?"

"Oh! Er, *maritozzi*," Stella said, as cheerily as she could.

"*Maritozzi*," said Mrs. Durant. "You can put it there on the table. You'll want the tray back, I suppose?"

"Umm, sure. I'm happy to wait."

Mrs. Durant called, more loudly, to reach those guests sunbathing on the lawn and collected in the courtyard. "Everyone, breakfast!"

Stella heard doors open and close, and some people wandered in from outside. Some familiar faces, but many people must have flown in just for the party, so she hadn't seen them in Aramezzo. The guests clustered around the table, suddenly set with plates and napkins. Stella spotted Louisa, accustomed to playing the supporting role, preparing the table.

The Durants' guests each took a *maritozzi* and then wandered away. Louisa, though, stayed close by, wiping crumbs and bits of fallen cream off the table.

In a soft voice, Stella asked, "How are you?"

Louisa shrugged. "It's pretty dim around here."

Stella nodded in understanding. "Of course. The grief."

"More the boredom, honestly. And the confusion. Everyone wants to leave, and we can't until the police give the green light. Which I hope is soon now that they have the guy."

"Right…" Stella hedged, trying to think of how to work what she needed to know into the conversation.

"Tripp, honey, you need to eat," Louisa brought a plate to her husband. He shook his head.

Louisa brought the plate back to the table. "He's hardly eating at all."

Guilty conscience, thought Stella. "Maybe it doesn't appeal to him. Not everyone loves cream."

"No," Louisa said. "I popped into the grocery store this morning to get the cereal he likes. He didn't eat that either."

Stella looked around. "How is Mrs. Lake? I'm sure Mrs. Stafford will ask me."

Louisa rolled her eyes.

Stella waited a beat, but it seemed that was her only answer.

"Well, Stella," said Mrs. Durant. "The *maritozzi* were a hit. I certainly thank you for stopping by. Most kind of you. You can send me the bill. We're here through the month." Under her breath, she muttered, "Or forever. Whichever comes last."

Stella's knees weakened. She knew the answer lay here, barely beyond her reach. She had to stall, to think of something even as her brain ran in all directions. "The costumes!" she yelped.

All eyes turned to her.

Mrs. Durant's eyes narrowed. "What about the costumes?"

"Just," Stella's thoughts tumbled. "I meant to say, earlier. They were amazing. I mean, how did you come up with such an innovative idea for a party?"

With a small smile, Mrs. Durant said, "Didn't I tell you already?"

Did she? Stella stammered, stretching her mouth into a strained smile, bobbing her head to the guests still left in the living room—Louisa, Tripp, the Durant girls, and Gillian, who entered from outside.

Mrs. Durant said, "I feel sure I did, but I've told the story so many times, it's hard to remember. We wanted to throw an old-style Carnevale party, but Micah wanted to invite her friends as part of their graduation celebration. She starts Emory in the fall, and who knows how many more times we'll be able to indulge her? So when she insisted Carnevale was too old-fashioned, they wanted a rave, we played up the compromise."

"Ingenious." Stella arranged her face into one of admiration. "Mrs. Stafford said that you were a theatrical force to be reckoned with."

"Back in the day," Mrs. Durant said evenly. "Now, Stella, if you don't mind, we've got to be getting back to—"

"What was your costume, Mrs. Durant? I don't remember."

"The Queen of Hearts."

"Oh, right." No glitter. But Stella knew she was onto something, something that had been tugging at her for so long, not even baking had freed it. All she knew was that it had something to do with Tripp. "And you, Tripp," she called over her shoulder as Mrs. Durant led her down the hallway. "I know I loved your costume but can't remember what it was."

"A magician," he said, flatly. They were all ready to see her off.

"Right! A magician! I loved that with the tuxedo and the top hat. I remember you saying it matched your..." Stella's voice trailed off. She looked at Louisa. Louisa had been in a bodysuit with a pink boa. How did that go with her husband's costume?

Stella's eyes widened. "Can I use your bathroom?" Mrs. Durant glared at Stella, who added, "I *really* need to go."

Mrs. Durant sighed in exasperation.

Stella crossed her legs and put on a pained look. "Please? It'll only take a sec."

Mrs. Durant looked panicked about what Stella might do on her Turkish rug. She seemed to decide that humoring Stella would be easier than dissuading her. Mrs. Durant pointed down the long hall to the end, past what Stella still considered the interview room. The door to the room was open, and Stella spied Mrs. Lake seated within. Though her eyes were closed, the rustle of her skirt and the twitch of her hand indicated she was awake.

For a moment, Stella thought about going in, but at an impatient sound from Mrs. Durant, she practically flew into the bathroom. With the door locked, she drew her phone out of her pocket and brought up the photos from the kitchen staff. There was the most recent one, the one she'd been studying, without Mrs. Lake or Louisa. But the one before that, in the background, with the benefit of zoom, Stella saw Mrs. Lake being shuffled off the lawn by Louisa. In a gold bunny costume.

Gold.

Stella zoomed in as much as she could without distortion, flipping back to other photos to examine different angles. Louisa always seemed just out of frame.

On purpose?

Louisa must be far smarter than she appeared. Maybe the whole "I can't manage my iPhone" bit was a ruse.

She couldn't be sure, but she thought the costume's sparkle came from glitter, not sequins.

Glitter to match her husband's costume.

And perhaps that's why she changed. Because she realized she might well have left glitter at the scene of the crime. So she threw on a backup outfit before the police came, probably explaining to everyone that the bunny costume made her feel exposed or was uncomfortable.

A bubble of realization rose in Stella's mind, popping with such force that she lost her breath.

A rabbit. Of course. A magician pulls a rabbit from its hat.

Magic. What was it Gillian said back when they met outside the flower shop? That Louisa used to do magic shows for neighborhood kids. Maybe that's why she'd chosen this costume, an homage to her old passion for illusion. Someone who had practiced sleight of hand could easily have lifted the phone from Mr. Lake.

The revelations began crashing like waves.

All the missing objects. Louisa was the gremlin, practicing. She put the items back when the housekeeping staff started being blamed. She'd been biding her time, for this moment. To get her freedom.

Not from the shackles of caring for Mrs. Lake. That must have paled in comparison to Mr. Lake's harassment.

She had the motive. Given that people expected her to check on Mrs. Lake, nobody would notice her ducking indoors. With Mrs. Lake's eyes closed, she could easily dart upstairs, place the phone she'd lifted earlier, plus the charger she'd brought, in her father-in-law's room.

The only question—was the bunny costume covered with glitter or sequins?

She had to find out.

She heard a noise outside in the hallway.

Quickly, she flushed the toilet and ran the water as if she'd washed her hands. She came out of the bathroom and plodded down the hallway, thinking. Mrs. Durant stood at the end of the hallway, one arm holding the tray and the other arm outstretched to corral Stella to the door. Before she could, Stella ducked into the room with Mrs. Lake. She poked her head out and said, "Mrs. Stafford will never forgive me if I don't give her regards to her old friend. I'll be only a moment."

As she entered the room, she heard a voice behind her, pitched so low she couldn't identify the speaker. "Don't worry, Chelsea, I'll get her out."

Mrs. Durant said, "You expect party crashers at a party, but post-party? Who raised this girl?"

"Hello, Mrs. Lake," Stella moved in front of the older woman. "I hope I'm not disturbing you."

Mrs. Lake opened her eyes. "Oh, hello, Stella. Hello, Louisa."

Oh no. Of all the bad luck.

Louisa.

How could Stella work the conversation to Louisa's contradicting costumes with Louisa present? Her mind raced and then her eyes landed on a plate with a smattering of crumbs. Stella smelled the cheesy, yeasty scent of pizza della Pasqua. Settling on the couch beside Mrs. Lake, Stella said, "I brought *maritozzi*. There may be one or two left. Can I bring you one?"

"No, thank you, dear. Louisa brought me these cookies earlier."

"Cookies, for breakfast?" mugged Stella to hide her confusion. Was Mrs. Lake touched in the head? Pizza della Pasqua could be confused for bread or even cake. But never cookies.

Mrs. Lake touched her belly. "I'm afraid it's all that I can handle with my medication in the morning."

"Of course. I hope they were good, at least."

"They were fine. Just a package of butter cookies. Nothing remarkable."

Stella tried not to let her mouth fall open. This was too specific to be a classification error. She prompted, "Butter cookies, you said?"

Louisa nodded quickly.

No matter how altered Mrs. Lake might be, Louisa had to know that those crumbs did not come from cookies. Butter or otherwise.

Stella stared at the plate.

And then stared at Louisa.

Before she could stop herself, the words tumbled out.

"You love her."

Louisa laughed nervously. "What do you mean?"

"You love her," Stella said simply. "There's only one place to get pizza della Pasqua around here this time of year, and that's Bar Cappellina. You made a special trip there to bring your mother-in-law back a treat she loved and didn't get to finish. You love her."

Louisa's laugh sounded like a cough. "Are you deaf? Those are butter cookies."

It didn't deserve a response and Stella offered none. Instead, she felt the ingredients falling into place, creating an understandable whole. She darted a glance toward Mrs. Lake's hands; her polish still scratched. Even though she engaged in almost no activity. "I see." She said. "I see it all now."

"Louisa, close the door." Mrs. Lake's voice held none of its former tremulousness.

"No, Judith. Don't."

"Louisa. Close the door."

Louisa sank into a chair, moaning quietly. "This can't be it."

Mrs. Lake frowned. "If you want something, done..." She rose quickly, sweeping to the door, closing it with an authoritative turn of the lock.

Stella's eyes widened, but she said nothing. Louisa continued to weep quietly. When Mrs. Lake returned to her chair, Stella said. "Yes. Now it makes sense."

"What do you think you see, dear?" Mrs. Lake said.

"All of it."

Louisa looked up, her face tear-streaked.

Stella said to Mrs. Lake, "You have a science background. Claire Stafford regards you as some sort of prodigy. And yet when I asked you about the charger, you asked if it was that thing you plug into a wall."

Mrs. Lake said nothing.

Stella then gestured to Mrs Lake's hands. "Your nail polish. Scratched."

"You can practice changing a battery a million times, but, as I discovered, you need to practice it with a room full of people downstairs to maintain steady hands."

Stella nodded. "Of course, you can buy a kit to make it easier. But...the paper trail."

"Those tools are for people who don't know what they're doing."

"So you use—"

"A flathead screwdriver. Badly, as you can see. At least when rushed." To Louisa, she said, "I told you we should have taken off the polish."

"You were right," Louisa sighed with a fond smile. "As always. But the pharmacy didn't have nail polish remover."

"What I don't get," Stella said, "is why you've faked a brain injury for this long?"

"I don't expect you to understand," Mrs. Lake said, and Louisa reached to put a hand on hers, squeezing it. "As much as I loved my husband when I married him, I hated him soon after. His not allowing me to pursue my career at a time when, as a woman in science, I required familial support.

His affairs. All of that paled in comparison to his daily acts of being a despicable human being."

"Amen," said Louisa.

Mrs. Lake put her free hand on top of Louisa's. "The brain injury gave me an out."

"Wouldn't it have been easier to leave him?'

Mrs. Lake and Louisa laughed. Louisa shook her head. "You didn't know Hollis very well, did you?"

"Well, no," confirmed Stella. "I mean, we barely crossed paths."

"I tried leaving. Once. He punished me for embarrassing him. It was the only time he hit me. His everyday abuse was bad enough. He threatened to leave me penniless if I tried again, would accuse me in court of being an alcoholic to deny me the one thing I had left. My children."

"But could he actually—" began Stella.

"No question," stated Louisa, flatly.

"His pockets and resources are deep," added Mrs. Lake.

"Even so, how did acting like you had a brain injury improve your situation?"

Mrs. Lake sighed. "I'm glad that isn't obvious to you, Stella. It means you've never had to hide in plain sight from a horrible man. You've never had to forcibly change the expectations, change the rules, in order to exist."

"Still," countered Stella. "Being bedridden for more than a decade."

Mrs. Lake and Louisa looked at each other and broke into peals of laughter. Mrs. Lake shook her head. "Bedridden? No such thing. Oh, the times we've had. Right, Louisa?"

Louisa numbered on her fingers, "Pilates, dance parties, the whole MasterClass series. Oh, and remember when we cooked along with the Great British Baking Show?"

"And had a different kind of tea each time!"

Their laughter broke off at a knock at the door.

"Louisa?" called Mrs. Durant. "It must be time to show Stella out?"

"In a minute!" Louisa responded.

Dumbfounded, Stella said, "But surely someone would have seen? Your staff? The housekeepers that got blamed for taking things?"

"Oh, I felt terrible about that," Louisa said, shaking her head. "As soon as I realized, I started sprinkling everything back into the house. That's all right as rain now."

Mrs. Lake said, "I compensate my staff well, Stella. And they appreciate it. The real concern was Louisa and Tripp's children. They're getting to an age where they'll get confused why Grammy is so active behind closed doors but like molasses everywhere else. A few months ago, Louisa and I had decided it was time to end the charade and orchestrate a 'recovery'. I could leave Hollis now. Louisa wouldn't let him divide me from my children."

"Never," Louisa said, emotion warming her words. "And I knew Tripp would agree. If Hollis cut you off, we would take you in. If he cut Tripp off in retribution, well, we'd downsize and figure it out. As long as we all have each other."

Stella guessed, "But then Mr. Lake started hitting on Louisa, which forced a new plan."

"You know that, too?" Judith Lake asked.

"It was the motive I came up with when I thought Tripp did it. Before I realized that Louisa had changed costumes and put that together with the glitter."

"That glitter," Mrs. Lake muttered. "I tried to brush it off, but it was stubborn and I started panicking that someone would come in. I had to hope I'd gotten enough that no one would notice. When I put the phone down, some of the glitter came off and I knew that trying to wipe it would only look more suspicious. Streaking, and then there'd be glitter on the floor, even more noticeable."

"Which is why you told me to change," said Louisa, fondly. "Always thinking ahead."

"I had to," Judith Lake's eyes blazed. "Hollis wanted to destroy the family I've given up everything to protect. I simply would not allow it."

Stella paused at the strength in Mrs. Lake's words. Finally, she said, "Tripp doesn't know? About any of this?"

Louisa shook her head. "No. He's such a good man but can't keep his emotions under wrap. He would have given everything away. This was our secret."

"And now yours," added Mrs. Lake. "But what will you do with it, I wonder?"

Stella thought for a moment. "There's an innocent man in jail. I'm guessing you slipped him the watch the night of the party?"

Louisa nodded. "It was our fail-safe. We'd hoped the police would rule the death a heart attack, but Judith knew there was a chance of blistering. In which case, we figured they'd most likely assume a house wiring problem; but if they decided it was murder, we wanted it to look like a robbery."

"How many fail-safes do you have?"

"Only one more," Mrs. Lake said. She reached into her purse.

Stella shouted and threw up her hands to protect her face. "Don't shoot!"

Mrs. Lake and Louisa exchanged glances. Mrs. Lake said, "And I thought you were rather clever." She pulled a tin of mints from her purse. "Would you like one?"

Stella shook her head rapidly, staring at the mints.

Mrs. Lake popped one into her mouth and then handed the tin to Louisa, who took one for herself. Then Mrs. Lake said, "How would shooting you help us, Stella? We can rationalize killing a monster. You are not only not a monster, but we'd be implicated immediately. Justifiably, I hasten to add. Even if we could get a gun into Italy, which, as you know, is not easy."

Concentrating on slowing her breathing, Stella said, "Then what is your last fail-safe?"

Mrs. Lake gestured at herself and Louisa, placidly sucking on mints. "I should think it would be obvious. Us."

Stella blinked. "What?"

With a sigh, as if disappointed in Stella, Louisa said, "What was my wrongdoing? I took my father-in-law's phone and gave it to my frail and ailing mother-in-law for safekeeping."

"But you're not frail and ailing," said Stella to Mrs. Lake.

"True. And if you insist on telling the authorities, well then, that jig will be up. Thank goodness. I've grown so tired of the charade. In which case, I guess we can chalk my recovery up to that glimmer of a chance the doctors always hoped for, but we never believed in."

"Love a miracle," Louisa smiled.

"Always," Mrs. Lake smiled back.

Stella felt herself growing angry. "Maybe Louisa can wheedle out of this one, but you, Mrs. Lake. Even if you have a miraculous recovery. You replaced the charger with a rigged one."

"Did I?" Mrs. Lake's eyes grew round with pretend wonder. "I certainly could. Make no mistake about that. Electricity is far simpler than anyone would assume."

Stella wanted to stamp her feet. "But you put that faulty charger and the phone in his room!"

Mrs. Lake nodded. "Indeed. A wifely task. Made the more difficult by the three flights of steps."

"A charger you knew to be faulty!" Stella felt they were going in circles.

"That will be hard to prove." Mrs. Lake nodded.

"The charger had no fingerprints on it."

"Exactly why it will be hard to prove."

Stella gritted her teeth in frustration. Her fear for herself evaporated in this moment of trying to get to the answer. "But if you put the charger in his room, it would have your fingerprints on it. Unless you cleaned them to hide what you did."

Mrs. Lake shrugged. "It was a masquerade ball, Stella. I was wearing gloves."

Stella remembered. "The phone case was missing!"

Mrs. Lake appeared genuinely confused when she said, "What phone case? Hollis never used one."

"Oh," Stella said. "But the battery! The phone battery, how will you explain—"

"That I changed my husband's phone battery for him at some point. Is that a crime?" Mrs. Lake shook her head. "Stella. Listen. Those deep pockets of Hollis's are now my deep pockets. I'm not worried. I can already guess the myriad of ways my army of attorneys will spin this. Perhaps that I gave my husband my charger since he misplaced his."

Slowly, Stella said, "But you're telling me everything. Now I know."

Mrs. Lake laughed. "What do you know? The ravings of a sick woman? Oh, Stella. I'm sorry, but I think no one will believe you. Try to tell people of this conversation and I'm afraid you'll lose all credibility."

Stella sat still.

"Stella, love. I admire your fortitude. Your tenacity. Not many could have seen through the elegance of this ruse. But you'll have to tender the same admiration for myself and Louisa. You can bring this to the police, and they will investigate it. But every connection is loose enough that they'll have to let us go. Now or later."

Stella fumed. At odds with her irritation, she acknowledged a begrudging respect for these women—their camaraderie, their fire, how they charted their own path. But they *killed* someone. Even if it were justified, she couldn't play the role of judge and jury. The internal battling made her scowl. Finally, she said, "An innocent man is in jail because of you."

"What? Who?" Louisa said. "Oh! Right. The vagrant."

"You didn't plant the exonerating evidence yet?" Mrs. Lake said.

"No, we can't have anyone find it before we're safely on the plane."

"Oh, right. Of course."

"Someone care to fill me in?" said Stella.

Louisa shrugged. "It's a fake. The Omega. I got it from a vendor in Times Square about a year ago. I figured it would come in handy for my illusions. I still have Hollis's real watch. We were going to plant it in his drawer on our way out of town. So we'll be in the air before anyone thinks to seek us out, but your man there will walk free."

"He doesn't owe you even one night in jail," Stella said.

"Well," said Mrs. Lake. "You don't owe us anything, either. I suspect there's nothing we can do to keep all this to yourself?"

"Part of me wants to," Stella admitted. "But a secret this big? How could I ever open up to anyone again? How could I live with myself?"

"Could you live with yourself if it meant we paid you enough to get back to New York? Perhaps your anguish would be attenuated by starting your own restaurant. On your financial terms."

"How did you know—"

"You're a curious person, Stella. Especially when you turned up the night of the murder, asking about chargers. Naturally, we asked questions about the person asking questions."

Stella nodded in thought. She hated herself for considering their offer, but she couldn't help it—she could get *out*. Now. Her own restaurant. Her own life back. Customers that she dealt with for a meal service, not for the length of a murder investigation. Without even selling the *casale*. The house would be a place to come home to.

Home.

She'd never thought of Aramezzo as home.

A war raged within her. Secure Mimmo's freedom but say nothing to the police about what she'd learned. Thus, securing her freedom. The opportunity to finally realize the dream she'd nursed since her first Easy

Bake Oven. *Her own restaurant.*

But…if she kept quiet…how could she stand her own company? Plus, this dark secret would lace every connection she'd ever make. That she'd known who killed a man, no matter how much anybody would have done the same, and said nothing.

"Stella?" Mrs. Lake prodded. "Our time is almost up. Chelsea will be hunting for the spare key to this office even now. She's wonderful, my Chelsea, but not fond of the unknown. Especially when it's under her roof."

"It's a tempting offer," Stella said, still imagining saying yes even as she imagined saying no. "But I can't accept. I have to go to the police."

Mrs. Lake nodded. "Your mother raised you well."

"I wouldn't go that far." Stella had a thought. "Listen, I need to do this. I can't keep your secret. But the good news for you is the police rarely listen to me. In that they never listen to me."

Mrs. Lake cocked her head to the side. "Whatever women do, they must do twice as well as men to be thought half as good. So says Charlotte Whitton, the first female mayor of a major Canadian city. Sometimes I think these times are changing, and sometimes I despair they ever will."

Stella rose. "I guess we're done here."

The women rose with her. "I suppose so."

"You're not going to stop me?"

Mrs. Lake smiled. "Stop a woman on a mission? Impossible."

Louisa added, "We accepted this as a possibility."

Mrs. Lake added, "An acceptance made all the easier because, though the next year or two could prove a challenge, it is so much better than hiding in the shadows."

nother warm spring evening.

Another dinner in Aramezzo's piazza.

Stella, being the first to arrive, scoped out a table and nabbed it. Adele came over, bringing menus and water. At someone dropping into the seat next to her with the scent of men's shampoo, Stella looked up, ready to greet Matteo.

"Oh. Ciao, Giancarlo." She adjusted her red bandana, finger catching in what was now a hole, not just a threadbare patch.

"Ciao, Stella. Matteo told me I might find you here."

"He did, did he?"

"Yes. I wanted to ask you. Now that the situation has settled down. Could I take you out this weekend?"

"On a . . . *date*?" Stella stammered. The last time someone asked her out on a date, the conversation had gone off the rails at about this moment. Her heart beat faster.

Giancarlo's slow grin spread across his face. "What else?"

A couple walking out of Bar Cappellina, arms around each other's waists, caught Stella's attention. Liliana's silky hair fell around Luca's face as he nuzzled her neck. Pulling her eyes away, Stella found her hands in her hair, pulling a curl, willing it to straighten. She found Giancarlo's eyes steady on her. She dropped her hands into her lap. "I would love to."

Giancarlo beamed. He reached for her hand, turning it over to stroke her palm as he brushed his lips over the space between her fingers and her wrist. Stella felt touched by the gesture, courtly and intimate at the same time. Giancarlo rose, "I'll leave you to your dinner. But I'll get your number from Matteo, if that's okay?"

Stella realized he still held her hand. "That's okay."

He grinned and leaned down, pressing his cheek against her own, whispering, "*Non vedo l'ora.*" And then, for reasons she didn't quite understand, he repeated it in English. "I can't wait."

Her breath vanished within her chest.

Giancarlo's eyes searched hers, as if he saw through her, into her. He stepped backward, eyes still on hers, lightly holding Stella's hand until he stepped far enough that it slipped from his grasp, floating back down. Stella watched him leave and then blinked, trying to get her bearings.

Feeling eyes on her, she turned and noticed Luca staring. Stella waved. He lifted his hand in an approximation of a wave, but his face stayed expressionless. Stella shifted uncomfortably.

"Stella! You're early for a change," Domenica said, settling into a chair while arranging her myriad colored scarves.

"I had nothing detaining me at home. I'm not baking."

"I know."

Stella frowned. "How can you know?"

Domenica touched Stella's cheek. "You're so pristine."

Laughing, Stella said, "I sure don't feel pristine. I feel like dirty laundry left in a pile for too long."

"Thank the Madonna you smell better than that," Matteo said, leaning to kiss first Domenica and then Stella's cheeks. "Not great, of course, but better than old laundry."

Stella scowled.

Matteo shook his head. "I'm teasing, of course. You smell like spring blossoms. Good enough to tempt any man." He gave Stella a knowing look. He must have passed Giancarlo on the street.

Stella ignored the look and reached for a menu. "So, what are we eating?"

Domenica batted her hand away. "Are you kidding? We've barely seen you. You will spill it and only then will we order."

Stella's eyes flicked longingly to the menu she'd memorized months before. "I've already told you what happened. What do you want to know?"

Domenica and Matteo exchanged glances. Matteo said, "You go first."

Domenica nodded. "When you told Captain Tribuzio the truth about the murder, how was he?"

"Dismissive."

"You had to argue to get him to listen?" Domenica looked at Matteo. "I guess you were right about that one."

"Honestly, I didn't have it in me to argue," Stella said. "I told him what happened at the villa. That Mrs. Lake and Louisa had admitted to the scheme. He told me he wouldn't tolerate my attention-getting behaviors. So I left."

"Stella, love," Domenica said. "How on earth did you control your temper?"

Stella smiled a beleaguered smile. "Turns out the antidote to indignation is exhaustion. Plus, I didn't feel the need to convince him. If the ladies got home because he sat on his hands, well...not on me."

"With your story, he must have at least figured out that you were the one responsible for finding that charger. Not Salvo." Matteo said, hopefully.

"Are you kidding? He told me I was piggybacking on Salvo's triumph."

"You didn't *tell* him?" Matteo sighed. "*Madonna mia*, Stella. The captain should know your role."

"Why?" Stella asked, raising her arms in what she suddenly realized was the universal Italian gesture for, "What are you gonna do?" She smiled at herself and then said, "I don't need the credit. I'm glad it's over.

What else you got?"

"But you deserve—" Matteo sputtered.

"You're not listening. I don't need recognition. Right now, I'd rather avoid it," Stella said. "Anyway, we often don't get what we deserve."

"Speaking of," Domenica said, "what do you know about the Lakes escaping back to the US?"

Stella shrugged. "I doubt I know more than you do. Tribuzio refused to even check the villa for the watch I told him was there. So he didn't know about it until Signor Durant called, saying the house cleaners had found it in Signor Lake's drawer. That's when the captain followed up on the rest. Found out from Signora Durant that her friend Judith experienced a sudden recovery from her long-standing brain trauma. Which she said everyone attributed to the shock jarring Signora Lake's brain back into action. Whatever the explained cause of the miracle, Signora Durant reported that after I left, Judith arranged for a private plane to meet them in Rome and fairly ran into the hired car."

"By the time the police arrived in Rome, the plane was over the ocean," Domenica said.

"Right. The police tried to put together an extradition order, but other than my report, which the captain had already downplayed, they didn't have enough to convince the State Department. The phone is fried. Local authorities had deemed the charger manipulated, but under close questioning, they admitted that the evidence for manipulation could be explained by the surge of electricity. So it's not enough."

"Louisa changing her costume?"

"Evidence of a woman who can't decide what to wear more than anything else. And the charger switch, from the outside, looks like the mistake of a dotty old woman," Stella said. "The whole thing was masterful."

Domenica nodded. "You sound as if you admire them. Should we worry about you?"

Stella chuckled in answer. Then she said, "You never know. The police are still trying to put together enough evidence. Maybe they'll succeed and Signora Lake will be called to account for her actions. But for now, she's living large. At least, as indicated from the photo I got of Signora Lake and Louisa at a Pure Barre class."

Matteo's mouth fell open. "You heard from them?"

"No, Claire Stafford sent it," Stella explained. "She and her husband were packing when they got wind of police pursuing the Lakes' flight— did I tell you they slept through my whole trip to the villa? Claire emailed me the photo along with a wire transfer to thank me for my service in a trying time."

"Generous?" Domenica asked.

"Very."

"Good," said Domenica and Matteo together.

"So that's it," Stella said. "You've got the whole scoop. Everything can go back to normal. I saw Mimmo this morning, complaining about the trash the Durant's guests left in the woods. So he seems unscathed."

"Speaking of back to normal. Marta and Leo," Matteo gestured to the couple with his chin as they strolled across the piazza, hand in hand.

"Yes," Stella said flatly. "I don't get what she sees in him. There are plenty of eligible guys who are solid, kind, smart human beings."

"Not in a small village, *cara*," countered Domenica.

"Oh, I don't know," Matteo said airily. "Stella might believe a village can supply the right number of good men."

"Matteo." Stella waggled a finger at him.

"What?" Domenica said. When no one responded, she said, "Ah. Giancarlo finally worked up the courage to ask Stella out."

"Domenica! Are you hacking my life now?" Stella asked with a grin.

"Yes, my dear, you are so endlessly fascinating, I spend my time poring over your emails." Domenica rolled her eyes. "I watched how Giancarlo walked away from the table, and I saw you in full blush. You're not the only one with deductive powers."

They laughed, and then Matteo nodded to Domenica. Domenica nodded back and pulled out a box. She pushed it toward Stella.

"What's this?" Stella asked.

"Open it," Matteo said.

"It's not my birthday," Stella protested, pulling the ribbon from the box.

"I should hope not," said Domenica. "Or our gesture loses all meaning."

Stella opened the box and pulled out a bandana made of a kind of gossamer material that glowed pale green in the fading sunlight.

"Your old ones are wearing out," Domenica said. "Don't get misty-eyed, it was no extravagance. We didn't buy it, I cut up one of my old scarves."

"Plus, you sewed the hem thing," Matteo reminded her.

"After that month sewing uniforms for the Coconut War, it wasn't a big deal."

"You made that up. There's no Coconut War." Matteo protested.

"Surely you've heard of the Coconut War. In Papua New Guinea. It was a brief war, to be sure, but—"

"It *is* an extravagance," Stella said softly, holding the bandana to her chest. "Thank you." She regarded her friends with shining eyes.

"It's our pleasure," Matteo said, leaning forward to touch her hand.

"You're welcome, *cara*," Domenica said. "And I have about a dozen more for you. I could only fit one in the box Matteo brought."

Stella tugged off the red bandana and tied the green material around her curls. The green of new oregano leaves, the green of young grapes, the green of Aramezzo's olive trees.

As Adele approached, Stella said, "Shoot, I haven't even *looked* at the menu." They all laughed.

"Glad to see you all here on a Friday," Adele said, pulling a pencil from behind her ear and readying it against her pad of paper. "What can I bring you?"

"I'll have the *pappardelle*." Stella announced.

"Did you see the chalkboard?" Adele asked, pointing at the easel propped beside the door of the restaurant. "Starting in spring, we have specials. Tonight, *strangozzi* with wild asparagus and *guanciale*."

Domenica said, "Nice try, Adele. Especially throwing in pork jowl, which our Stella can't usually resist. But she'll have the *pappardelle*."

Stella said nothing.

Matteo said, "Stella?"

Slowly, Stella said, "Do you know what I love about Umbrian food? It doesn't pretend to be fancy. It's exactly what it looks like—simple, rustic, a little bit domesticated and a little bit wild. The food here is honest and it's delicious and no matter where you're from, it tastes of home."

Domenica and Matteo exchanged glances while Adele tapped her pad with the pencil.

"I'll have the special," Stella said with a smile. "Change of season. Change of bandana. I get it now. There's no time like the present."

I HOPE YOU ENJOYED YOUR VISIT TO UMBRIA, THE GREEN HEART OF ITALY!

More mystery is already brewing in Aramezzo; look for book four in the *Murder in an Italian Village* series coming soon!

Don't want to miss a clue? Sign up for my monthly newsletter, *The Grapevine* (michelledamiani.com/thegrapevine), and you'll be the first to know when the next book is available.

As a welcome to *The Grapevine*, you'll receive **Santa Lucia**, my best-selling novel set in Santa Lucia—where Stella has a great aunt who is married to the mayor. The books will eventually cross, so now is the time to discover Santa Lucia!

Along with top-secret book news and deals, and your free copy of *Santa Lucia*, every month you'll receive expert travel tips, delicious recipes, and book reviews for your next wanderlust read.

Hope to welcome you soon!

— Michelle
michelledamiani.com

BRUTTI MA BUONI

These nut-filled quasi-meringues hail from the Piedmont, though every region has put their own spin on it. In Tuscany, the recipe shifted and grew more rarified. There, the egg white, sugar, and nut batter gets a turn on the stove-top, which create caramelized notes. Tuscan brutti ma buoni are delicious, but the recipe is fussy and messy. Stella— who has no time for fuss and mess what with guests and mysteries—uses the more basic version, and thinks you should too.

This batter comes together in fifteen minutes, leaving you, dear reader and baker, ample time to while away the afternoon with a cookie and a good book.

INGREDIENTS FOR 3 DOZEN *BRUTTI MA BUONI*

150 grams of egg whites

300 grams of granulated sugar

500 grams of nuts (virtually any kind will do, so experiment! Roasting brings out the toasty earthiness of nuts, but you can use raw nuts if you'd prefer), chopped by hand or in a food processor until in fairly small, uneven pieces. You'll want some fine pieces to absorb into the egg white, and some toothiness from larger pieces, about the size of a pea.

a dash of salt

a teaspoon of vanilla or another flavor

---

1) Heat oven to 160°C/340°F.

2) Line three cookie sheet with parchment paper.

3) Whip egg whites until very stiff peaks form. At the end, add the salt and the flavoring.

4) Mix the egg whites with the ground nuts and the sugar.

5) Once combined, form into balls about the size of a ping-pong ball and place on cookie sheet. Leave plenty of space for the cookies to expand.

6) Bake for 20 to 25 minutes, until firm and dry.

7) Leave on cookie sheets for a few minutes to finish firming up.

8) Remove to a rack to cool.

Buon appetito!